A BLOW FOR FREEDOM

Jessica could  s actually kissing and dismaying, w l her blood was arms slipped aroun o her tiptoes in order to respond more fully to his kisses.

"Remarkable," he said, when he at least released her.

"How dare you, sir!" she demanded, all her outrage returning.

When his only response was a wider grin, Jessica's hand formed a fist almost of its own accord, arcing back and then forward again in an upward right cross to Sir Brian's firm jaw that would have done boxing champion Gentleman Jackson proud.

Hands on her hips, Jessica looked down at where Sir Brian lay on his backside in the soft dirt of the rose garden and declared, "Some of us refuse to be exploited, sir."

Little did Jessica know that the battle had only just begun. . . .

THE BATTLING BLUESTOCKING

THE
BATTLING
BLUESTOCKING

AMANDA SCOTT

A SIGNET BOOK

NEW AMERICAN LIBRARY

FOR
Susan B. Steele
Lady Extraordinary

NAL BOOKS ARE AVAILABLE AT QUANTITY DISCOUNTS WHEN USED
TO PROMOTE PRODUCTS OR SERVICES. FOR INFORMATION PLEASE
WRITE TO PREMIUM MARKETING DIVISION, NEW AMERICAN
LIBRARY, 1633 BROADWAY, NEW YORK, NEW YORK 10019.

SIGNET TRADEMARK REG. U.S. PAT. OFF. AND FOREIGN COUNTRIES
REGISTERED TRADEMARK—MARCA REGISTRADA
HECHO EN CHICAGO, U.S.A.

SIGNET, SIGNET CLASSIC, MENTOR, PLUME, MERIDIAN and NAL
BOOKS are published by New American Library
1633 Broadway, New York, New York 10019

First Printing, July 1985

1 2 3 4 5 6 7 8 9

PRINTED IN THE UNITED STATES OF AMERICA

1

"STAND AND DELIVER!"

The dreaded command rang out above the whistling of crisp spring winds that swept across the treeless heights of the rugged Cornish cliffs. Neither the distant roar of the mighty Atlantic as it crashed against the rocky shore far below, nor the clatter and jingle of wheels, harness, and plunging hoofbeats as the coachman struggled to bring his startled team under control again succeeded in muffling the words. The command was easily heard and understood by each of the three occupants inside the crested red-plush-lined carriage that until that moment had been moving at a smooth, distance-eating pace along the high, winding cliff road from St. Ives toward Zennor Head.

"Merciful heavens, Cyril, do something!" exclaimed the elder of the two fashionably attired young ladies within, a fragile, pink-cheeked, blond-haired woman in a pomona-green carriage gown and matching spencer, who, despite the fact that she was rapidly approaching her thirtieth year, was still very pretty. " 'Tis highwaymen!" she cried. "We shall be murdered!" With one slim yellow-gloved hand clutching Lord Gordon's plump arm, Lady Gordon grabbed agitatedly with the other for a strap to steady herself just as the coachman finally regained command of his team and the carriage lurched to a complete halt.

In the momentary period of what, after so much commotion, seemed to be utter silence, Lord Gordon removed his lady's hand before it could wrinkle his elegant dark blue sleeve, gave the hand a pat, and with a loud "harrumph" advised her in his customary pompous tones to leave everything to him. "Best thing under such circumstances is to keep a still tongue, Georgeanne, and do precisely as we're told. Less chance that way of anyone's coming to grief."

From the forward seat, the younger lady, who had shown none of her sister's agitation, flicked Lord Gordon a look laced with icy contempt. Of slightly darker coloring and built upon more generous lines than Lady Gordon, she was attired in a chinchilla-trimmed gray wool traveling dress. Her soft light brown hair had been neatly arranged under a delightful straw bonnet decorated with gay pink ribbons that exactly matched her pleated bodice and the elegant French gloves that came into view now as she withdrew her slender hands from the large chinchilla muff resting in her lap. Miss Jessica Sutton-Drew was well accustomed to hearing her many admirers employ such terms as dazzling, magnificent, and splendid to describe her beauty, but Lord Gordon was not one who discovered much to be admired beyond her fine features, elegant carriage, and voluptuous figure, for the lovely Miss Sutton-Drew, though generally of a cheerful, humorous disposition, often found it difficult to conceal her scorn for her pompous brother-in-law.

"I believe," she said in a carefully even tone, as she removed her gloves with quick, precise movements, "that you would truly advise poor Georgie to submit to whatever outrageous demands these villains might make of her, Cyril, without so much as lifting one of your perfectly manicured fingertips to protect her."

Miss Sutton-Drew's meaning was abundantly clear, and Lord Gordon, his round face flooding with color, found it impossible to meet the steady gaze of her clear gray eyes. Nervously he lifted a plump hand to pluck at the thick dark side whiskers framing his countenance.

"Upon my word, Jessica," he muttered, "I wish you will not be so vulgar. A properly bred gentlewoman should know nothing about such matters."

"How absurd you are, Cyril," Miss Sutton-Drew retorted, glancing toward the coach's landward window as she slipped her bare hands into the warmth of the large chinchilla muff once again. "What you really mean to say is that a proper spinster should *profess* a lack of such knowledge. I assure you, however, that having arrived at the age of six-and-twenty, there is little I do not know about the more unfortunate ways of men. Indeed, being a child of rather more than average intelligence, and being most fortunately blessed with an aunt who consented to answer those questions which my parents considered improper for a daughter of theirs to ask, I daresay there was little I did not understand about a good many so-called unmentionable things by the time I was thirteen or so."

She had not shifted her gaze away from the window, and just then Lady Gordon, who had been staring fixedly out the same window, started and gave a little shriek, clutching at her breast in that region where she supposed her heart was to be found.

"I see one of them!" she cried. "The embankment hid him before, but oh, he is coming this way! I feel sure I shall suffer a spasm just like one of Mama's if that awful man should so much as speak to me, Cyril. You must do something."

Miss Sutton-Drew paid scant heed to her sister's distress, but her own attitude at once became more alert, and she straightened her shoulders slightly as her rosy lips compressed themselves into lines of determination. Lord Gordon also straightened, nervously puffing out his cheeks and continuing in an absentminded way to pat his wife's hand as he, too, peered anxiously toward the coach windows.

Suddenly the sunlight on that side of the coach was obscured by a large bay horse, and although his nearness made it impossible to get a good look at the rider's face, a golden-brown-leather-clad arm came into view as the coach door was unceremoniously jerked open.

"Right ho, me hearties," sang out the voice they had heard moments earlier. "Hand over the gewgaws all right and tight now. I've me pops aimed right at yer fashionable hearts, but it'd go clean agin me grain t' 'ave t' shoot ye, and that's a fac'."

Lady Gordon gave another cry and shrank against her husband, who was already reaching for his purse. Miss Sutton-Drew frowned at him, then spoke calmly to the highwayman.

"Since your idiotic horse is not only fidgeting but is much too close to the carriage to allow you to see us clearly," she said, her voice carrying easily, "I doubt very much that your aim would be true. Therefore, I see no good reason to comply with your demands."

"Jessica!" her sister and brother-in-law protested as one.

Miss Sutton-Drew ignored them, keeping her attention riveted upon the highwayman. He said nothing at first, then muttered something that sounded like an oath, and she saw his left knee move slightly.

"Back, Sailor. Easy, boy." The horse moved obediently, backing nearly to the high embankment that edged the side of the roadbed, and a moment later the occupants of the coach had an unobstructed view of the masked highwayman. Youthfully slim and broad-shouldered, he was dressed in tan riding breeches and the golden-brown leather jacket over a rough blue plaid shirt. He wore no proper neckcloth, but the dark blue mask tied around the lower half of his face, covering his nose, mouth, and chin, looked very much like a sort of kerchief that men of the lower orders generally wore knotted haphazardly around their necks. The mask did nothing to conceal his eyes, which were dark blue, or the straight bushy eyebrows above them. A dun-colored slouch hat had been pulled tightly down over medium brown hair, until even the Cornish wind seemed unable to dislodge it, and although a strong gust made an attempt just then to whip the mask from the highwayman's face, it was unsuccessful. Jessica noted that the lower half of the mask had been tucked carefully into the tightly fastened collar of his shirt.

The man sat easily in his saddle, one hand holding his reins, the other a silver-mounted pistol, the sight of which made Miss Sutton-Drew's eyes narrow, just as the slight change in his rough accent and tone had done seconds earlier when he had spoken to his horse. The hand holding the pistol trembled a little, but he steadied it and spoke again in his rustic accent. "Now ye see it, me dear, so thar kin be no mistake. So if ye'll all jest be so kind as t'—"

The explosion and the highwayman's shout of pained astonishment came together. His pistol fell to the ground, where it discharged harmlessly, while he clapped the hand that had been holding it to his left shoulder. Above his mask the skin around his dark blue eyes tightened and turned a sickly shade of gray-white. Dark red blood began almost immediately to ooze between his fingers where they pressed against the small neat hole in the upper sleeve of his leather jacket, and the highwayman swayed slightly in his saddle. Seconds later, making a visible effort to regain his dignity, he drew a long, steadying breath and glared accusingly into the dim interior of the coach.

Lord and Lady Gordon, who had both nearly jumped out of their skins at the sound of the shot, were now wrinkling their noses at the distinct and unpleasant odor of burning fur. Only Miss Sutton-Drew appeared unaffected either by what had transpired or by the odd smell. With complete calm she removed both hands from her chinchilla muff. A lacy pink handkerchief in the left one was put to use to extinguish one or two tiny sparks still glowing at the edges of the small black hole that had appeared so suddenly in the center of the muff, while the little silver-and-gilt pistol in her right hand pointed steadily at the highwayman's broad chest.

"Do not do anything hastily," she said in a conversational tone. "There is another bullet in this pistol." She paused long enough to dampen a corner of the lacy handkerchief with the tip of her dainty tongue and to rub the charred bit of the muff again before continuing, "I should advise you to call in your henchmen, Mr. Highwayman. Order them to relinquish their weapons and prepare to be haled directly before the nearest justice of the peace."

The highwayman was still staring at her in astonishment, but he straightened a little at her words, his eyes reflecting both pain and something else. Not fear, Jessica thought, regarding him closely. More like a hint of amusement mixed with perhaps a touch of apprehension.

His voice was well enough under control, however. "You've only my . . . meself t' deal with, m'lady. No cohorts. D'ye mind if I stanch the flow of claret from me poor shoulder afore we trot along? I'd not wish t' inconvenience ye by perishing before yer lovely eyes."

The impudence was somehow appealing, and Jessica's lips twitched, but she managed to retain her composure. "Certainly you may do what is necessary," she said. "But please attempt nothing foolish. I assure you I shall have less compunction about using this pistol a second time than I had the first. Perhaps," she added, "my brother-in-law's guard may be of some assistance to you. He certainly was of little enough use to us."

The coach swayed a little as one of the men on the box moved to comply with her wishes, and the highwayman's horse started, flinging up his head and beginning to back when his master's knees clamped involuntarily against his flanks. Jessica's hand tightened on her pistol, then relaxed again when the animal was brought under immediate control. Another gust of the crisp spring wind plastered the highwayman's mask against his face just then, and she noted a jawline so rigid that she knew he must be clenching his teeth against the pain caused by his horse's sudden movement.

"Please allow Peters to assist you," she said gently.

"No need, ma'am," he muttered. Withdrawing a large white handkerchief from an inside pocket, he wadded it inside his sleeve, against his shoulder, then fastened the front of his jacket. "Snug enough now," he said. "I'll do. 'Tisn't far, after all."

Lord Gordon, who had been indignantly observing the exchange between his intrepid young sister-in-law and the would-be highwayman, chose this moment to assert his rank and authority.

"You'll soon regret having had the temerity to hold up the Gordon coach, my man," he declared pompously before turning his attention to the spindly guard, waiting hesitantly in the roadway for further orders. "Peters," barked his lordship impatiently, "unmask that fiend and tie his hands behind him. Then you may deposit him with the nearest magistrate. I believe 'tis Sir Brian Gregory at Shaldon Park."

"It is, indeed," the highwayman informed him on a rueful note, then added more hastily as the guard began reluctantly to approach him, "I say, my lord, I'll go along with your man willingly enough, but I beg you'll allow me to retain the use of my hands. It'd cause me a devilish amount of unnecessary pain to have them tied behind me, I assure you. And," he added, again with that odd mixture of amusement and wariness in his eyes, "no doubt you'll think it odd, but you may believe me when I say it will be easier for your man there to see to the business if he allows me to retain my mask as well."

"Poppycock," snapped Lord Gordon. "Why, I never

heard of such a preposterous thing. Retain that damn-fool mask? Rubbish. Rubbish, I say. Have it off him at once, Peters. And tie his hands as well, else he's like to overpower you along the road.''

The hapless Peters glanced uncertainly at his master, then back at the tall youth on the big bay horse. The guard didn't say a word, but it was clear enough to Jessica that the poor man was wondering just how his master expected him to snatch a mask from a face several feet above his reach if the wearer of the mask refused to cooperate. Her ready sense of humor was tickled, and she glanced at her sister, half-expecting to encounter a similar reaction. Instead, Lady Gordon's eyes were narrowed, though her fear seemed to have dissipated. As if sensing Jessica's steady gaze, she turned. There was curiosity in the gray-green eyes beneath the thick dark lashes so much like Jessica's own, but Lady Gordon said nothing.

Lord Gordon harrumphed again and parted his full pink lips as if to speak, but Jessica forestalled him before he could bark at the poor bewildered guard again.

"Really, Cyril, what do you expect Peters to do? He can hardly drag the man from his horse. Or perhaps you will order me to shoot him again if he refuses to take off that mask.''

"I'd as lief you did no such thing, ma'am.'' The highwayman's accent had improved steadily, and he spoke now as he had a moment before in what Jessica suspected to be his normal voice. It revealed the youthfulness she had begun to suspect earlier, but also a breeding above what one might expect in a normal highwayman. Her curiosity increased accordingly.

Lord Gordon, having demanded to know where his guard's shotgun had got to and having been told that since there had never been a lick of trouble before when they visited St. Ives, he had not thought it worth the trouble to bring it, was sputtering about the evils of the servant population and the rights of persons traveling the king's highroads. When he went on to declaim about the absurdity of a highwayman's having the audacity to make demands of his captors, Jessica, regarding the highwayman in a measuring way, interrupted the spate calmly.

"Will you give me your solemn word that you will not attempt to escape us if we leave your hands free?" she asked.

"Word of a . . . that is, of course I do," he responded, checking himself.

Jessica was certain he had been about to reveal himself. His prompt reply put her forcibly in mind of her father whenever he said "word of a gentleman" or, more precisely, "word of a Sutton-Drew." It was not the sort of response one expected from a man of common breeding. Indeed, it was a gentleman's response.

She turned complacently to her brother-in-law. "There, Cyril, you see how easily the matter is arranged. He has agreed to accompany us without further ado."

"Us!" Lord Gordon was astounded. "Upon my word, Jessica, what are you talking about? Peters will see this villain into the magistrate's hands whilst I escort you and my lady safely back to Gordon Hall. Presently, after I have completely refreshed myself, I shall go along to Shaldon Park to see that proper charges are lodged against this . . . this person."

"Nonsense, Cyril. Peters has no horse, so unless you mean for him to ride pillion behind the highwayman, he will have to walk, for the highwayman is wounded and cannot do so. Besides," she added, noting the now undisguised amusement lighting the highwayman's eyes, "I captured him with no help whatsoever from you and yours, and I mean to see him safely disposed. I've not the slightest intention of leaving such an important matter as this is your man Peters' hands. So, do order your coachman to drive on, if you please," she added as Cyril stared at her, his mouth unbecomingly agape. "And you," she said firmly to the horseman, "since you seem to know the way, perhaps you will ride just ahead of the coach. I am counting upon you to do nothing rash, but I fear I shall have to trust your good word in the matter, for I do not choose to give my pistol into Peters' keeping. His judgment, I believe, is not very acute."

"No need, miss," the guard volunteered. "I've got his pistol." He held it out to show her, having picked it up from where it lay upon the ground.

"Yes, well, that's very good, Peters," she replied

kindly. "I'm sure you will be careful not to let it discharge again."

"No, miss . . . that is . . ." He regarded the pistol ruefully. "I doubt it had but the one shot."

"Too true," agreed the highwayman, abandoning further pretense with a sigh. "I was a gudgeon not to bring a second pistol, but I never thought I should need to shoot it at all, you see. Do you suppose we could go now, ma'am? I promise I shall do nothing to alarm anyone, but I'd as lief arrive at Shaldon Park with at least a shred of my dignity intact, and I'm already as weak as a cat."

Jessica agreed, and a moment later Lord Gordon signaled his coachman to drive on, but as the coach lurched forward, he turned his pent-up fury on his sister-in-law.

"Upon my word, Jessica, I never heard of such a thing. What your esteemed father would say to all this, I'm sure I have no idea. A young woman concealing a loaded pistol about her person! Whatever is the world coming to, I wonder."

Lady Gordon chuckled, her equanimity completely restored. "Since dearest Papa himself gave Jessica that pistol because of all her traveling about from one relative to another, I doubt he would say much more than that she has been stirring the stewpot again," she said, grinning at her sister. "I'd forgotten it is your habit to carry it in your muff, however."

"Well," said Lord Gordon indignantly, rounding upon her before Jessica could reply, "your papa may use such a vulgar expression, though I've certainly never heard him do so, but it ill becomes you to let such words fall from your lips, Georgeanne." His brows were heavily furrowed. "I don't know how it is that you so often forget yourself when your sister makes her annual visit to us, but I cannot help but think her influence upon you is a deleterious one. Unless you take care to resist that influence, I shall find myself forced in future to consider refusing to allow you the pleasure of her company."

"Oh, no, Cyril!" her ladyship exclaimed, turning beseeching eyes up toward his stern ones. "I'm sure I beg your pardon if I said anything to offend you. I shall take good care not to do so again."

Lord Gordon patted her hand comfortingly but stiffened when Jessica's musical laughter rippled through the coach.

"Don't be a peagoose, Georgie," she said. "Cyril is merely ruffling his feathers because he is put out with me at the moment. And it is patently unfair of you, sir," she added, shaking her head at him, "to threaten poor Georgie like that when what you really wish to do is to come to cuffs with me. Not that you ever win such confrontations, of course. Nonetheless, you know perfectly well that, despite our differences, you look forward to my annual visits simply because your servants are never so efficient or your household so well run as when I am present to see to those things for you. Confess now that you were put out this year when I delayed my arrival in order to devote the time necessary to reorganize Madeleine's household to acccommodate the new heir."

It was Jessica's habit each year to leave her fond parents to care for each other at the family home in Gloucestershire, in order to engage in a tour of certain other relatives' homes. She was happiest when she felt needed, and her talents for organization and basic housekeeping were generally much admired by those who exploited them. Lord Gordon, however, had a preference for more submissive females, and much as he might enjoy the fruits of her efficiency, he could not approve of Jessica's forthright manner of speech.

"Nonsense," he retorted now as color suffused his jowly cheeks. "I am persuaded that your younger sister appreciated your assistance after suffering through the dreadful ordeal of childbirth, but it is surely coming it a bit strong to suggest that you reorganized the Earl of Porth's entire household. You overrate your abilities. Furthermore, you've not the slightest sense of delicacy, and if you encourage Madeleine to flout Porth's authority the way you continually encourage Georgeanne to flout mine, I am certain the man was glad to see the back of you." After that promising start, and pointedly ignoring a weak mumur of protest from his wife, he plunged with renewed vigor into a full-scale diatribe, describing in detail his sister-in-law's shortcomings and how he'd have dealt with them if he'd been so unfortunate as to have had the raising of her.

Jessica heard him out meekly, merely donning her pink gloves before inserting her hands once again into the huge chinchilla muff, and regarding Lord Gordon with wide, solemn eyes. When he had finished, she gave that characteristic little shake of her head and favored him with an admiring look.

"It is the most amazing thing, Cyril," she said earnestly, "but you never seem to lose yourself in verbiage, no matter how furious you get. When I lose my temper, I always seem to get my tongue tangled just when I want to make my most telling point. Papa does, too. You deliver a far better scold than he does, doesn't he, Georgie?" She turned to her sister for confirmation of that interesting fact, but poor Lady Gordon, appalled to find herself included in such a discussion, merely shrank back into her corner. Jessica smiled encouragingly, but her gray eyes glittered with suppressed anger.

"It is quite all right, my dear," she said. "I understand perfectly why you go in such awe of him. So much sound and fury. You never did react well to blustering. No doubt it is only when you see his little rages directed at me that you can recognize them for the simple expulsions of overheated air that they really are." An indignant gasp from her brother-in-law drew her attention, and she bit her lower lip ruefully. "I should not have said that, Cyril. It was not at all becoming of me. One day this wretched temper of mine will be my undoing, but you really have no right to scold me in such a fashion. I am of age, you know, and you have no authority over me. However, we shall not quarrel anymore today, so you may be calm. I am persuaded that it cannot be at all good for your health . . . all that blood rushing to your face like that. Oh, look," she added as the coach passed between a pair of tall stone-mounted wrought-iron gates, flanked by enormous yew hedges, and past a staring, ruddy-cheeked lodge keeper, "I do believe we must have arrived at Shaldon Park."

Though he was quite puffed up with offended indignation, Lord Gordon was momentarily diverted by Jessica's words and cast a glance out the window. The respite was a brief one, however, and he soon renewed his tirade, assuring her that as master of the house in which she was presently residing, he did indeed have every right to scold, and adding a catalog of Jessica's misbehavior over the past five or six years' worth of visits to Gordon Hall. Though she did not interrupt, she paid not the slightest heed to him now, fixing her interest instead upon the lovely hedge-protected park through which they were passing and upon the distant occasionally glimpsed view, beyond the tall, thick hedges and a wide variety of flowering and deciduous trees, of the gray Atlantic, which had become visible again as a result of their having been traveling steadily uphill. A few moments later, she enjoyed a brief view of gray water from either window, for Shaldon Park was located just at the point where Cornwall narrows before flaring into the rounded hook known as Land's End or, more properly, the Penwith Peninsula. The neck of the peninsula being a mere four miles wide at that point, visitors to Shaldon Park were thus rewarded on clear days and from specific vantage points with a spectacular view of the Atlantic to the north and west and the English Channel to the south.

"Tell me about Sir Brian Gregory," Jessica said, suddenly curious to know more about the man who owned Shaldon Park.

Since she had cut into his lecture mid-sentence, Lord Gordon looked more offended than ever, but because he could not resist puffing off his knowledge of the local gentry, he responded more temperately than might otherwise have been the case.

"Undoubtedly the wealthiest landowner in this part of Cornwall," he said grandly. "Owns a dozen mines here, in Devon, and in Somerset, plus a plantation—sugar, I believe—in the Indies."

"Goodness," Jessica said, properly impressed. "Have I ever had the privilege of meeting this King Midas?"

Lord Gordon frowned in disapproval of her levity, but his lady shook her head. "I cannot think that you have," she replied, "for he was abroad when you visited us last year, and I think he was nearly always gone to London for the Season just prior to your annual visit to us. I know he generally departs several weeks before we do. He does occasionally favor us with a call, and twice he has accepted invitations to dine, but we rarely meet him in London, and being a bachelor, he does not entertain here. He's very handsome," she added with a sidelong glance at her husband. "At least, I think he is."

"Rubbish," pronounced her spouse. "Man's a fine rider to the hounds . . . A Melton man, you know . . . keeps a snug little box in Leicestershire. Excellent seat. But he pays scant heed to the proper mode of fashion. Dresses all by guess. Not the sort of fellow to attract the ladies at all." Lord Gordon smoothed his coat with a finicking finger as if to punctuate his statement.

"My goodness, Cyril," Jessica murmured dulcetly, "how well you understand our sex."

"Bound to," he replied, puffing out his cheeks. "Been on the town since I don't know when. A goodly number of years—must be twenty by now, I expect. Fancy I ought to know a point more than the devil."

"Indeed." She smiled at him sweetly, winked at her startled sister, then leaned forward to peer out the window, hoping to catch a view of the house that went with the beautiful park. Dusky pink wild roses were budding along the roadside, and daisies waved their cheerful heads in a nearby grassy meadow. Then, just ahead and above them on the hillside, loomed the house. It was built in the Palladian style of mellow South Somerset sandstone from the Hamdon Hall quarries, its broad central facade domed in white Luxulyanite, an attractive porphyritic granite quarried from the Cornish village which gave it its name. The two flanking wings boasted white colonnades of the same sun-glinting granite.

Jessica expelled a little sigh of satisfaction. The house was exactly as she had hoped it would be, a jewel set off by the flower-filled park surrounding it. As they drew nearer, the carriage wheels crunched on gravel, and she could see a well-tended drive circling a smoothly scythed lawn, in the center of which was a white marble unicorn, rampant, hooves raised in what appeared to be an enthusiastic welcome to approaching guests. A moment later they drew to a halt before sweeping steps that led to the portico, and glancing back at the unicorn, Jessica observed that his left eye was closed in an unmistakable wink. That little bit of whimsy made her more curious than ever to meet the owner of Shaldon Park.

2

"YOU LADIES WILL remain in the carriage whilst I attend to this matter," Lord Gordon stated firmly as a gray-livery-clad flunky ran down the broad granite steps to open the door of the coach.

Ignoring him, Jessica accepted the aid of the flunky and descended to the gravel drive. A statuesque young woman, she was broad of shoulder and hip and narrow of waist, and nearly as tall as the lad who assisted her. Twitching her gray wool skirt into place, she straightened her hat, settled her muff on her left arm, ignored her brother-in-law's indignant muttering, and turned to see where the highwayman had gone.

He had managed to dismount unassisted and was presently looping his reins through a ring at the top of a white post set into the ground near the bottom left of the steps. He glanced up as she watched him, but he was not looking at her. Instead, he seemed to be watching the flunky, who was now assisting Lady Gordon from the coach. Lord Gordon followed a moment later, and the youth turned his attention to the highwayman. Jessica saw the lad's eyes widen, but he looked quickly away again, almost, she thought, as if he had received some sort of signal. She looked again at the highwayman, but he returned her look blandly with nothing more than a slight twinkle in his eyes.

"Shall we go in?" he asked, gesturing to the others to lead the way.

"Seems to me you're in a dashed almighty hurry," Lord Gordon told him suspiciously.

"Only to have the matter over and done," was the response.

"You'll be hanging from a gallows once this is over and done, my lad," his lordship informed him roundly. "I

18

shouldn't think you'd be in such a headlong rush to reach that end."

"Oh, I'll wager it won't come to that, my lord," the highwayman returned with an ironic little chuckle.

He seemed momentarily more sure of himself, Jessica thought, her curiosity by now thoroughly aroused. There was a hint of cockiness now, too, and the attitude was no longer appealing. Indeed, what had appeared to be boyish impudence before now seemed little more than insolence, and it was beginning to irritate Miss Sutton-Drew.

They moved up the steps toward the tall, highly polished double doors that marked the entrance to the house. There was no need to knock, of course, for their arrival had been noted by those within, and the doors swung wide as they drew near. A stately butler admitted them, informing Lord Gordon that Sir Brian was in his bookroom and would receive them at once. Jessica noticed that the highwayman slouched a little and kept his head turned away from the butler. However, if that worthy thought it odd that he was admitting a masked man with a bloodstained jacket to his master's house, he gave no sign of it, merely requesting that they take seats in the drawing room, off the hall to the right, while he went to inform his master of their arrival.

The drawing room, like the entry hall, was elegantly appointed. Jessica mused that despite Lord Gordon's condemnation of his mode of dress, Sir Brian's house showed no sign of not being well-tended. Blue velvet curtains hung at tall diamond-paned windows on two sides of the room. The front windows overlooked the drive and the lawn with the winking unicorn, and those at the side overlooked ornamental shrubbery and neatly tended formal flowerbeds. The furnishings appeared to be mostly Sheraton, from the striped blue-and-silver-silk-covered mahogany settee facing the fireplace to the slim-legged side chairs near the wall. Several tables, including a splendid satinwood sideboard banded with rosewood inlays, also stood near the walls, which were papered in a suble pattern of blue pinstripes set wide apart on a cream background. A series of blue-gray-and-pink Aubusson carpets covered the highly polished wood floor, while silver accessories and bowls of brilliantly colored flowers completed the decor.

The room appeared to be lived in and homey, despite the formality of most of the furniture.

Adding to the casual air was a leather-bound book that had been left open on the settee. Jessica picked it up and shut it as she took her seat. If the person reading it lost his place, so much the better, she thought. Maybe next time he would mark his place properly instead of taking the risk of damaging the book. It was a good one, though, one of her favorites, *Marmion* by Walter Scott. She preferred the Gothic romances that her father and many others so heartily disapproved of, but she loved good poetry, too. She wondered if Sir Brian had been reading the book.

"You might as well take off that mask now," Lord Gordon said testily, glaring at the highwayman, who had been watching Jessica.

The masked man hesitated indecisively for a moment, but then with a darting glance at Lady Gordon, he shook his head. "Not yet, I think," he said, adding, "By Jove, though, with your leave, I will take a seat. I seem to have gone a trifle weak at the knees."

He looked dangerously pale, Jessica thought, and the light of amusement had vanished completely from his eyes. As he sank with obvious gratitude onto one of the side chairs, he watched the door leading into the hall, and it seemed to Jessica that the apprehension she had noted earlier had manifestly increased.

Lady Gordon sat down upon the settee beside Jessica, and his lordship moved toward one of the tall front windows. He peered outside for a brief moment before turning back and addressing the room at large.

"I say, where is Gregory? His man said he would be with us immediately. I cannot like attending to this sort of business with ladies present. I don't know what I can have been thinking of to allow the two of you to accompany me."

The highwayman regarded him over his mask, a glint of amusement returning to his eyes for the moment. "Can't say I noticed that you were given a deal of choice in the matter, my lord."

"That's enough of your impudence, my lad. You'll be singing a different tune once Sir Brian has you in charge, I daresay."

The highwayman fell silent, clearly giving consideration to his lordship's words. Then he said in a more subdued tone, "I wager you're in the right of it, my lord. Moreover, something tells me I shall do better without the mask, as you suggested earlier." So saying, with his right hand he first pulled off the disreputable slouch hat, dropping it onto the floor beside him and attempting to smooth his tousled hair. Then, with the same hand, he reached back and, not without some difficulty, loosened the knot holding the mask in place, letting it fall forward, then pulling it from his shirt collar and dropping it on the hat. Lady Gordon gasped at the sight of the handsome young face thus revealed, and the highwayman smiled ruefully at her. "I was afraid you might recognize me, ma'am. We met some months ago, did we not?"

Jessica stared at her sister in amazement, but before Lady Gordon could speak, the door opened from the hall and the butler announced Sir Brian Gregory.

As she turned to take her first look at the owner of Shaldon Park, Jessica noted that the highwayman's rueful smile had lingered, but this time it seemed to be directed at the man just entering the room. A look passed between the two, and Sir Brian's dark eyes narrowed slightly, but otherwise he seemed only mildly surprised as he looked over the persons waiting to speak to him.

Her brother-in-law's strictures notwithstanding, Jessica liked the look of her host very much. He was certainly no dandy, and she doubted very much if even the Corinthian set would claim him to its membership, unless of course he was indeed the very apt sportsman that Lord Gordon seemed to think he was.

He appeared to be some five or six years older than she was herself, and he was a good deal taller, too, well over six feet, with broad, muscular shoulders and slim hips. His dark brown riding coat had clearly been cut for comfort rather than style, and though his shirt was white and clean, the breeches he wore above polished top boots were scarcely what her mother would have decreed as proper attire to greet ladies in his drawing room. He wore no jewelry except for a carved emerald signet ring upon his right hand. Nonetheless, she agreed with her sister that the man had the sort of looks that she liked best. His dark blond hair looked thick and windswept without appearing to have been coaxed and bullied into the style, and his face, framed by smooth side whiskers, was deeply tanned, with strong, firmly etched features. The nose was straight and well-shaped, the chin square with an almost stubborn look to it, and the lips twitching now with a touch of humor that also lit his deep brown eyes. The man seemed to radiate an arrogant vitality that appealed to Miss Sutton-Drew deeply.

He glanced around at the group, then spoke over his shoulder to the hovering butler. "That will be all, Fairby." The voice was low-pitched with a nearly regal tone to it that reflected the arrogance Jessica had seen in the way he carried himself. Clearly, she thought, he had rapidly determined by Lord Gordon's purposeful expression that his visitors were in no expectation of being served any refreshment. As the butler shut the door, Sir Brian flicked another, oddly penetrating glance around the room. This time it paused as he acknowledged Lord and Lady Gordon with a brief word and a nod, passed over Jessica, and came to rest upon the young man in the side chair.

"Well, Andrew, Fairby neglected to inform me that you were part of the group awaiting me."

"I don't think he saw me," the young man replied carefully.

"Dear me, he must be getting older than I'd suspected," Sir Brian said. "I should think that the fact that your shoulder appears to be dripping blood all over my house ought to have impressed itself upon him."

"A slight exaggeration, sir. I've got blood on my coat, that's all. A mere flesh wound, I assure you. It scarcely troubles me at the moment."

"Well, it troubles me, young man. How came you by it?"

The others had been staring in astonishment at the two men during this interchange, but Lord Gordon found his voice at last. "What's this?" he demanded. "Do you know this young ruffian, Sir Brian?"

"I know this young gentleman," Sir Brian corrected gently, without taking his eyes from the would-be highwayman. "He is my nephew, Andrew Liskeard. My elder sister's child," he added, "though he was bereft of both parents some years ago." His jaw tightened slightly. "What!" Lord Gordon looked disbelievingly from one to the other. "But he held us up on the St. Ives cliff road. He's no more than a common highwayman, sir."

Though Sir Brian did turn politely when his lordship spoke, his expression was bland, and he took the news without so much as a blink. But when he turned back to his nephew, Jessica noted an ominous glitter in his eyes that made her glad he was not looking at her.

"Is that true?" he asked the young man quietly.

Andrew shifted slightly in his chair as though he would get to his feet, but looking at his uncle, he changed his mind, merely straightening self-consciously where he sat. He swallowed and ran a nervous tongue over his lower lip before replying, "It's true enough. But I took care that no one recognized me, though Dolby at the lodge knew Sailor, I think, and young Michael recognized us both out front. They won't split though, and it was merely for a wager, Uncle Brian. I scarcely need to tell you there was no harm intended."

"A wager?" Again the words were spoken quietly. Sir Brian had not moved any nearer, nor had his position changed. He still stood just a few feet from the hall door, and he appeared to be relaxed enough to stand where he was all day if necessary. Indeed, there was nothing specific about his appearance to indicate that he was hearing anything beyond the ordinary. Yet there was something in the air, some aura emanating from the tall, broad-shouldered gentleman that once again made Jessica glad that she was not the one required to answer his questions.

Andrew's attention was focused solely upon his uncle now, and Jessica was a little surprised to note that his tone became more confident as he explained the wager. "It was Barney Howard, sir. You know . . . old Northumberland's nephew." Sir Brian nodded. "Well, we have both been invited to join the same club at school, the Scalawags. You belonged when you were up, did you not?" Again Sir Brian nodded, and Andrew's confidence visibly gained strength. "I thought so. Well, the thing of it was that we each had to accomplish three unusual feats, the sort of nonsensical stunts we, none of us, would have thought of doing otherwise. Nothing but the merest bobbery, I assure you, but the things we had to do were written down on white cards by the old boys, and we each chose three cards. The wager was extra, that I would accomplish my three before Barney accomplishes his. Stopping a coach on the king's road was my third," he added, unable to avoid a touch of pride in his voice, though his expression remained wary.

"Well, upon my word," said Lord Gordon, staring.

"You may well say so, my lord," agreed Sir Brian without taking his stern gaze from his nephew.

"This certainly puts a different light on the matter," Lord Gordon said with a sapient air. "Of course, the moment I realized he was related to you, sir, I knew there must be some logical explanation."

"Did you indeed, my lord?" This time Sir Brian did glance at his lordship, but his look was an enigmatic one, and Lord Gordon clearly chose to assume that they were in complete agreement.

He chuckled ponderously. "Certainly. Quite a prank, I must say. Imagine the daring of it all. The danger. Why, it takes a real man to pull off such a feat. A bit foolish, perhaps, but then, we were all young and foolish at one time, were we not, Sir Brian?"

"I suppose we were," Sir Brian agreed evenly. "Do I take this to mean then, my lord, that you no longer wish to prefer charges? I assume that is why you came to me in the first place, since you seem not to have known of my relationship with your highwayman?"

"Prefer charges!" Andrew exclaimed before Lord Gordon could speak. "I should think not." He grinned at his lordship, all his confidence and that cocky arrogance restored. "I knew how it would be the moment I explained," he said. Then he turned to his uncle. "You must see that it was just a lark, sir. I was afraid I'd be dished if I took off my mask before I got home, because I was certain Lady Gordon would recognize me, and once the other lady had shot me, I feared that when they realized I was your nephew, they might haul me off to some other J.P. before I could explain thiings. Fearing, you know, that *you* might prefer charges against *her* for shooting me. Only I was persuaded you would do nothin·

of the sort, and since I'm the only one who suffered"— he indicated his injured shoulder with an insouciant gesture—"why, there's no harm done to speak of, is there?"

"Surely not, my young friend," Lord Gordon assured him. "A good prank. A jolly good lark, indeed."

Jessica had been listening to the interchange with gathering indignation, and she could no longer contain herself. Glaring at her brother-in-law, she informed him flatly that she could not believe her ears. "How can you stand there and behave as if nothing out of the ordinary has occurred here?" she demanded.

"Be silent, Jessica," Lord Gordon commanded, drawing himself up and hooking a thumb in his waistcoat pocket. "I told you this was no affair for a lady to concern herself with. 'Tis a matter between gentlemen, a mere prank, and not something anyone would expect you to understand. There is nothing more to be said and no reason for us to occupy more of Sir Brian's time."

"On the contrary," Jessica countered, "there is still a great deal to be said, Cyril. I might have expected you to drop the matter this easily, but I cannot do so. It is all very well and good for you and this young prankster of yours to insist that there was no harm done, but that was through no fault of his. And, for that matter, I cannot agree that there was no harm. Lady Gordon," she informed Sir Brian, getting to her feet in order not to have to speak over her shoulder to him, "was frightened out of her wits. Had she been with child, she might well have miscarried."

Sir Brian was regarding her now with a good deal more interest than he had hitherto shown, but when he spoke, it was still in that quiet, even tone. "Is she with child, Miss . . . ?"

"Jessica Sutton-Drew," she supplied. "I am Lady Gordon's sister, visiting from Gloucestershire. And, no, sir, she is not to my knowledge with child, but that is beside the point."

"I disagree. It would have been very much to the point, had she been with child."

"Please, Jessica," Lord Gordon pleaded, giving up any attempt to bully her. "This conversation is not at all seemly."

"I apologize if I've offended your sensibilities again, Cyril," she responded promptly. "It would perhaps have been better if I had offered your weak heart as a possibility instead."

"Does Lord Gordon have a weak heart?" Sir Brian inquired.

"No, he does not," Jessica replied, incurably honest. The light of amusement in her host's eyes reminded her forcibly of the same light seen earlier in his nephew's, and for a scant second she felt a response in her own before anger took over. "That does not matter in the slightest, sir. Your idiotish nephew had no way to know that such a condition did not exist. Furthermore, his pistol was loaded, and when I shot him, he dropped it, causing it to discharge. It was through chance only that no one was injured or even killed."

"I agree that it was careless of him to drop his pistol," Sir Brian acknowledged. "It was truly you who shot him?"

"I did."

"I see. Then he must have been very careless, indeed." He glanced again at his nephew.

Andrew grinned at him. "No carelessness, sir. She had her pistol hidden in that great muff she carries. I never so much as had an inkling."

"You must be a most redoubtable young woman, Miss Sutton-Drew. Have you your pistol by you now?"

"I have."

"May I see it?"

Jessica reached into the muff and removed the little pistol from the pocket which accommodated it. Sir Brian stepped forward to take it from her, and she noted absently that the carving of his signet ring was that of a unicorn's head.

"Have a care, sir," she warned as he turned the pistol to examine it. "It is still loaded."

"I see that it is," he responded. "A nice little weapon. Did you intend to kill your highwayman?"

"If I had intended to kill him, sir, he would be dead." Jessica looked Sir Brian straight in the eye. "My father would not allow me to carry that pistol until I could shoot whatever I aimed at. I do not miss easily, and your nephew made a good target. What do you intend to do about this, Sir Brian?"

In reply he glanced again at his nephew, who gazed back at him confidently. "What do you wish me to do, Miss Sutton-Drew?" Some of Andrew's confidence faded, but not enough of it to suit Jessica.

"If he were a man of common stock, Sir Brian, he would hang for his little prank."

"That possibility certainly exists, ma'am. But you do not answer my question."

"Here now, Jessica," Lord Gordon interposed hastily, "enough is enough. 'Twas naught more than a boy's prank, and no harm done. We'll drop the matter here and now, if you please."

"But I do not please, Cyril. All this nonsense merely serves to prove how right I was to insist that Georgeanne and I accompany you to Shaldon Park. You and Sir Brian here seem perfectly willing to sweep the whole business under the nearest carpet, and that young jackanapes is sitting there just as pleased as can be with himself. He has no idea of the harm he might have done."

Andrew looked at her in protest. "Here, I say, ma'am, I'm dreadfully sorry if I frightened you."

"Pooh," Jessica retorted. "You know perfectly well that I was not in the least frightened. Not that you gave such a likelihood the smallest vestige of a thought. But I believe in equality," she went on, turning to face Sir Brian again. "Generally that term seems to suggest a belief in raising the lower orders above their stations. That is not my meaning. Certainly not in this instance. But it is patently unfair, sir, that a farmer's son who did what your nephew did today—whether as a prank or not—would hang for his mischief, while you and my brother-in-law merely applaud Andrew's behavior as a very good joke."

"You may safely believe, Miss Sutton-Drew, that I do not so regard his behavior," Sir Brian said quietly.

"But you are glad that my brother-in-law has decided not to prefer charges, are you not?"

"I cannot deny that."

"Well, you will be disappointed then, Sir Brian, for I fully intend to prefer those charges myself."

"Jessica!" exploded Lord Gordon. "I forbid you to do any such thing."

"You have no right to forbid me, Cyril. It is rather my right as an English citizen to prefer charges against any felon who assaults me. Is that not so, Sir Brian?"

"Here now, Miss Sutton-Drew, you can't do such a shabby thing," protested Andrew, sitting up quickly, then wincing at the pain the movement caused him. "It was only a prank. My word on it."

"You deserve a hard lesson, young man," Jessica said, regarding him sternly. "I have no patience with wagers and pranks when they endanger others. Even to endanger yourself is, in my opinion, not only not the least bit manly but witless besides. You did something you ought not to have done, and you deserve to face the natural consequences of your actions."

"Jessica, for God's sake!"

"But, I say, Miss Sutton—"

"Silence, Andrew."

Jessica regarded Sir Brian steadily. "No doubt, as his uncle, you will refuse to proceed, sir, so perhaps we should seek out another magistrate. It would be unfair to expect you to deal with this."

"You underestimate me, Miss Sutton-Drew," he replied, returning her look with equal steadiness. He was still standing quite near her, and though she decided it was no doubt nothing more than his height, there was something nearly overpowering about that nearness. It sent shivers up and down her spine, while at the same time there was a contrasting warmth deep within her. She gave herself a shake, realizing that he was still speaking, that he had just said something about his sense of honor. "I agree that Andrew must face the consequences of his actions," he told her, still looking deeply into her eyes, "and though I readily admit that I had intended those consequences to be little more than a few warm minutes on the carpet in my bookroom, there is a great deal of truth in what you say."

"Look here, Sir Brian," protested Lord Gordon, his man-to-man smile a little forced. "My sister-in-law simply don't understand these matters between gentlemen. Boy's merely growing into a man. Certain rituals, don't you know? Things women never comprehend."

Jessica turned on him indignantly, but the quiet voice intruded before she could vent her indignation.

"Miss Sutton-Drew makes some telling points, my lord," Sir Brian said, facing Lord Gordon directly. "The consequences of one's actions must be confronted, and I am sure that you and I would never wish our position in life to protect us against those consequences when we deserve to face them."

"N-no, of course not," his lordship replied doubtfully. "But surely, sir, you cannot intend—"

"I intend that Andrew's wounds shall be properly seen to," Sir Brian told him firmly. "Then, since formal charges have been preferred against him, he will be taken to the jail cell near my stables and clapped into irons until I convene the assize court in two weeks' time."

"Good lord, man! You'll never turn him over to a jury. 'Twould be to condemn the lad to death." Lord Gordon turned again to plead with Jessica. "Use your head, Jessica. You cannot want such a thing."

Indeed, she did not want such a thing, but Jessica did not for a moment believe that young Andrew would be put to death. Once he was identified as Sir Brian's nephew, it was doubtful a jury could be found that would sentence him to death. Nonetheless, she was certain the experience of being locked up and taken to trial would bring home to the lad, as nothing else could, the seriousness of his actions. She did not put these thoughts all into words, but she made it perfectly clear to both her brother-in-law and Sir Brian that she had no intention of withdrawing her charges.

As they prepared at last to take their departure, Sir Brian returned Jessica's pistol to her. She slipped it back into the little pocket in her muff and turned away.

"Oh, Miss Sutton-Drew, before you leave, there is one more thing."

She turned toward him again, her gaze rising to meet his. "Yes, Sir Brian?"

"I may have some more questions to put to you about this little matter before it reaches the assize court. May I have leave to call upon you at Gordon Hall one afternoon?"

His expression was unreadable, but once again she

sensed some underlying emotion. Not anger this time, but something that was perhaps even more dangerous. Something that made her conscious, once again, of that warmth deep within her. She gave a little shake of her head, as if to clear it, then returned her steady gaze to his.

"If you wish to call, sir, I should not be unwilling to receive you," she said calmly.

Some moments later, in the carriage, Jessica was completely oblivious as Lord Gordon expostulated upon her impudence in insisting upon pressing charges against the nephew of the wealthiest man in all Cornwall. Instead, she found her thoughts focusing upon that man himself. To say that Sir Brian Gregory had surprised her was to put the matter mildly. However, amazed as she was that he had agreed to proceed against his nephew, she reserved her judgment, for it occurred to her that he might have done so merely to humor her or to prevent her from lodging her charges with another magistrate. Nonetheless, or perhaps even as a result of such thoughts, she could not help suspecting that Sir Brian might be one of those rarest of creatures, a sensible man.

Since the days of her come-out years before, Jessica had learned to accept the effect her beauty had upon others, and even to accept having a good many eligible gentlemen of the *beau monde* practically worship at her feet. She had not once, however, had the slightest inclination to accept any of their most charming advances, for she consistently found the men who pursued her to be both boring and shallow, as well as shockingly easy to intimidate with her forthright manners. Though she secretly yearned for romance, still she tended to despise the stupider heroines in the Gothic literature she so enjoyed reading, and she truly believed she was happiest when running other people's lives and households. For some years she had cheerfully made the spring-and-summer circuit from one relative to another, feeling sincere pride in the thought that she was contributing something worthwhile to each of their lives and firmly insisting to herself that she was wise not to clutter her own life with romantic nonsense.

She felt a sense of responsibility toward each of those relatives, too. Her younger sister, Madeleine, had always depended upon her and never more so than after the difficult birth of her first child. And despite Lord Gordon's caustic words, she knew that Madeleine's husband, the wealthy young Earl of Porth, had greatly appreciated Jessica's assistance. The earl was one of the very few gentlemen besides her father for whom Jessica had any respect at all. She suspected that Lord Gordon realized that fact and was a bit jealous. He was also jealous of her influence upon his wife. Georgeanne always displayed more courage when Jessica was at hand to support her, and Jessica believed it was not at all good for Lord Gordon always to have his own way about things.

From Gordon Hall her annual round of relations would take her to London, where she looked forward to spending the Season with her mother's fascinating spinster sister, the Lady Susan Peel. Thinking of Lady Susan always brought a smile to Jessica's lips, for Lady Susan customarily provided the greatest test of Jessica's skills. Not that her household required any particular attention. Not at all. Lady Susan's housekeeper, Mrs. Birdlip, was a veritable jewel, and she was ably assisted by Bates, Lady Susan's elderly butler. But neither Mrs. Birdlip nor Bates had any influence whatsoever with their mistress beyond the confines of the house itself. And having acquired, despite her solid position in the highest rank of the *beau monde,* a formidable reputation as a bluestocking, Lady Susan was active in every worthy cause going in the metropolis, sometimes more active than her niece thought she ought to be. At the moment, according to Lady Susan's letters, she was deeply involved in the defense of a bookseller who had been unfairly charged with libel, which cause seemed to her niece to be fairly harmless. Nonetheless, Jessica always left London for home feeling a little as if she had left a bomb behind her just waiting to explode. So far nothing dreadful had happened, but her visits to the tall, elegant house on the southwest corner of Hanover Square were never dull.

All these thoughts passed through her head now as the carriage rolled smoothly through the thriving hamlet of Marazion and over Raginnis Hill toward the cliffs above Mount Bay, where Gordon Hall was located. For once, Jessica paid scant attention to the breathtaking view and little at all to the cries of the gannets and cormorants that populated the area. Instead she told herself that hers was a busy, complete life, that there was still precious little room in it for romance. Then she felt a rush of warmth to her face as it occurred to her that such a train of thought was an odd one to have been started merely as a result of meeting the master of Shaldon Park.

3

THE NEXT TWO days passed slowly for Jessica. She amused herself by assisting the housekeeper and several maids in turning out all the storage closets and trunks on the third floor of Gordon Hall and in supervising the thorough beating of a wealth of carpets, tapestries, and down comforters. For relaxation she joined her sister in her boudoir for a comfortable coze or strolled with her through the extensive and magnificent gardens, protected from the harsh winds sweeping in from the sea by tall boxwood and yew hedges, and from the sun's harmful rays by a becoming straw picture hat tied under her firm, rounded chin with lavender ribbons.

But no matter how assiduously she kept herself occupied, her thoughts kept returning to Shaldon Park and the two men who dwelt there. The more she thought about young Andrew, the more she began to think she must have been carried away by her unpredictable temper. Though it was quite true that he had behaved foolishly and without thought for the consequences, and just as true that a man of lesser rank would surely suffer the harshest penalty of the law, it was also true that Andrew had merely behaved in a manner consistent with his age and sex. There had been no malice behind his actions. It was likewise true that she would undeniably have refused to press charges against a man of lower rank who, also meaning no harm, had behaved in a similar fashion.

In fact, Miss Sutton-Drew's conscience was bothering her. She was beginning to suspect that what at the time had seemed to be a perfectly rational course of action had actually been nothing more than a reaction to Lord Gordon's immediate acceptance of the nature of things. The thought was a lowering one. Nevertheless, Jessica began to believe that if Andrew had shown proper remorse for his actions, and if Lord Gordon had been the one adamantly demanding justice, she would most likely have championed Sir Brian's nephew. With the assistance of hindsight she was able to acknowledge that what she had seen as brash cockiness on Andrew's part was much more likely to have been mere bravado and the result of uncertainty. She remembered the apprehension she had seen in his eyes whenever his uncle had been mentioned, followed by the growing confidence when Sir Brian had remained so calm. She remembered, too, the fading of that confidence when Sir Brian had taken her part in the discussion. Indeed, as she told herself more and more often in those two days, what she had seen had been a boy uncertain of the probable adult response to his actions, a mere boy whom she had condemned to a trial and possible death, very likely out of spite toward her pompous brother-in-law. Not liking the light in which she saw herself as these thoughts repeated themselves over and over in her head, Jessica began to wonder what was keeping Sir Brian from paying his promised call.

By the morning of the third day she had reached the point of attempting to decide whether she ought to order out her sister's carriage and return to Shaldon Park. The mental vision of Andrew wearing irons and sitting in a dank cell redolent of stable odors nearly decided her in favor of such an outing, but the rather mind-shaking notion that Andrew might not be her sole reason for wishing to meet Sir Brian again stopped her cold. It was a ridiculous notion. Sir Brian was merely a man like any other man. She had no reason for thinking otherwise. Still, the notion nagged at her until she gave up all thought of visiting Shaldon Park. Sir Brian had mentioned that he would not convene the assize court for two weeks, so if he did not come to call within another day or so, there would still be ample time for her to swallow her pride and tell Lord Gordon to inform him that she had decided to drop the charges. It would certainly not hurt Andrew to cool his heels for another two days.

Nevertheless there was relief in her eyes that very afternoon when her ladyship's butler entered the cozy yellow morning room on the second floor of Gordon Hall to inform Miss Sutton-Drew that Sir Brian Gregory awaited her pleasure in the first-floor drawing room.

"Thank you, Borthwick. I shall go down to him at once." She arose from the comfortable armchair near the window and set the book she had been reading down upon a side table after carefully marking her place with a striped ribbon. Then, with a quick, appraising glance in the gilt-framed mirror above the chimneypiece, she decided, after smoothing a strand of light brown hair back into place in the coil at the crown of her head and twisting one of the tendrils in front of her shapely ears into a tighter curl, that her appearance was satisfactory. Shaking out the skirts of her pale blue afternoon frock, she descended the wide stairway to the first floor. Sir Brian turned from one of the red-and-white-draped drawing room windows when she entered.

"Good afternoon, Miss Sutton-Drew," he said. "Will your sister be joining us?"

"Good afternoon, sir," she replied, smiling. "She is resting, and there is no need to disturb her, for I am well beyond the age of needing a chaperon, I assure you."

"I am delighted to hear you say so. I was just admiring the gardens. They appear to be in magnificent form at the moment."

Jessica recognized the hint, telling herself that he no doubt wished to discuss his nephew where there would be the least likelihood of their being overheard. It could not be very pleasant for him to realize that a good part of Cornwall probably already knew he harbored a felon in his household.

"Would you like to walk outside, sir?" she asked. "The gardens are indeed very pleasant, and it was clear from our visit to your home that you appreciate natural beauty."

He looked directly at her. "I do, indeed, Miss Sutton-Drew." There was a little pause during which Jessica sought unsuccessfully for something witty to say before his expression relaxed into a smile and his dark brown eyes began to twinkle. "I should very much like to walk in the gardens," he said.

"As you wish, sir." She turned quickly so that he would

not see the color she felt rushing to her face, but she was aware of him walking behind her as she led the way down the wide, curving stairway to the ground floor and through a large salon decorated in green, blue, and white, colors which seemed to make the room almost an extension of the lovely garden beyond the French doors on its far side. Jessica could hear Sir Brian's footsteps behind her. She even seemed to be aware of his breathing. The sensation was an odd one. She could not remember ever having been so conscious of a man's nearness as she was of his. Anticipating the very moment when he would step past her to open the French doors, she moved aside as though he had spoken to her, and the flesh on her left arm seemed to prickle as his passing stirred the air near it. Jessica looked down at her arm, expecting to see goose bumps, but it looked perfectly normal. Looking up again, she found Sir Brian grinning as he waited for her to pass through the open door.

"Something wrong?" he asked. She shook her head quickly and moved past him, almost skipping down the flagstone steps of the broad terrace in her hurry to regain control of herself. He followed behind her at a leisurely pace, and she was forced to wait for him on the privet-lined gravel path at the bottom of the steps. As she took stock of herself, she realized that her breathing seemed perfectly normal and that there seemed to be no sensation such as that of blood racing through her veins or of her heart pounding against her chest. She was being a ninny, she decided. In a state merely because she was nervous of revealing how foolishly she had behaved over the matter of Andrew.

"Shall we walk through the rose garden?" she suggested. "Because the outer hedges protect it from the wind, we get an early spring here, and many of our roses are in full bloom." Her voice was perfectly steady, and assured that she was in full control of herself once more, she looked up into the deep brown eyes above hers with gathering confidence. When she realized he had been waiting for her to look up, her confidence suffered a slight setback and she looked away again, self-consciously awaiting his reply.

With a chuckle in his voice Sir Brian agreed that a stroll

through the rose garden would be very pleasant. Then, except for the sound of their feet upon the gravel, silence descended between them as they walked along the path, which was separated from the soft, well-cultivated soil of the gardens by a single-layer brick-and-masonry edging as well as by the low, neatly trimmed privet hedges that framed each bed. The silence grew, and Jessica, with a clear knowledge that she was avoiding the topic on both their minds, occasionally pointed out one or another of the more magnificent blooms. Each time she spoke, however, the silence, instead of breaking, seemed to grow and deepen, until finally Sir Brian cleared his throat and spoke firmly.

"I had a purpose in coming here today, Miss Sutton-Drew."

"I know you did, sir," she replied, relieved despite herself that he had finally brought matters to a head. "You want to hear more about the episode the other day, and I confess I have a few things I wish to say on that subject myself."

"Yes, I've not the slightest doubt of that," he agreed. "You certainly must have realized by now that I cannot possibly prosecute my nephew for what was clearly a prank and nothing more. I must say that I admire those principles of yours that prompted you, however unwisely, to bring Andrew to book for his actions, but while I agree that fear of prosecution has no doubt provided the lad with a well-deserved lesson, I am likewise certain that you have come to your senses by now and realize that your brother-in-law was quite right in wishing to drop the matter."

Whether it was his unfortunate choice of words, the mention of Lord Gordon's wishes, or simply the arrogance he displayed in daring to assume anything whatsoever about her thought processes, Jessica found her temper rising and all her good intentions fleeing before her. Instead of agreeing that she had been wrong, as she had fully intended to do, she heard herself telling him that he was in error.

"I haven't the slightest intention of withdrawing my charges against your idiotish nephew, sir," she stated indignantly.

"You are merely being obstinate, Miss Sutton-Drew."

"How dare you!"

But Sir Brian had a temper of his own, and although he did not raise his voice, she could not doubt from the spark in his eye and the visible control he exerted over himself that he was very angry indeed. In the moments that followed, Jess_a began to feel much as if she were someone else watching from a short distance away while two people argued with each other. They had come to a halt on the pathway, and after some moments of point and counterpoint, facing him, hand on her hips, Jessica heard herself telling him, her voice adrip with icy scorn, that his precious nephew deserved whatever was coming to him.

"As you choose, Miss Equal Justice," Sir Brian snapped, glaring back at her. "And once the jury finds him guilty, will you insist that I sentence him to hang for his dastardly misdeeds, or will you be satisfied if I merely banish him forever to my West Indian estates?"

Instead of being abashed by his words, as he so clearly expected her to be, Jessica seized upon them. "Estates, indeed," she retorted. "I have heard of your *estates*, Sir Brian. Plantations. Sugar plantations, undoubtedly manned by slave labor. And here in England you own mines—dozens of them in three counties, my brother-in-law said—and no doubt every one of them worked by women and children, exploited so that you and your nephew might live high and well. I had not thought it out previously, sir, but I know now what kind of man you are, and I ought to have realized that you can have little sense of true justice and would therefore defend your wretched nephew, no matter how depraved he might be. No," she commanded fiercely when he opened his mouth to speak, "do not say a word. It will do you no good at all, for I must tell you that I, like my aunt, the Lady Susan Peel, and our good friend the Duke of Grosvenor, am a member of the Africa Institute and am therefore determined to do all I can to eliminate human exploitation altogether. There is nothing you can say now, sir, that will effect a change in my determination to pursue this matter. I have no wish to see your nephew hanged, but I have likewise no doubt whatsoever that you can prevent that from happening in the unlikely event that a jury ever recommends such a course. Until that moment, I do wish him to know what it would be like to be someone other than who he is, perhaps one of your own mine workers!"

Initially, Sir Brian's eyes had flashed and his lips had tightened in response to Jessica's tirade, but as she had gone on, her tone blistering, his expression had begun to relax, and when she finished, the look on his face was one of wry admiration.

"By heaven," he said slowly, shaking his head. "I never thought I'd meet a woman like you. All beauty and fire, with strong principles, as well. Precisely the sort of wench I've searched for all my life and given up hope of finding. You are truly remarkable, my dear, and must forgive me if I take a liberty. I cannot help myself." And with those words, to Miss Sutten-Drew's outraged astonishment, Sir Brian took her firmly into his arms and kissed her soundly. Though she struggled briefly, scarcely a moment passed before Jessica found her attention diverted by the incredible warmth and softness of his lips upon hers and felt her body responding to his as though it were guided by some entity beyond herself.

As soon as he felt the movement of that magnificent body against his own, Sir Brian relaxed his hold on her sufficiently to allow one hand to move caressingly across her shoulders and then, tantalizingly down her spine. His fingers seemed almost to be playing some sort of tune upon her body, a tune to which her every nerve responded. As his hand moved gently to the curve of her waist, his lips became more demanding, and Jessica suddenly felt as if her entire body were swelling, growing too big for the gown she wore. She felt dizzy, too, as though all her blood were rushing to her head, and once again she seemed to be watching the scene from afar as her arms slipped around him and she rose up onto her tiptoes in order to respond more fully to his kisses.

A moment later, his hands now gentle on her shoulders, Sir Brian set Jessica back upon her heels. For a long moment she stared at his broad chest, still feeling dizzy and a little disoriented. Then, almost shyly, she looked up. She was flushed, and her lips were still parted in a near-childlike epxression of wonder. Sir Brian grinned, and his dark eyes began to dance.

"Remarkable, indeed," he said.

"Oh!" All her outrage returned, and the memory of their argument with it, as deeper color flooded her countenance. "How dare you, sir!" she demanded. When his only response was a wider grin, Jessica's ready temper leapt beyond control. Her hand formed a fist almost of its own accord, arcing back and then forward again in an upward right cross to Sir Brian's firm jaw that would have done boxing champion Gentleman Jackson proud at the height of his career. Indeed, her fury seemed to lend the full strength of her body to that one blow, and, catching him completely off guard as it did, it staggered Sir Brian, causing him to take several steps backward, whereupon, catching his heel against one of the bricks lining the pathway, he fell victim to the law of gravity, pitched over the low privet hedge, and landed solidly upon his backside in the soft dirt of the rose garden, the lower part of his legs coming to rest atop the hedge.

Glaring down at him with her hands now upon her hips, totally unaware that she had accomplished anything out of the ordinary, Jessica informed him roundly that she only hoped he might have learned a good lesson. "Some of us," she added militantly, "refuse to be exploited, sir!"

And with that as a parting shot, she turned upon her heel and strode back to the house. At the top of the terrace steps she turned to see that Sir Brian was still sitting in the rose garden where she had left him, though he had changed his position slightly. Having extricated his feet from the hedge, he had hunched up his knees and was presently resting his forearms upon them as he watched her. Remnants of the astonishment that had invaded his countenance at the moment of impact with the soft dirt lingered until he realized that she had turned to look at him. For a long moment he regarded her steadily, measuringly. Then he grinned again. With an angry flounce Jessica turned and entered the house, hurrying up to her own bedchamber and entering it with an immeasurable sense of gratitude that she had managed to do so without encountering anyone on the way.

Pouring cool water from the ewer into her china basin, she sponged her heated face until her senses ceased to reel, and within a half-hour she had recovered her equanimity sufficiently to ring for Mellin, her tirewoman, to assist her in changing her gown, and then to go about her usual business. Thus it was that she was able to greet, albeit with somewhat studied calm, the information, conveyed to the first-floor drawing room directly after supper, that Mr. Andrew Liskeard was below, inquiring to know whether Miss Sutton-Drew was at home to late callers.

Lord Gordon looked up from a stack of estate papers he had been perusing as he sipped his after-dinner port. "Andrew Liskeard?" He turned to regard his sister-in-law curiously. "Did Borthwick say Andrew Liskeard?"

"He did, Cyril," she replied, "thought I've no more notion than you have of what Mr. Liskeard can be doing here. To the best of my knowledge, he should still be in irons."

"Well, I daresay I'm the one who's wanted," Lord Gordon declared, setting down his glass of port and preparing to raise himself from the comfortable chair. "Odd that Borthwick announced him to you, Jessica. Very odd. I shall speak to him."

"Never mind, Cyril. If Mr. Liskeard is indeed below, it is I whom he has come to see. No doubt his uncle sent him. I doubt he has another pistol by him, but if I have need of you, I shall send Borthwick to fetch you." She smiled sweetly at him, nodded at her sister, who was looking from one to the other of them in bewilderment, and took herself off to meet Andrew Liskeard. She assumed his uncle had sent him in hopes of swaying her from her course, and she was determined to be as firm with the boy as she had been with the man. Indeed, her temper was slightly ruffled at the thought that Sir Brian might think she could be so easily dissuaded that a mere lad scarcely dry behind the ears could accomplish it.

Andrew awaited her in the garden saloon, and when she entered, he took two steps toward her, then hesitated, watching her warily. "I . . . I hoped you would see me," he said hastily.

There was no sign of the cocky arrogance that had irritated her earlier. Instead, his expression put her so forcibly in mind of a mischievous puppy who knows it had done wrong and isn't sure whether or not it is to be kicked that Jessica felt her temper melting away.

"I hope you are completely recovered from your wound," she said gently.

He moved his left arm easily. "Scarcely a twinge, ma'am, assure you."

Jessica nodded, glad he had not been seriously injured. "Why did you wish to see me?"

"To apologize," he answered. "I realize that I was a complete gudgeon, that what I did could have had serious consequences. You were right to be as angry as you were with me."

"I daresay your uncle knows you are here," she said conversationally.

"He sent me." The young man met her steady gaze. "I would have come anyway, Miss Sutton-Drew. I've had a deal of time to think, over these past few days, and it didn't take Uncle Brian's orders to bring me here. I hope you believe that."

"I do," she said, smiling at him. He went on, earnestly explaining the l son he had learned and assuring her just as earnestly that besides leaving him to the discomfort of a jail cell for three days' time, his uncle has torn a proper strip off him for his prank, but Jessica listened with only half an ear. It occurred to her that although she ought to have been angry that Sir Brian had acted in opposition to her wishes, she was in fact relieved that the responsibility for Andrew's fate was no longer laid upon her doorstep.

"And I had the devil's own time finding *Marmion* again, because one of the housemaids put it back on the wrong bookshelf after you'd closed it," Andrew concluded, breaking into her thoughts. Then, after a brief pause, he said, "So what shall I tell him?"

"Tell whom? I'm frightfully sorry, Andrew," she apologized. "I'm afraid something distracted me."

He smiled a little forlornly. "Uncle Brian said the decision is still up to you, ma'am. About the assizes."

"You mean he still means to have you up on my charges unless I formally withdraw them?"

"Of course, ma'am. It's the law, and Uncle Brian sets great store by the law. I can tell you," he added ruefully and with a reminiscent gleam in his eye, "that I wish I had realized how much store he sets by it before I ever got myself involved in this tangle."

Jessica let out a long breath, unsure as to how this turn of events affected her. But as she was examining her own feelings, she suddenly realized that her companion was regarding her with a great deal of anxiety. "Oh, Andrew, forgive me," she said quickly, compassionately. "Of course I shall withdraw the charge. I never meant it, you know. Not once I realized you were not a hardened criminal. I'm afraid I was guilty of the very prejudice—in reverse, you know—that I accused your uncle and Lord Gordon of harboring. And then my dreadful temper got the better of me, and . . . well, that is all quite unimportant to you, is it not? You will tell your uncle for me to do as he thinks best in the matter. I do hope he was not too harsh with you."

Andrew grinned, looking not unlike his uncle when he did so. "To say that he was mad as fire, ma'am, would still be to understate the case. I could scarcely stand upon my feet when he had done with me." Noting her shocked expression, he added hastily, "No, no, my uncle ceased long ago to punish me physically for my misdeeds. Which is fortunate indeed, since I am a deal too old for whipping and he has the good fortune to be one of the foremost amateur pugilists in England. The reason I found it difficult to stand is simply that he has a way with words that turns my knees to pudding. And he doesn't even raise his voice."

Andrew grimaced at the memory of his private confrontation with his uncle, but once again Jessica's thoughts had wandered. She, too, was remembering such a confrontation, and the information that Sir Brian was thought to be an outstanding man in the ring brought a smile to her lips as the vision of him thumping to his backside in the rose garden danced merrily through her mind.

Andrew left some moments later, and Jessica returned to the first-floor drawing room to report to Lord and Lady Gordon that she had agreed to withdraw her charge. Lord Gordon expressed vociferous approval, and her ladyship also appeared to be relieved. Jessica wondered what Sir Brian's reaction would be.

She expected that he might call the next day to extend his gratitude, and when he did not, she began to watch the post, thinking he might send a note. When none was forthcoming, she began to wonder whether she would see him again at all. Possibly, she thought, he would simply remove to London, where the annual social Season was soon to get under way. The thought, since she did not intend to go to the metropolis for some weeks yet herself, was a rather daunting one.

In order to restore her senses to their usual calm state, she decided some three or four days after Andrew's visit to accompany her sister to visit some of the Gordon tenants. There had been an outbreak of measles in one family, and Lady Gordon meant to take baskets of food and assure herself that the physician from Marazion had visited the household. The young mother, looking worn and bedraggled, greeted the two women with sincere gratitude and informed her ladyship that Dr. Hallworthy had indeed been to call and had given her all the proper instructions. Since she seemed to be more concerned about her husband's comfort in a household of sick children than about the children themselves, Lady Gordon was reassured that none of the invalids was in any particular danger and climbed back into the carriage beside Jessica with a cheerful smile.

"There, that's done, then," she said.

Jessica chuckled. "The role of Lady Bountiful becomes you, Georgie."

"I enjoy it," replied her sister frankly. "You remember how I used to beg to go with Mama whenever she visited the tenants. You hated it. Said they ought to do for each other and not depend so much upon their landlord."

"I know better now," Jessica said. "I used to believe that things would be better if the lower classes refused to be dependent upon their betters, if they stood on their own. But I'm no longer so certain that that is true. Now I fight to make the men in control do right by their dependents."

"Do you really, Jess? I thought you mostly spent your time in London trying to keep Aunt Susan out of the briars."

Grinning, Jessica admitted the truth of her sister's statement. "I suppose I do spend most of my time that way. But I doubt anyone could be in Aunt Susan's company for very long before learning that there is a great deal of good left to be done in this world of ours. I've scarcely the energy she seems to have, or the motivation, but there are times when I wish I could be as involved as she is in something I believed in.''

"Well, I know that Papa certainly thinks Aunt Susan is a deal too busy. I've heard him give thanks time out of number for the fact that Grandpapa had the good sense to arrange his marriage with Mama and not with her elder sister. Really, Jess, everyone agrees that you would do better to go to more parties and fewer meetings of the Africa Institute and the Society to End the Employment of Climbing Boys. Those groups rarely accomplish anything.''

"I think they will accomplish a great deal in time, Georgie.''

They rode in silence for some moments, and Jessica stared idly out the window at the passing countryside. They were on the cliff road traveling now along the southwest side of Mount's Bay. The view of the rolling blue waters of the bay below was wonderful and one of which Jessica never grew tired. The steady rocking of the carriage and the rhythmic movement of the distant water became almost hypnotic, so when the carriage suddenly lurched to a stop, Jessica started much as though she had been sharply wakened from a nap. Lady Gordon reached for a strap to steady herself, paling as the memory of the highwayman only days before flashed through her mind. Jessica, watching her, knew exactly what she was thinking, but hearing a feminine voice among those raised outside, was able to comfort her.

"That is no highwayman, Georgie. Something is going forward, no doubt in the road itself, which is why we have come to a halt. I'll see what it is.''

"Oh, Jess, do you think you should?''

"Don't be a goose. If Peters has come out without his blunderbuss again, which I very much doubt after the tongue-lashing Cyril gave him, rest assured that I have not.'' Smugly she hefted the chinchilla muff, which had been skillfully mended so that no sign of the tiny bullet hole remained. "Lady Bountiful, meet Lady Intrepid.''

Grinning at the sally, Georgeanne relaxed against the plush squabs. "Very well, dearest, but do nothing foolish, I beg you.''

"I won't.'' Pushing open the door, Jessica let down the

steps for herself and descended to the road to see that there was indeed a contretemps going forward. A burly man was confronting a young girl smack in the middle of the road, and there was no way, with the cliff on one side and the ditch on the other, by which the coach might pass unless the pair were to move. Just as that thought passed through Jessica's mind, the man grabbed the young girl by the arm, pushing her toward the cliff.

"Here, stop that before you push her right over!" Jessica cried without thinking.

The man turned toward her, glaring. "And just who the de'il d'ye think ye might be?" he demanded.

"That is no concern of yours," Jessica replied, "but I suggest that you take your hands from that young lady. I can plainly see that she is no relation of yours, so you can have no right to be manhandling her on a public road."

The girl looked at her gratefully. Blond, blue-eyed, and petite, she was well dressed and appeared to be a gentlewoman with approximately seventeen summers to her credit, while the man was rough-clad, middle-aged, and clearly of the working class. The girl, ignoring the fact that the man still held her arm in a cruel grip, spoke to Jessica.

"He works in one of my father's mines, ma'am, and he is displeased with the conditions there. He accosted me here on the road in hopes of using me to convince my father to effect changes at the mine." Her voice was cultured and gentle, but the sound of it seemed to exacerbate the miner's temper.

He gave her a shake. "What's between us is between us, missy, so you shut yer yap, and jest be lettin' these folks move on by."

Jessica stepped forward to interfere, her attention so focused upon the pair in the roadway that she quite failed to hear approaching hoofbeats. The sound of the quiet voice behind her arrested her midstep, however.

"Take nothing from that muff except your hand, my girl," Sir Brian warned her sternly.

4

TAKING A DEEP breath to steady her nerves, Jessica turned to see that both Sir Brian and Andrew Liskeard had ridden up behind the coach. Sir Brian dismounted and handed his reins to his nephew without taking his eyes from Jessica.

"Good day to you, sir," she said. "Our coach could not pass, so I got down to see if there was some difficulty, and discovered this fellow browbeating that young lady."

" 'Ere now," protested the burly miner, "this b'ain't no affair o' yourn. Jest git on about yer business 'n leave me t' mine."

Jessica whirled on him. "You have no business to accost this lady, my good man. If you have a grievance, there are surely more proper ways by which you can make it known."

"Now, lookee 'ere, me fine lady, ye've no right t' go puttin' yer nose inta other folks' affairs, so unless—"

"Hayle, isn't it?" interposed Sir Brian quietly.

The miner snapped around, lifting his fists. "Aye, 'n what if it is? Ye'd best keep yer nose clean, too, me fine gent, 'er I'll gi'e ye pepper."

Sir Brian stepped in front of Jessica. "I shouldn't attempt it if I were you." His voice was very soft, but whether it was as a result of his words or something in his attitude, the burly man dropped his fists and adopted a sulky expression. After a brief silence Sir Brian continued calmly, "I thought I'd recognized you. A good many of my men have a high regard for your judgment, Hayle. If there is a problem at St. Erth mines, I'm certain Sir Warren will listen to anything you have to say to the purpose, but not if you inconvenience his daughter."

The calm tone had its effect, though the miner remained truculent. "Fac' is, 'e don't listen. Mine's unsafe, 'n 'e knows it. Thought maybe Miss Janet 'ere could make 'im listen if she unnerstood the trouble. Didn't mean t' frighten t' lass.''

Stepping forward impulsively, Jessica opened her mouth to protest that it had looked very much to her as though the man's primary purpose had been to frighten the wits out of the girl, but Sir Brian's firm hand upon her shoulder silenced her even before he spoke.

''I'm certain you had no such intention,'' he said, still in that calm tone. ''But you did frighten her, nevertheless. If you feel that you cannot get a fair hearing at St. Erth, come and talk to me. You'll find me at Shaldon Park nearly any evening until I leave for London. If you can convince me that a problem truly exists, I will speak to Sir Warren for you.''

The miner regarded him searchingly for a long moment. Then he grunted, ''Fair enow. I'll come, right soon.'' With that, to Jessica's amazement, he turned on his heel and strode away.

Young Janet ran up to Sir Brian and took his hand, squeezing it. ''Oh, thank you, sir. I cannot tell you how that man frightened me.''

''Then perhaps you might tell me how it comes about that you are wandering upon a public road unattended, Miss St. Erth.'' His tone was stern now, and she looked up at him, her soft pink lips forming an O.

''I . . . I have been visiting a friend near Mousehole,'' she said hesitantly. ''My maid was to have come with me, but she had the toothache and was feeling poorly, so I left her at home. I do not ride, you see, but it is not a long walk. I never thought . . .'' Her voice faded away entirely when Sir Brian's expression did not soften. ''Must you tell Papa?'' she asked in a small voice, her eyes very wide. ''He will be in such a taking, for he is very strict about that sort of thing, you know.''

Sir Brian appeared to consider the matter for a moment or two, while young Janet regarded him anxiously. At last the firm line of his lips softened. ''I think you have learned a good lesson from this incident,'' he said then, ''so if you do not care to mention the incident to your father, I see no reason why I should do so.''

''Oh, no, I shall say nothing at all!''

"Excellent. Then my nephew and I shall see you safely home. You know Mr. Liskeard, I trust?"

She blushed rosily and cast a shy glance toward Andrew, still sitting astride Sailor. "Oh, yes," she said.

"Good. Andrew, take her up before you and start toward St. Erth's. I shall overtake you in a few moments."

Andrew agreed with alacrity, and a few moments later Sir Brian drew Jessica a little away from the coach. "You are lucky I came along when I did," he said quietly.

"Why?" she asked. "It must always be pleasant to see you, sir, but since I had my sister's coachman and an armed guard with me, not to mention my pistol, I was scarcely in any danger. I daresay that amongst us all, we should have convinced that idiotish man to unhand Miss St. Erth without your assistance."

"If you had been so foolish as to let that fellow see your pistol, you might have lived to be very sorry for it, my girl," was the curt response. "I doubt he would have thought much of it, and then what would you have done? Would you have shot him down where he stood?"

Jessica had been enjoying herself. It had not occurred to her that she might have had any difficulty rescuing Janet St. Erth from the miner, but Sir Brian's question gave her food for thought. It also made her a little uncomfortable. The truth was that she didn't think she could have shot the miner. Certainly not while Miss St. Erth stood so close to him. She looked up at Sir Brian uncertainly, aware that her knees felt a little weak.

"There was still the guard, sir."

"True, but the mistake you made was in challenging Hayle in the first place. You attacked him and his actions, instead of trying to discover why he was accosting Miss St. Erth. He was bound to react violently."

"Well, I could scarcely pass by such a scene, even if they hadn't been blocking the road."

"Exactly why I said it was lucky Andrew and I came along."

The regal arrogance was there again, in both his tone and stance, making Jessica long to slap him. But his nearness was having its usual effect upon her, as well, and the mixture of feelings was confusing. She glared at him.

"I don't know what you accomplished," she retorted,

"except to delay whatever violence that man is capable of. I would not have let him hurt that poor girl, so you did nothing more in that respect than I'd have done myself. You just led him to believe you might be able to help him. He'll be angrier than ever when he discovers you're no more than another mine owner."

"He knows who I am," Sir Brian said.

"Well, then he must have seen that he was outnumbered, because I can't believe he thinks he can get any help from another such as his own master."

Sir Brian made no further attempt to convince her, merely giving her a straight look that added to her discomfiture before handing her back into the carriage. Then, pausing only long enough pay his respects to Lady Gordon, he mounted his horse and rode off after Andrew and Miss St. Erth. Jessica watched him go, then nearly snapped off poor Lady Gordon's nose a moment later for remarking that Sir Brian's arrival had been most timely.

It was not until some time later, when she was safely alone in her own bedchamber, that Jessica allowed herself to consider the episode more objectively. Very few moments of thought were necessary before she came to the conclusion that Sir Brian had indeed defused an explosive situation. Remembering how easily Hayle's aggressive attitude had fired her own quick temper, she realized that at the very least an undignified shouting match would have arisen from their confrontation. At the worst there might well have been violence. Instead, Sir Brian had managed to effect a peaceful outcome. Of course, there might still be trouble if he could do nothing to help Hayle, but he had at least seen to it that Miss St. Erth would say nothing to her father about being accosted. That had been rather clever of him, she thought.

She had more than one reason to think about Sir Brian in the weeks ahead, for both he and his nephew became frequent visitors at Gordon Hall, and even accepted an occasional invitation to dine, a fact which gratified Lord and Lady Gordon rather more than it pleased Jessica. She had expected to find her first meeting with Sir Brian after the business with Hayle to be a trifle strained, but it was not. Sir Brian was perfectly affable, soon putting her at ease with his charming ways.

Miss Sutton-Drew was rapidly becoming convinced that Sir Brian had indeed determined to fix her interest in himself, and she was wary of him as a result. He certainly did not seem to be the sort of worshipful puppy she had met so often before, nor—which would have been much worse—was he a fool. Still, she had long since convinced herself that she was destined to be a spinster, and she tended to question the motives of anyone who appeared to encourage her in the pursuit of any other course. As a consequence she kept her distance as much as she was able to do so. Nonetheless, she was aware of Sir Brian no matter how many other people were in the room when he was present. He stirred something within her, and she seemed to have no defenses against whatever it was.

She heard nothing further about Miss St. Erth or the man Hayle, and finally, when her curiosity could bear it no longer, she asked Andrew if he knew anything about the matter. He had begun treating Gordon Hall nearly as a second home, just as though he had never had the temerity to hold up his lordship's carriage, and that afternoon he had come alone, complaining that there was nothing to do at home because his uncle was busy with the assizes. Jessica bore him off to sit upon a stone bench on the windward side of the tall yew hedges, where they could watch the waves roll in on the beach far below, before she put her question to him.

"Oh, Uncle Brian took care of that business," Andrew replied glibly. "Sir Warren's got some devilish nipcheese notions, but everything is all right and tight now. I have seen Janet . . . that is, Miss St. Erth, a time or two since that day, you know, and she tells me Hayle sought her out, once matters were in hand, to apologize for his rudeness."

"Goodness, that must have surprised her," Jessica said, smiling vaguely but thinking of Sir Brian, wondering how he had managed to make a man like Sir Warren attend to the dangers of his mine.

"Well, I daresay," Andrew went on, unaware of her wandering thoughts, "but she is so full of plans for her first Season in London, you know, that she really said very little about it. Isn't it odd, Miss Sutton-Drew, how girls one once thought of as pests grow up to be rather dashing and pretty?"

"Miss St. Erth is certainly pretty," Jessica agreed absently.

"Well, I should say so," he returned with fervor. He then went on to read Jessica a catalog of the girl's points, much as he might have done for a favorite horse, but she managed to keep her countenance and to pretend to listen with keen interest. It occurred to her that she might well be subjected to many such discussions until Lady St. Erth bore her charming daughter off to London, since Andrew had fallen into the habit of calling at Gordon Hall almost daily. However, within two days an event occurred that put Miss St. Erth straight out of the lad's head.

Jessica was returning to the house from the stables, having ridden out with her groom for some well-needed exercise, when she heard the quick clatter of hooves on the drive. Turning, she beheld young Mr. Liskeard astride Sailor, balancing what appeared to be a pile of wet laundry across the saddle bow before him. As he drew to a halt beside her, the pile of laundry moved.

"Andrew, what on earth!"

The lad was frowning anxiously. "It's a lady, Miss Sutton-Drew, a young lady. I discovered her, exhausted, lying all aheap on the beach near the south end of Mount's Bay. She must have nearly drowned."

"Merciful heavens. Who is she?"

"I haven't the faintest idea. I can't seem to make her understand a word I say to her, and she hasn't spoken. Where shall I take her, Miss Sutton-Drew? I can't take her home. We're all men there. It wouldn't be proper. I thought perhaps Lady Gordon—"

"Good gracious, Andrew, you should have taken the poor thing to the nearest inn. Bring her inside quickly. We've got to get her warmed up before she catches her death."

With Andrew carrying the stranger, Jessica led the way into the house, directing the housekeeper to show young Mr. Liskeard to a bedchamber where he could desposit his burden and to cause a fire to be kindled there. "Also, you had better find the poor thing some dry clothes, Mrs. Borthwick, and some warm broth, perhaps."

Just then the young woman stirred in Andrew's arms and opened her eyes. They were brown, a few shades lighter than her damp hair. Her skin was darkly tanned, and she appeared to be quite slim, though rather full-bosomed. Her lips were full and well-shaped. As she looked around the entryway of Gordon Hall, her eyes seemed to widen with fear and her lips parted to emit a low cry.

"You're safe," Andrew said gently.

She gazed up at him, then stared at Jessica, then at plump Mrs. Borthwick, before she began to struggle weakly in Andrew's arms.

"Be still," he said. "You are safe."

She did not seem to understand him at all, and a moment later, in a high-pitched, nearly wailing voice, she spoke rapidly. It was the others' turn to stare, for the words pouring from her mouth were, to their ears, at any rate, complete gibberish.

Lady Gordon rushed into the hallway from the garden saloon. "What on earth . . . ?" She looked first at Andrew's burden and then at Jessica.

"I haven't the faintest notion," the latter replied. "Andrew found this young woman on the beach. She is wet and cold, so he brought her here, knowing we would help her. Unfortunately she does not appear to be English and does not seem to understand what we say to her."

"Well, she still needs to get dry and warm," Lady Gordon said firmly. "Take her upstairs, Andrew. Mrs. Borthwick will show you. Perhaps if you soothe her the way one would soothe a wild bird, it would help."

He nodded gratefully, then began to murmur soft nonsense to the girl as he followed Mrs. Borthwick up the wide stairway. The girl seemed to settle more quietly into his arms as he spoke.

Jessica looked at her sister. "You handled that very well, Georgie."

Lady Gordon straightened a little, smiling. "Yes, I did, did I not? I expect it comes of playing Lady Bountiful so often. One learns what to do in certain circumstances."

"You speak as though a refugee washing up on the beach is a common occurrence," Jessica teased.

"No, of course not," Georgeanne said with dignity. "It is simply a matter of using one's common sense and doing the most important thing first. It was perfectly clear that the most important thing was to get the poor creature dry and warm with some nourishing English food in her."

"You are a good person, Georgie, but something feels odd in all this."

"Time enough to sort it out once she's on her feet again," Lady Gordon said practically. Then, with a spark of mischief in her eye, she added, "Perhaps you ought to seek Sir Brian's advice in the matter."

"Don't be ridic—" Jessica broke off when she noticed her sister's laughing eyes. "You rogue, Georgie. You know how I detest receiving advice from that man."

"Or from anyone else," her ladyship pointed out with sisterly bluntness. "I have frequently noted, however, that Sir Brian quite enjoys being asked for advice. Or have you not observed that fact?"

"He has a habit of thrusting it upon one whether one asks it or not," Jessica replied, not without a touch of tartness in her tone.

"I expect it comes of being a justice of the peace and deciding other people's lives for them," said Lady Gordon placidly, "and since he will learn about this business soon enough, you might as well be prepared."

Jessica smiled at her. For once she didn't think she would mind at all hearing what Sir Brian would have to say. It was a puzzling situation. Andrew, when he came downstairs again, agreed with her.

"Uncle Brian will know what to do," he said. "But I think before I ask him, I shall just ride round to the nearest villages to see if I can discover any information that will help us."

Whether he discovered anything or not, Jessica had no way of knowing, for he did not return that day to Gordon Hall. The stranger slept most of the afternoon and was still asleep that evening when Borthwick announced Sir Brian.

They had gathered, as was their custom, in the first-floor drawing room after supper. Lord Gordon sat near the cheerful little fire, a glass of port and a branch of working candles on the low parquetry table beside him and the ever-present stack of estate papers in his lap. Lady Gordon, in a chair on the opposite side of the parquetry table from her husband, worked diligently at her tapestry frame, chatting all the while with her sister, who was attempting to convince a square of cardboard, a pile of gaily colored ribbons, and some yellow netting that they ought somehow to form themselves into the exact sort of elegant reticule pictured in the copy of *La Belle Assemblée* that rested upon the settee beside her. The instructions which accompanied the drawing in the fashionable magazine repeated from time to time the assurance that the pattern in question was simple enough to enable the most inexperienced hand to achieve excellent results. So far Miss Sutton-Drew had failed to achieve anything remotely resembling the exquisite drawing. She looked up with undisguised relief when Borthwick announced Sir Brian.

That gentleman had condescended to honor them by wearing evening attire instead of his usual riding dress, and he looked more precise than Jessica had yet seen him, in black trousers and coat, well-polished half-boots, a white shirt, and embroidered waistcoat. He was not dressed nearly so fashionably as Lord Gordon, who sported padded shoulders and a wasp waist to his dark blue coat, worn over yellow cossack trousers that, in Jessica's opinion, merely gave his lordship the unfortunate appearance of a plump toby jug. By comparison, Sir Brian's height and regal carriage gave him an air of elegance that no tailor would ever achieve for Lord Gordon.

The dark brown eyes met hers immediately, and the tall broad-shouldered gentleman smiled. It fascinated her to watch the way the smile lit his eyes as well as his face. In repose his strong features looked almost harsh, but when he smiled, they softened dramatically. Feeling a glow of gentle warmth, Jessica smiled back, little realizing that her own countenance altered nearly as much as his, making her look younger and more vulnerable, while adding a gentleness to her features that was otherwise concealed by her air of dignity.

Lord Gordon set aside his papers and took snuff. "Welcome," he said, carefully dusting his sleeve. "I daresay you've heard all about our latest excitement. To be sure, you must have done, for young Andrew was no doubt full of his discovery when he returned to Shaldon Park."

"He was," replied Sir Brian. "Good evening, Lady

Gordon. I trust my nephew's imposition upon your good nature has caused no serious problems."

"No, indeed, sir," she answered, blushing a little. "How could she, when she has scarcely wakened since Mrs. Borthwick tucked her up in bed? Do sit down, sir. Cyril, pour out a glass of port for Sir Brian."

"You relieve my mind considerably, ma'am," Sir Brian said, accepting the glass offered by his lordship and taking a seat on the settee next to Jessica, grinning at her when she scrambled in a most undignified fashion to clear away the magazine as well as the odd bits and pieces of her project to make room for him.

"Were you concerned about our young stranger?" his lordship inquired, frowning a little at his sister-in-law. "I cannot think why you should be. Pretty young thing."

"I don't doubt it," Sir Brian replied, smiling slightly at him. "You would be well advised to place a guard at her door, however."

"A guard! Well, upon my word, sir. Surely you don't think that poor young thing is in any danger?"

Lady Gordon's hand flew to her mouth. "Oh, dear," she murmured.

"Nothing of the sort," Sir Brian said. "It is rather the reverse, I fear. You know nothing of her antecedents, after all. This may be no more than a rather complex ploy with your silver as the target, ma'am."

"Oh, surely not," protested her ladyship. "Why, you haven't seen her, sir. She cannot be more than eighteen at the most. And so innocent and helpless. Why, she does not even speak English. Mrs. Borthwick quite despaired of being able to communicate with her, though she did somehow manage to elicit the information that the poor child's name is Kara—Kara Boo is what Mrs. Borthwick thought she said, though we cannot help but think that a trifle unlikely. I believe most of their communication is accomplished through the use of hand signals, you know."

"No doubt." Sir Brian's tone was dry, and he turned to Jessica. "What do you think of the refugee, Miss Sutton-Drew?"

"So far I have no reason to form any judgment at all, sir," Jessica returned primly.

"I doubt that would stop you," he murmured in an

undertone, his eyes dancing. "Will you ride with me tomorrow?"

Color flooded her cheeks, but as Lord Gordon chose that particular moment to demand to know what Sir Brian would advise him to do in the situation, she was spared the necessity of an immediate reply.

"I should do what I could to discover more about her origins," Sir Brian told his lordship. "And I should certainly do whatever was necessary to protect my own, in the event that your Kara is a thief or worse."

Lord Gordon tut-tutted and Lady Gordon protested that she could not imagine that the poor young thing upstairs might be a danger to anyone. During the ensuing conversation Jessica was able to compose herself, so that by the time Sir Brian arose to take his departure, she had herself well in hand. When he bent near to inform her that he would call for her at ten the following morning, she replied calmly that it would be her pleasure to ride with him.

When he had gone, Lord Gordon commented with a touch of pride that they had been seeing quite a lot of that gentleman of late. "Stroke of luck when young Andrew chose our coach to hold up, what?"

His wife, with a twinkling look at her sister, agreed that it was indeed a stroke of luck and then deftly changed the subject. Jessica, attempting to sort out the tangle of cardboard, ribbons, and netting that she had jumbled together in order to make room for Sir Brian to sit beside her, had no idea what to think. All she knew in that moment was that she was looking forward with more than ordinary pleasurable anticipation to riding with him the following morning.

Accordingly, she was dressed in her lavender riding habit and ready to go long before the appointed hour, so when Mrs. Borthwick informed her that the young person upstairs would no doubt like to sit for a spell in the garden, Jessica volunteered to accompany her there. The housekeeper brought Kara down immediately, indicating with hand signals that she was to go along with Miss Sutton-Drew. The girl, attired in a serviceable blue gown that no doubt belonged to one of the maidservants, and wearing her hair combed simply back behind her ears to fall in dark brown waves to her slim waist, seemed not in the least averse to accompanying Jessica. Within a few moments they were seated side by side upon a stone bench at one side of the path in the rose garden.

Trying to keep her interest inconspicuous, Jessica casually loosened the jacket of her riding habit and looked Kara over carefully while the girl feasted her eyes upon the beauty of the garden. She was very pretty and, Jessica mused, she scarcely looked like a thief. Still, it seemed odd that she spoke no English at all. And whatever language she did speak was nothing like any Jessica had ever heard. The girl turned and smiled at her, and Jessica smiled back. It occurred to her then that it was exceedingly awkward not being able to converse with her. When she saw Sir Brian descending the terrace steps a moment or so later, she leapt quickly to her feet.

"Good morning, sir," she called with more enthusiasm than he was accustomed to hearing in her voice. "You are in good time to meet our guest. I cannot introduce you properly, of course, for I do not know her full name, and I must agree with my sister that Mrs. Borthwick's suggestion seems improbable. As to that, I suppose Kara would be as unable to pronounce your name as she seems to be to say any of ours. Still, you can at least have a look at her and see for yourself how pretty she is." His understanding smile telling her better than words would have done that she sounded perfectly demented, Jessica gathered her dignity and turned toward the girl, who was watching Sir Brian's approach with wary interest. "This is Sir Brian Gregory, Kara," Jessica enunciated carefully, pointing at him.

The girl murmured something, then gave a sad shake of her head, as though the foreign sounds were too much for her unpracticed tongue to imitate. Then, with a regal air that surpassed Sir Brian's at his most arrogant, she held up her hand to him.

"I believe she expects me to kiss her hand," he said in an aside to Jessica as he nodded to the girl.

"Or perhaps to kneel before her," she suggested with a wicked gleam in her eye. He shot her a speaking look, and she chuckled. "She certainly does have an air about her. Even Mrs. Borthwick, though she still refers to her as young Kara, or more simply as 'that young person,' treats her with respect to her face.''

"And Borthwick?"

Jessica chuckled again. "Doesn't pay her any heed at all. She might as well be so much air as far as he is concerned. I cannot recall a single instance when he has referred to her at all.''

"I see." His expression was serious, but he said nothing else, beyond asking her if she was ready to depart, and Jessica nodded, surprised that he did not see the humor she saw in the situation. She was further surprised when he indicated to Kara that she was to accompany them inside. It would have been more logical, as Jessica saw matters, to have left her to enjoy the warmth of the garden while they followed the path around the house to the stables.

Mrs. Borthwick met them in the hall and took charge of Kara, saying she had some nice broth waiting upstairs for her. Borthwick approached them just then to see if either Sir Brian or Jessica had orders for him, and Jessica watched curiously as Sir Brian took him to one side and spoke quietly with him. She could not overhear their conversation, but she saw grim respect dawning in Borthwick's eyes as he nodded in reply to something Sir Brian said. A moment later Sir Brian turned back to her.

"Ready?"

She made a face at him. "Hours ago."

"I'm glad to hear it," he told her, looking down into her eyes, an enigmatic expression in his own.

Instantly, all thought of the strange girl vanished, and Jessica felt only warm and alive and excited about the ride ahead. She could not reach the stables quickly enough, and even the fact that her groom rode close behind them could not spoil the sudden magic of the morning for her.

5

THE RIDE WAS everything Jessica had expected it to be and more. When she put her heels to her mount on a long, straight patch of greensward, Sir Brian responded instantly and with enthusiasm, turning the run into a race and beating her by a horse's length. She drew up beside him, laughing.

"That was wonderful!"

He grinned at her but said nothing, merely giving his horse its head and moving on at a walk. They rode for some time in companionable silence until they came to a gate. As soon as she saw it, Jessica turned in her saddle and signaled her groom to ride ahead and open it for them. But Sir Brian, giving her a look, waved the lad away and, leaning down from his saddle, swung the gate back easily himself. With a courtly gesture, he indicated that Jessica should precede him, then followed her, leaving the groom to shut the gate behind them.

Strangely, it did not bother Jessica at all to have her order so casually countermanded. Nor did it disturb her independent spirit some moments later as they rode through a shady wood, when Sir Brian insisted that she fasten the jacket of her riding habit despite the fact that she told him she wasn't the least bit chilly.

"It is not good to allow yourself to become overheated and then to cool off so rapidly," he said gently.

Both the tone and the look that accompanied his words lit that familiar warm flame inside her again, and she looked away, flushing slightly, but feeling a strange sense of security that she could not remember having felt before. As she obediently fastened the spencer to her throat, the notion occurred to her that she might perhaps learn to trust the large man riding beside her to take care of her, that she might no longer have to take that burden entirely to herself if she would but allow herself to follow his lead. It was a notion that was foreign to her, however, for even her parents had encouraged her to depend upon herself. If anything, Jessica mused, she took care of other people. No one but Jessica took care of Jessica. She stole a glance at her companion. He was looking straight ahead, but there was a distinct twinkle in his eye. No doubt she was merely fantasizing, she told herself firmly.

Searching for a safe topic of conversation, she gestured at last toward the stitching on his saddle blanket. "Why does your crest feature a unicorn's head?" she asked.

Sir Brian chuckled. "Mere whimsy," he told her. "My esteemed ancestor, the first baronet, was so astonished to be granted a title that he took the unicorn, that most incredible of medieval beasts, as his signet. No doubt his attitude and the fact that his descendants likewise refuse to refine too much upon the business is the reason no further titles have been granted."

Conversation between them proceeded easily after that, and they nearly lost track of the time, returning to Gordon Hall at last to find Andrew awaiting them impatiently, a middle-aged swarthy-looking man in dark trousers and a duffel coat beside him.

"Miss Sutton-Drew, Uncle Brian, I think I have found someone who can help us solve the riddle of Kara," Andrew said, walking quickly toward them as they dismounted in the stableyard. "You'll never guess what happened."

"But you will tell us, no doubt," Sir Brian said, handing his reins to the groom and glancing at Jessica to see if she was ready to go into the house. "Perhaps your tale might wait until we have at least gone inside, out of the sun?"

"Oh, yes, of course," Andrew replied, abashed. "I didn't mean to fall on your necks in such a fashion. Oh," he added, as an afterthought, "this is Ling Chow. He is Malaysian." His last words were spoken in such a tone as to show that he considered the information to be of great importance, but Sir Brian merely shook the man's hand and introduced Miss Sutton-Drew before leading the way into the garden saloon.

Jessica rang for refreshments, and suggested that they

all take seats. Then she spoke to Andrew. "You were going to tell us how you met Mr. Chow," she said.

"Beg pardon, miss," interposed the stranger softly. "Is Ling, Mr. Ling. In this country, people say Oriental names backward."

"How interesting, Mr. Ling. Do forgive my ignorance. Did I hear Andrew say you are Malaysian?"

"Yes, miss, from Malay peninsula. China, you know."

"No. That is, I didn't know," she confessed. "I fear that geography is not a favorite subject of mine, and I can never keep the Oriental countries straight in my mind."

"Nor I," Andrew said, laughing as he accepted a glass of Madeira from a tray Borthwick held out to him just then. "Uncle Brian is always telling me I should study harder."

Jessica noted that Andrew's words caused Ling Chow to look speculatively at the tall gentleman, but following his glance, she encountered Sir Brian's smiling eyes and promptly turned her own gaze back to Andrew.

"Where did you encounter Mr. Ling? I believe you suggested he might shed some light on our mystery."

"Indeed, ma'am," Andrew agreed, "it was the oddest thing. I have been visiting all the villages hereabouts, you know, hoping to learn something to the purpose—though I don't mind telling you, I had nearly thrown in the towel— and I was strolling down the street in Mousehole watching the fishermen repairing their nets, when dashed if Mr. Ling and another gentleman didn't step straight out of the doorway just ahead of me. They seemed to be speaking the same language that Kara speaks, and I thought . . . well, the fact is, I imposed upon Mr. Ling here to come along to try what he could do."

"How kind of you," Jessica said to Ling Chow. Then, turning to Borthwick, who had stepped back after serving the others to stand beside Sir Brian's chair, she requested that he relay her compliments to Miss Kara and ask her to step down to the garden saloon.

"At once, Miss Jessica."

She glanced again at Sir Brian, but he was watching Ling Chow, an enigmatic expression on his face. He had not said a word since entering the garden saloon, and she found herself wondering what he thought of this turn of events. Certainly his expression told her nothing at all.

Borthwick brought Kara to them some moments later. They were followed by both Lord and Lady Gordon, who, having heard that a man was present who might be able to communicate with their guest, were all agog to discover whether he might be successful or not. Kara entered the room ahead of them, smiled at Andrew and Jessica, then looked curiously at Ling Chow. The dark man, having been presented to Lord and Lady Gordon, hesitated briefly, glancing at Jessica as if for permission to begin, but then he spoke a few syllables of the same sort of gibberish they had heard from the girl earlier. Kara's eyes lit up and she took two or three steps toward him, replying in a stream of babble.

"Well, upon my word!" exclaimed Lord Gordon, impressed.

Jessica looked again at Sir Brian. This time he looked back at her, lifting one eyebrow. She smiled. Then, realizing the others had paused in their exchange, she turned to Ling Chow.

"Can you understand her, Mr. Ling?"

"Indeed, missy, but I not know if I believe what I hear."

"What did she say?" demanded Andrew.

"She say her name Kara Boo. Say also that she a princess."

"Well, upon my word!"

"A princess! By Jove." Andrew looked at Kara in awe, then turned his gaze upon his uncle and Jessica in turn. "What do you think about that?"

"Amazing," said Sir Brian, his tone a trifle dry.

"I vow, I don't know what to say," said Lady Gordon in astonishment. "Just think, a real princess in my house."

" 'Good gracious' will do for a start," said Jessica.

"Well, what else did she say?" Andrew said, ignoring the others and regarding Kara with widened eyes.

"She say she come from Javasu, near south of peninsula of Malay. She Malaysian princess, but actually born in China."

His audience seeming utterly captivated, Ling Chow went on asking questions of the girl and translating. Her tale was that one day while she was walking in her private gardens attended by her women, a number of men from the crew of a pirate vessel had scaled the garden walls, and she had been captured, bound and gagged, and carried off to their ship.

Subsequently she had been sold by the pirates into slavery, first to the captain of a brig, from which ship she had been transferred to another, an American slave ship. There, Ling explained, she had at least found company for a brief period in the society of a few more female slaves, though after five weeks' cruising, those unfortunates had been sold off at some unknown port. Kara, however, had been kept aboard the slave ship for another three months, suffering untold dangers and indignities, until, nearing land, and preferring death to slavery, she had jumped overboard and swum to shore, where, providentially, Andrew had discovered her, exhausted and near death upon the rocky beach.

"Well, upon my word," said Lord Gordon for the third time. "Lucky for her young Andrew came along, ain't it?"

"By Jove," murmured Andrew in agreement.

"That is truly a remarkable story," Jessica said. "Tell me, Mr. Ling, did she actually say she has been aboard a slave ship?"

He nodded. "She say that, miss."

"Pray, ask her what that ship was like. I confess to a rather morbid curiosity about such things."

Lady Gordon protested that they, none of them, wished to hear the gruesome details, but none of the others supported her, and Jessica persisted. Ling Chow relayed her question, listened to agitated gibberish for some moments, then turned back to Jessica. "She say most unpleasant. Much beatings and suffering. Many women and men with very black skin."

"But what sort of accommodations had they?" Jessica inquired. "I have heard dreadful tales about the conditions aboard those ships. Ask her if such tales are actually true."

Again there was a brief exchange of the gibberish. "She say rooms very small and cramped. Women often forced to stay with crew in crew quarters because no room in slave quarters." He shot an oblique glance at the astounded Andrew, than added, "Princess most fortunate in that she suffer less than most. Manage to protect virtue."

Andrew's relief was evident, and the dark man went on, "Last few months she even have room to self."

"I see." Jessica regarded Kara steadily. The girl sat quietly, regarding her hands, which were folded in her lap. "It must have been most uncomfortable for her, nonetheless."

"By Jove, Miss Jessica, that is to put the matter quite mildly indeed," Andrew said, shoving a hand through his hair. "Imagine the courage it must have taken to jump off a ship like that. She's damn . . . that is, she's dashed fortunate to know how to swim."

"Indeed, she is," Jessica agreed. "She seems to be very tired now, as well," she added when the "princess" yawned delicately behind one hand. "Perhaps Mrs. Borthwick—"

"Nonsense," interposed Lord Gordon. "Georgeanne shall take her up herself. A real princess oughtn't to be relegated to the housekeeper's care. Where on earth have your manners gone begging, Jessica?"

She apologized, being careful not to meet Sir Brian's eye. A few moments later, both Lord and Lady Gordon had gone off with their guest, and Andrew agreed immediately when his uncle suggested that he might like to escort Ling Chow back to Mousehole. Within moments afterward Jessica found herself alone in the garden saloon with Sir Brian.

"I believe," he said musingly, "that we should all learn to trust the instincts of a good butler. They are generally infallible. Though I suspect," he added, his eyes twinkling, "that after that little display you find the Princess Kara Boo from Javasu as difficult to swallow as I do."

She looked up at him. "Well, I am nearly certain she is a fraud, but I said nothing for I am persuaded that Cyril will not listen to me. It was the slave ship, you see."

"Ah, I confess I wondered what tipped you off, considering your lamentable lack of proper grounding in geography. Did you never learn the use of globes in your schoolroom, my girl?"

"No, only our sister Madeleine was ever interested in such stuff. I'm afraid Georgie and I are both disgustingly insular. I collect, however, that Malay is not in or near China?''

"Not noticeably, I'm afraid." He grinned. "The slender peninsula our Ling Chow mentioned so glibly is, if anything, part of Siam. Malay is a small country at the very tip of that peninsula and is actually much nearer Borneo and Sumatra than China. What mistake did she make about the slave ship?''

"They are nothing like what she described, I fear. I once saw a model of one that the Duke of Grosvenor possesses, you see. The slaves, hundreds of them, are chained together and forced to lie stretched out next to each other in dark, dreadful holding areas between decks. There is not room even to walk amongst them, the duke said, and the filth is unimaginable. If Kara had been exposed to anything at all like that, she must have mentioned it, don't you agree?''

"Indeed." He regarded her searchingly for a moment or two, and she thought he was about to say something more about the slave ship or perhaps ask something about her association with the Africa Institute, but he did not. Instead he said, "We seem to have a small problem."

"What shall we do, sir? Neither Cyril nor Andrew will take our word against hers and Mr. Ling's unless we can provide them with irrefutable evidence. Cyril has no great opinion of the Africa Institute, you know. He thinks my Aunt Susan is nothing but a mischief-maker bluestocking, and he will never believe that I can know more about any subject than he does himself. And Andrew is completely taken in by that girl. He thinks she's wonderful and beautiful and—''

"In a word, the boy is smitten," Sir Brian inserted dryly.

"Yes, he is, and he is very young," she pointed out.

"He'll age. The important thing now is to expose those two. I wonder what the purpose is behind all this nonsense?''

"You suspect they are confederates? I suppose it *is* rather odd to have two persons here on our own little peninsula who speak Malaysian.''

"If it is Malaysian. I suspect that it is no more than the

gibberish it sounds like, and there are not two persons, my dear, but three. Remember, Andrew said he overheard two men talking. There may be even more." He frowned a little, thinking. "I believe our best course is to keep our counsel until I can manage a thorough investigation into the matter."

"Should I not speak to Andrew?"

"And say what? If he can believe that a wench with brown hair and hazel eyes is a Chinese Malaysian princess, such small facts as we might present to him of geography and ship's architecture will scarcely influence his thinking. With any luck he will become disenchanted with the girl herself before we are forced to disillusion him."

He seemed confident that such a disenchantment was likely, but Jessica was not so certain, and when she saw Andrew the following day, the lad showed not the slightest sign of weakening in his admiration for his courageous princess.

"I have been walking in the garden with Kara," he confessed when he entered the garden saloon to find Jessica reading her book. "You may think she ought to have had a maid with her, but I assure you that I would never step beyond the bounds of propriety with her, Miss Sutton-Drew. Nor would she allow such a thing. And I know I ought to have come round properly to the front entrance from the stables, but I am beginning to feel quite at home here, you know. Pray do not hesitate to tell me, however, if you believe I have erred."

Jessica smiled at him, trying to remember him as a cocksure highwayman and failing. At the moment he looked so much the beseeching little boy. "You are welcome no matter what door you choose to use, Andrew," she told him. "I know that both my sister and brother-in-law are pleased to have you treat their home as your own." That was perfectly true. Lord Gordon had been congratulating himself again only that morning upon his good fortune in having had his coach held up by a wealthy young man who deposited beautiful and no-doubt wealthy princesses upon his doorstep. Her eyes gleamed in appreciation of the memory. "Where is Kara now?" she asked.

"Oh, she came inside by way of the hall door. I think she was a trifle weary. She may be worried too, you know."

"Oh, how so?"

"Well, when I escorted Ling Chow back to Mousehole yesterday, he told me some dashed appalling things. Did you know that the princess has no rights to speak of under English law? If she were a young child, she could seek the crown's protection and thus be accorded the rights of any English subject, but she is not a child, and those men from the slave ship are probably searching for her right now. If they were to take her back to the ship, there is no law that would stop them."

"Dear me, how unfortunate."

"You may well say so, ma'am. And Ling Chow says the princess's father is the wealthiest man in all Malaysia. She is accustomed to being treated with the greatest civility and respect. I say, do you suppose I ought to marry her?"

"What?" Jessica nearly choked, but the boy was in earnest. "On no account must you do such a thing," she told him.

"Well, I think it may be my duty, you know. I found her, and I ought to protect her, particularly if there is no practicable way by which she might safely be restored to her family. Bestowing my name upon her would turn the trick though, would it not? Lord Gordon said it would, when I asked him about it. If she were my wife, she would have all the protection English law can afford her."

"Andrew, did Ling Chow suggest this course to you?"

"Not at all. That is, he did say that the only way she could become an English subject would be if she were to marry one, but he certainly didn't suggest that I marry her. I thought of that myself. By Jove, Miss Jessica, I wish I could discuss the matter with her. I have been teaching her English, you know, but she still cannot carry on a proper conversation, and I don't understand a word of her language."

"None of us does," Jessica said with a wry twist of her lips. "Look here, Andrew, before you discuss that subject again with his lordship or anyone else, I think you should ask your uncle what he thinks about it."

"Well, I don't think he will like the notion at all, but if

you think I should discuss it with him, I will. However, ma'am," he added more firmly, "despite what he says, if I come to believe that nothing else will protect her from being carried off again by those slavers, I shall have to do my duty by her."

During the next few days Jessica racked her brain for a way by which the young man could be brought to see his princess in a truer light. At first, she placed her dependence upon Sir Brian, thinking he would succeed easily in convincing Andrew that there was no need to marry Kara. However, Sir Brian failed and, according to Andrew, merely lost his temper when the suggestion was made to him and roundly informed his nephew that the princess was a fraud. Since he still had no clear-cut evidence to provide, however, Andrew flatly disbelieved him, telling Jessica it was absurd to expect Ling Chow—a mere foreigner, after all—to have a better notion of geography than either she or Andrew himself had, or to assume that there was not more than one style of slave ship sailing the seas. His allegiance to Kara thus became stronger than ever, and Jessica realized that it would take a concerted effort now to persuade him of his error.

The assizes were still in session, and she saw nothing of Sir Brian, which was frustrating in the extreme, since she would have very much enjoyed telling him what she thought of the way he had mishandled Andrew. If Cyril was actually encouraging the lad to consider marriage, she knew it would take a subtle approach indeed to convince him that Kara was a fraud. It would be particularly helpful, she decided, if Andrew were to be the one to expose the Malaysian plot. In order to accomplish that end, she determined to throw them together as much as possible, knowing it would be extremely difficult for the young woman to maintain her imposture if she were forced to be continually in his company. She told Andrew, as well, that he ought to invite Ling Chow to call as often as possible so that he might communicate better with his princess. Andrew agreed with alacrity, and in the days that followed, Jessica began to note the signs of strain on the lovely young girl's face. Ling Chow, too, showed a tendency to speak more curtly and, she noticed, a trifle more grammatically. If anyone ought to notice a slipping accent, she told herself with a mischievous smile, it would surely be Andrew, who as a would-be highwayman had had similar problems himself not long since.

The assizes were adjourned at last, but several days passed before Sir Brian came to call, and when he did, he chose a moment when Ling Chow, Kara, and Andrew were all in the garden. Jessica and Lady Gordon were enjoying a comfortable coze in the cheerful morning room when he was announced, and they both went down to the drawing room to greet him.

"Where is Gordon?" he asked without ceremony.

"Why, I daresay he is in his bookroom, sir," her ladyship replied. "He left word that he is not to be disturbed, but I can send Borthwick to fetch him if you wish to see him particularly."

"I think he will wish to hear what I've got to say," Sir Brian told her, smiling slightly. He turned to Jessica. "Is Andrew here? He said he meant to come."

"Yes, they are in the garden."

"The 'princess,' too?"

"And Ling Chow."

"Delightful. Please, my lady, ask his lordship to join us in the garden saloon." Moments later, Lord Gordon joined the others, and Sir Brian greeted him with a brief nod. "Good day, my lord. I doubt you would relish missing this. The others will be in from the garden in a trice. The admirable Borthwick sent a footman to fetch them."

"Upon my word, sir, is there to be an announcement forthcoming? Young Andrew mentioned his intentions to me, but I didn't know he'd popped the question already. Dashed fine choice, if you ask me. A real princess, and wealthy to boot if that Ling Chow has his facts straight."

Sir Brian's expression hardened noticeably, but his attention was diverted when Andrew, Kara, and Ling Chow entered from the garden. He turned toward them, his lips firming into a straight line as he watched their approach.

Andrew eyes him warily, and there was a touch of defiance in his voice when he greeted him. "The footman said you wanted to speak to us."

"I do, indeed, lad, but first there are some introductions to be made. I believe you are slightly, but only slightly, acquainted with Miss Mary Wilcox of Witheridge." He gestured toward Kara, who gasped, then collapsed into the nearest chair, clutching at her bosom and staring at him in dismay.

Andrew's eyes widened with shock. "No! That cannot be. It cannot!"

"It is quite true," his uncle informed him flatly. "Your princess is no more than a wench from Devonshire looking to snare a rich young husband. She and her cohorts, such as your friend Ling Chow, here . . ." He broke off long enough to turn a sharp look upon the fellow. "His real name, by the way, is Charlie Dawson, and he is an erstwhile miner from the same general area as Miss Wilcox. The two of them, along with a third man named Richards, tried to pull off the same stunt over in Almondsbury only a month ago. I have spoken to people there who will quite willingly identify her, including the parents of another young fool who would have married her in order to offer the protection of his name against her mythical slavers. I've talked to members of her family as well. Your princess is unmasked, Andrew."

"Well, upon my word!" exclaimed Lord Gordon. "To have taken us all in like that. 'Tis a clever piece of work you've done, sir, to unmask these villains. To think the princess you rescued was naught but a common Devonshire wench, after all, young Andrew. Fair gammoned us all, she did. Lucky for you your uncle kept his wits about him, ain't it?"

Flushing with mortification, Andrew glared wretchedly at Lord Gordon and the others, then turned on his heels and strode out of the room.

"Oh, dear," murmured Lady Gordon compassionately. "The poor boy."

"He'll get over it," Sir Brian said in a harsh voice.

"Will you take this pair in charge?" Lord Gordon asked hopefully.

"There is no charge. As yet, I fear they've broken no law. However," Sir Brian added, turning a gimlet eye upon the hapless girl and her cohort, "I would strongly advise you both to have a care about playing this game in future. Others might not be so lenient toward you as we are prepared to be."

"Kin we go?" the erstwhile Ling Chow demanded in a surly tone.

"You may."

"Come on then, Molly," the man said, taking her arm in a bruising grip, hauling her unceremoniously out of the chair, and fairly pushing her out of the room ahead of him.

Jessica turned to face Sir Brian. "May I have a private word with you?" she asked in chilled tones.

"Of course." His good humor seemed to be restored by the departure of Mary Wilcox and Charlie Dawson, and he returned her cool look with a smile. Then, turning to the others, he begged their indulgence. "If you will excuse us," he said smoothly, "Miss Jessica and I will be in the garden."

Lord Gordon gave beaming approval, and her ladyship's eyes twinkled, but Jessica's expression did not soften. For once, even Sir Brian's nearness as he leaned past her to open the French doors did not affect her. He walked beside her buoyantly, his expression one of satisfaction. Clearly he was pleased with himself and expected applause and perhaps even a modicum of gratitude for his efforts. But Jessica had no intention of accommodating him. She was furious, and she waited only until they had reached the bottom of the terrace steps before rounding on him.

"How could you do such a thing?" she demanded.

Sir Brian regarded her quizzically. "I told you I meant to expose that lot for the villains they are. I thought I had done well to unmask them so quickly, considering how crowded my calendar has been of late."

"But to have presented the facts of the matter in such a public way! To have humiliated Andrew like that. It was cruel, sir. I did not realize you could be so insensitive."

He frowned, taken aback by her criticism, and a look of resentment crossed his face. "Andrew will recover, and I could see no reason, once I had the facts, not to make them known. I am sorry if I offended your sensibility, ma'am. I seem to do that rather often. First with my estates in the

Indies and my mines here, then by helping you out on the road, and now with my handling of this little affair. No doubt you would have managed things with far more dexterity if I had just kept out of it.''

"Well, I *was* handling them with dexterity until you chose to lose your idiotish temper and rip up at him over his wishing to marry that stupid girl,'' she informed him bluntly. "And I believed I had made a recovery, too, despite the awkwardness occasioned by your precipitate disclosure of the fraud. He was well on the way to discovering for himself that his princess was no such thing. But that is beside the point now,'' she added hotly. "I should certainly have chosen a more delicate way to disclose to him the facts you discovered than to blurt them out in front of Cyril and Georgie and the rest. There was no need to humiliate Andrew like that in front of all of us. He is young and very sensitive.''

"Then the sooner he grows up, the better it will be for him.'' His resentment was nearly tactile, and Jessica fought an impulse to take a step away from him. Suddenly he shrugged. "Perhaps Andrew is not the only one who needs to grow up. Good day to you, Miss Sutton-Drew.''

To her frustrated astonishment, he turned his back upon her and strode angrily away. There being nothing she could do to stop him, Jessica walked slowly up to the house, but she could not pretend to be very surprised when she heard from Lord Gordon a day or two later that Sir Brian had departed for London, taking his nephew with him.

6

FOR A WEEK longer Jessica kicked her heels in Cornwall, but her thoughts were often in London with Sir Brian. She found herself wondering what he was doing at a particular moment and whether or not he was still angry with her. Her own anger had dissipated very soon after she had returned to the house from the garden.

She still believed that she had been right to take him to task for his ham-handed mismanagement of a delicate situation, but she had learned in the short time she had known him that he was unaccustomed to criticism of any kind, particularly from a mere female—and one, moreover, whom he no doubt believed to take the same delight in spurning his amorous advances as she took in criticizing his management of everything from his West Indian estates and West Country mines to his nephew's sensibilities. Perhaps she had been too critical, she told herself. She had certainly let her feelings about persons who exploited other persons be known. But then, when he had unmasked the pair of villains who had been exploiting them all, she had criticized his handling of the matter instead of congratulating him upon his successful investigation.

He had clearly expected to please her, perhaps even to impress her. Was it any wonder, then, that he had resented her displeasure? As the days passed slowly by, she discovered that she missed his company. And Andrew's too, of course, she told herself firmly. But after all, she had seen a good deal of Andrew the previous week. Of his uncle she had seen nothing at all until he had walked into Gordon Hall to rout the would-be princess. Remembering the moment his name had been announced that day, Jessica remembered, too, the excitement she had felt and the way he had smiled that gentle little smile at her when she had walked into the drawing room with her sister.

Giving herself an admonitory shake each time that particular line of thought plagued her, Jessica would firmly put all notions of Sir Brian from her mind and plunge more heartily than ever into the preparations for removal to the metropolis.

The day of departure arrived at last. Lord Gordon fussed pompously all through breakfast, and Lady Gordon wondered vaguely from time to time what there was of any importance that might have been left undone. When she wondered for the third time whether her woman might not have forgotten to put her favorite French perfume into her dressing case, Jessica laughed at her.

"Don't put yourself in a taking, Georgie. Your dresser is a very efficient woman, and has very likely remembered a good many things that have never so much as crossed your mind."

"Very true," Lord Gordon said testily as he forked a pile of scrambled eggs into his mouth. He chewed quickly, swallowed, then observed that if anything *had* been forgotten, a replacement could always be purchased in London, like as not. "Daresay you'll be wasting the ready as you generally do, my love, and won't wear half of the stuff you're taking with you. Upon my word, I've already ordered two coaches for the baggage alone."

"Well, you might just as well order up a third, Cyril," Jessica told him, "not for baggage but for servants, for Georgie decided this morning that, besides her dresser, your man, and my Mellin, she wants to take two of the housemaids and the youngest footman along."

"Upon my word," his lordship muttered, "we're going to look like an army caravan before you've done. That's five carriages, plus our own."

"We could put black plumes up and hire a mute and pretend we're a funeral cortege," Jessica said wickedly.

"Jess, don't even suggest such a thing," her sister expostulated. "I'm sure even to mention funerals must be bad luck."

Jessica apologized, saying she didn't know what sort of giddiness had overcome her, and applied her attention to her breakfast. Later, in the lead coach, however, she found her spirits rising with every passing mile. Never since the days of her come-out had she looked forward to her

London visit with such enthusiasm. Since Lord Gordon did not believe in rapid travel, however, the journey occupied four days' time. They stopped the first night in Exeter, the second in Salisbury, and the third at a charming little inn in Woking, but by early afternoon of the fourth day, the coach was rolling along under warm, sunny skies through the cobbled streets of London. They traveled through Knightsbridge, up Piccadilly to Bond Street, then along Conduit Street to George Street, and finally drew up before Lady Susan Peel's tall, elegantly appointed house on the southwest corner of Hanover Square.

The house was built of brown brick with red-brick lintels and window dressings, and a roof of glazed tile. Its porch and cornices displayed magnificent Portland stonework; however, the main architectural feature of Lady Susan's house as well as that of its neighbors was the way the windows of each floor were made to look as though they were connected to those above and below in long vertical strips by means of connecting "aprons" of rusticated stone. The windows themselves were glazed with Crown glass from Newcastle, which had a sheen on the surface and a faint bluish tinge that gave them the look of polished mirrors.

Jessica loved the house and its setting. The square was beautiful, its central wrought-iron-railed garden lushly green and mellowed with age, and the view down George Street, boasting as it did the magnificent projection of the portico of St. George's Church across the way, she thought particularly pleasant. She let out a little sigh of pleasure as a Gordon footman opened the carriage door, let down the steps, and assisted her to alight.

Lord Gordon also expressed relief at the journey's end. "Upon my word, here we are at last. You must be glad you will soon be able to refresh yourself, my dear. Not that it's more than a skip and a jump to Duke Street from here. Though it is not my habit, I can tell you, I am looking forward to a bit of a catnap before dinner."

Looking up at the house as her maid and baggage were set down upon the flagway from two of the coaches following in their wake, Jessica realized that someone had been set to watch for her arrival, for a number of green-liveried servants emerged at once and hurried down the stone steps to deal with her boxes and trunks. Turning back to the carriage, she said her good-byes and thanked her sister and brother-in-law for their hospitality.

"Well, but you must come to visit us in Duke Street, too, Jess," her sister insisted.

"Of course I shall. But I'll give you and Cyril a day or so to find your feet before I do. No doubt Aunt Susan will have made a good many plans for my entertainment."

Lady Gordon wrinkled her little nose. "Not merely the Africa Institute and climbing boys this year, Jessica. Do try to take part in more of the Season's activities. I'm sure I can get vouchers for Almack's if you'd attend one of the subscription balls with me."

Laughing, Jessica shook her head. "Almack's is much too staid and stuffy for Aunt Susan's taste," she said, thus dismissing that Olympus of the social world, "and I shouldn't know how to behave at such an affair anymore, Georgie, so don't expect to cozen me into going. We don't live so completely out of the way as you seem to think, but I shan't go to Almack's."

A moment later she left them and ascended the front steps to the entrance of the house. It was not the porter but Bates himself, Lady Susan's slim, elderly butler, who awaited her, his wrinkled countenance beaming beneath his shining white-fringed pate.

"Miss Jessica, how good to see you again. I trust your journey was a pleasant one."

She agreed that the journey had been very pleasant, and he ushered her into the two-story entry hall, the floor of which was paved with Purbeck stone laid in squares with little diamonds of black Namur marble at the crossing of the joints. The hall boasted a gay rococo ceiling, and the cream-colored plaster walls were arrayed with a variety of wrought-iron lamp-holders, link extinguishers, and candle sconces. The woodwork had been fashionably painted to match the walls, but the sweeping mahogany handrailing and uncarpeted stairs at the left rear of the hall, as well as the first-floor gallery rail above, had been left their natural color and polished to a high gloss.

"How is my aunt, Bates?" Jessica inquired as he waved a pair of footmen carrying one of her trunks toward the stairs.

"In the pink, miss. Entertaining a guest at the moment, but she said to show you up directly you arrived."

"Oh, but I should change my dress first. I cannot go to her in all my dirt."

"Nonsense, Miss Jessica. Her ladyship won't mind a bit of travel dust, but she said I was not to let you disappear upstairs without first stepping in to see her."

"Very well, then," Jessica agreed smiling. "I daresay my poor Mellin won't have my gowns unpacked or pressed for a good while yet. You may take me to her ladyship."

She paused to greet Mrs. Birdlip, Lady Susan's plump and smiling housekeeper, then followed Bates up the wide stairs and around the right side of the gallery to the elegant green-and-gray drawing room. It hadn't occurred to her amidst the bustling activity of the entry hall to ask who her aunt's guest was, for she had merely assumed the person to be one of the ladies or gentlemen who pursued the same interests as Lady Susan. Therefore it came as a profound shock to her to see Sir Brian Gregory getting casually to his feet as Bates spoke her name and she stepped across the threshold.

Jessica stopped just inside the doorway as a myriad of emotions threatened to make her dizzy. Sir Brian, having shot a speaking glance at the chinchilla muff, which she carried on her left arm, was now smiling at her in a knowing way, and it occurred to her that he seemed very much at home in her aunt's house. But she was too stunned to return the smile and not by any means certain that she wanted to do so. Not, at least, until she sorted out the feelings warring through her body. The smile and the odd light in his eyes seemed to indicate that he had quite forgotten the difficulties attending their last meeting, but she had not. On the other hand, she was sincerely delighted to see him and none the less so that he no longer seemed to be angry with her. But what on earth was he doing in Lady Susan's drawing room?

As these thoughts passed through Jessica's head, her aunt stood up, speaking rapidly in her musical voice and moving to greet her. "Jessica, dear child, how perfectly enchanting you look. That shade of gray matches your eyes and is particularly becoming to you, and how well the chinchilla trim sets off your hair. Oh, my dear, how delighted I am to see you again."

Presently enjoying her later middle years, Lady Susan was nearly as tall as her niece, but willowy, and she moved with elegant grace. Her graying blond hair was piled atop her head in a style that might have looked haphazard had she not carried it off with such an air of dignity. Golden tendrils caressed her ears and the back of her long neck, softening her expression. She wore a cream-colored afternoon gown that was high of neck and long of sleeve but which showed every sign of having been designed by a modiste of the very first stare. Lady Susan spent her considerable wealth on many worthy causes, but she did not stint herself. Though her house was more than a hundred years old, it was generally in an excellent state of repair, furnished with taste and elegance, and it boasted a number of modern conveniences, not the leaast of which was the valve closet in the basement near the kitchen. And Lady Susan herself was always dressed in the first style of elegance.

Jessica kissed her aunt's sweet-smelling powdered cheek. "I'm very glad to be here, ma'am. You've even managed nice weather for me. The square looked perfectly lovely when we arrived, being so green and so full of flowers this year."

"Yes, and only wait until you see my gardens," her aunt agreed, regarding her fondly. But then she recollected herself with a little gesture of dismay. "But we are neglecting my guest. I understand you have previously made Sir Brian's acquaintance, my dear."

"Yes, indeed," Jessica replied, moving forward to greet him properly. "How do you do, sir?"

"Very well, Miss Jessica. London agrees with me." Unthinkingly, she had held out her right hand, and he promptly took it between his own, giving it a gentle squeeze. She was very conscious of the warmth of his touch, even through her glove, and as she looked up, his eyes met hers, and he smiled the intimate little smile she remembered so well. A lock of the dark blond hair had fallen across his brow, and Jessica's hand twitched in his as she experienced a strong desire to smooth it back into place.

Determined not to fall victim to his ready charm at least until she had some definition of his present intentions, she straightened, withdrawing her hand and trying to gather her customary dignity around her. Her gray eyes narrowed slightly, challenging him. "And your nephew, sir?" she asked. "Does London agree with him, as well?"

"I'm thankful to say it does, ma'am. By the greatest gift of providence, Lady St. Erth and her charming daughter arrived in town not two days after we did." He smiled at her, and this time Jessica responded without hesitation.

"Then he has recovered his—"

"His balance?" His eyes quizzed her, and she could feel warmth invading her cheeks when she realized her aunt probably didn't have the slightest notion what they were talking about. "It would be better, perhaps, to say that he emerged from the sulks with quite satisfactory speed and is presently enjoying his customary sunny temperament."

"I suppose that is the way *you* would describe matters, sir," she said tartly before turning to Lady Susan with an apologetic smile. "Sir Brian's nephew suffered a disturbance of the heart before they left Cornwall," she explained.

"Oh, yes, Sir Brian has told me all about that scandalous business," Lady Susan said as she took her seat again, her expressive blue eyes positively sparkling with indignation. "Dreadful the way some folks take to deception as a way of life. And such a shame that young men must always be so vulnerable to the charms of that sort of woman. But sit down, my dear, sit down."

Realizing that she had underestimated Sir Brian, Jessica turned toward him once she had taken a seat upon one of the comfortable settees that littered the pleasant drawing room. Laying her muff beside her, she removed her gloves as she spoke. "Have you known my aunt long, sir? I do not believe you mentioned the acquaintance when we were in Cornwall."

"Sir Brian has expressed an interest in the Africa

Institute," her ladyship informed her. "He came to see me about a week ago to discover more about our work, and he has been a frequent visitor since." She smiled at him. "As I told him, what with Mr. Hatchard's troubles, as well as all the other little projects we constantly have in train, we need all the assistance we can find."

"Mr. Hatchard? He is the bookseller you wrote to me about, is he not? Owns that delightful shop in Piccadilly."

"Indeed, my dear. The same. It is a most unfortunate circumstance. All on account of the Institute's wretched annual report. He published it, you see, at the end of the year. And now there is such a furor, you wouldn't believe."

"Gracious, but what could he have published that was so dreadful? I vow, ma'am, your letters were never very clear on the subject."

"It was not Hatchard's doing, precisely," Sir Brian put in. "He merely printed what had been submitted to him by the directors of the Institute. Unfortunately, the report included an account from Antigua describing the case of an aide-de-camp to the governor, Sir James Leith. Briefly, the aide is said to have flogged a female slave who was with child. The woman then complained to the governor, who reprimanded his aide, who, in turn, is said to have flogged the woman again. The governor then very properly dismissed the aide-de-camp from his service, whereupon the insolent fellow returned his uniform by dressing up one of his slave boys in it and sending him, mounted upon a donkey, to Sir James."

"Not the most tactful thing to have done under the circumstances, certainly," put in Lady Susan. "Naturally, Sir James was prodigiously displeased. He ordered an indictment of the aide-de-camp to be presented to the grand jury of the island, but they refused to sanction prosecution. Typical of them, I'm afraid."

"Indeed, you may be right about that, my lady," Sir Brian said quietly.

"But what had Mr. Hatchard to do with any of this?" Jessica wanted to know.

"Well," said Sir Brian, "unfortunately, the island's judicial records make no reference to the matter. Therefore, the island's legislature has brought an action against Hatchard for libel. They say they will drop the matter only if the Institute reveals the identity of its informant."

"Which, of course, we have refused to do," said Lady Susan matter-of-factly.

"But if Mr. Hatchard is in trouble through no particular fault of his own—"

"Mr. Hatchard is in no extreme danger," her ladyship said firmly, "whereas our informant would be in danger of his very life."

"That is true, you know," said Sir Brian gently.

They discussed the matter for some moments longer before Sir Brian took his leave of them and Jessica found herself alone with her aunt.

"I do hope you are not fatigued," Lady Susan said, hugging her. "I want to hear all about the family and everything you have been doing since I last saw you."

"Goodness, ma'am, that will take weeks!"

"Then so be it. I particularly wish to hear about that charming young man who just left us. He may choose to think I believe he has a sincere interest in the Institute— for that matter, he may very well be sincere—but he has talked of little other than your beautiful self throughout most of his frequent visits to this house, my dear. You have certainly made a conquest there. And not the sort you usually attract, either. A far superior specimen this time. I congratulate you. What do you think of him?"

"I am not at all certain what I think, to be perfectly frank," Jessica informed her with a rueful smile. "He told me only the second time we met that I was the exact sort of woman for whom he had been searching all his life. It smacked a bit of Cheltenham dramatics, ma'am. I could hardly believe he was sincere. But I must admit his visits to Gordon Hall before he left Cornwall were frequent enough to make me believe he was actually attempting to fix my interest. Then, after that unfortunate business with the fake princess, he left rather abruptly and in a temper. I believed he would want nothing further to do with me."

"Well, he has clearly recovered his good humor," her ladyship pointed out dryly. "I think he is perfectly charming."

"He has certainly shown that he does not hold a

grudge," Jessica agreed, "but I cannot think his interest in the Institute is anything more than a possible attempt to impress me. I accused him of being an exploiter of human flesh, you see, and I think the charge rankled. But it is true, ma'am. Sir Brian is not only a mine owner who employs women and children in those dreadful holes, he is also the owner of vast sugar plantations in the West Indies —a slave owner, in fact. For him to join the Institute must be a contradiction to all he believes. We know well that such men think only of profit and nothing of the sad condition to which they reduce the people they exploit. He may be charming, but he is also the embodiment of all we most abhor, ma'am."

"Oh, not of *all* we abhor, Jessica, my love. And with the Institute's constant need for both money and influence— particularly at the moment, when both are needed to assist poor Mr. Hatchard with his defense—I think we must do all in our power not to alienate Sir Brian, who is willing to provide both. I have accepted his offer to help us, and I hope you will not object to the fact that I also accepted his offer to escort us to Lady Jersey's drum tomorrow evening."

"Lady Jersey!" Jessica exclaimed, astonished. She remembered her ladyship well, for Lady Jersey was one of the leaders of London's social world, an incurable gossip who had earned the sobriquet of "Silence," onetime mistress of the Regent himself, if what Jessica had heard during her come-out was true, and certainly a most formidable dame. "Why, ma'am, I thought you had eschewed such entertainments as hers for all time."

"Well, you are quite out then, for I should never be so foolish as to say I will *never* do something," announced her ladyship, looking virtuously down her slender nose. "Besides, it has occurred to me that perhaps it would be wise to get back into the social way of things, and fortunately I had not yet remembered to send my regrets when Sir Brian chanced to suggest the outing. The people of the *beau monde*," she added hastily, "have a great deal of money, my dear and most spend it foolishly. Sir Brian is quite right in that I ought to be using what influence I still have in that world to convince them to spend it where it is most needed."

There was little to be said in opposition to such logical reasoning, and Jessica made no further attempt to dissuade her, despite the fact that she suggested Sir Brian might have other motives for suggesting the outing. The two ladies spent the evening comfortably at home, enjoying each other's company and conversation. The only thing to mar their comfort was the fact that the drawing-room chimney smoked dreadfully, but once Jessica had convinced Lady Susan that she was quite warm enough without a fire, the difficulty was soon remedied by causing the fire to be extinguished and the windows flung open long enough to air out the room. In her own bedchamber, later, however, Jessica was dismayed to be told by her maid that it had also been necessary to extinguish the fire in that room.

"Chimney smokes something fierce, Miss Jessica," said the wiry Mellin in a disgusted tone, wiping her hands on her frilly apron. "Seems such a well-run house, too, but that chimney's a disgrace, and not at all what we're accustomed to."

At breakfast the following morning, Jessica brought the subject up again. "Really, Aunt Susan, you cannot leave these chimneys as they are. Why, the one in my bed-chamber, according to Mellin, is in even more wretched condition than the one in the drawing room. No doubt you've been too busy to attend to the matter yourself, but Bates or Mrs. Birdlip should certainly have seen to it. I'll arrange with one of them to hire a sweep at once."

"No, Jessica," her aunt said firmly. "I won't have one in my house. Awful men who terrorize children to make them climb up into the chimneys to clean them. The chimneys can stay as they are. Summer is nearly upon us, and heaven knows we won't need the fires then. We can simply wrap up a little warmer if we need to in the meantime."

Jessica dropped the subject, knowing that what her aunt said about the harsh methods employed by the chimney sweeps was perfectly true. She had heard enough horror stories to know that they made life miserable for their so-called apprentices, starving and beating them in the name of service to the community.

The two ladies spent that afternoon receiving callers,

and after the last of these had departed, repaired to their bedchambers to prepare for the evening ahead. Sir Brian called for them at nine o'clock, and though he greeted Lady Susan with his usual charm, he seemed to have eyes only for Jessica.

She had dressed carefully and was looking particularly magnificent in an evening gown of magenta silk, trimmed with silver lace, her hair arranged in an intricate array of plaits and coils piled atop her head to give her added height. It was a style she rarely affected, for the simple reason that it generally gave her the appearance of towering over most of the men of her acquaintance. But it was a becoming style, and she knew she would be safe in allowing Mellin to create the effect on this particular occasion.

The drum was only the first of many such activities, however, for once Lady Susan made up her mind to do anything, she did it with a will. Jessica soon found herself involved in such a whirlwind of activities that even her sister laughingly predicted that she was overdoing it.

"I find it most entertaining," Lady Gordon said as they enjoyed a dish of bohea together one drizzly afternoon in Duke Street, "that you and Aunt Susan of all people are hobnobbing with the *beau monde* instead of sitting through stuffy dinners with the likes of Mr. Grey-Bennett or Mr. Wilberforce and their reformers. I look to see you both at the next assembly at Almack's, dear Jess."

Jessica had laughingly denied the likelihood of such a thing coming to pass, but though she did not go to Almack's, she attended a good many entertainments that her busy aunt had hitherto stigmatized as frivolous wastes of one's valuable time. Instead of the dinners with politicians, and meetings of the Institute or the Society to End the Employment of Climbing Boys or any of the other similar societies of which her aunt was an avid and active member, Jessica found herself enjoying routs and balls, masquerades, Venetian breakfasts, and dinner parties with such people as Lady Jersey, the Cowpers, the Princess Esterhazy, or Lady Prodmore, the latter being a wealthy social climber with a number of annoying affectations, not the least of which in Jessica's opinion was a small black page named Albert. It rather shocked Jessica that her aunt would encourage the notice of a woman like Lady Prodmore, particularly when she discovered that the woman had informed Lady Susan that Albert was not merely a servant but was, in fact, her personal property, a slave purchased two years before in France. However, Lady Susan informed her niece bluntly that if the woman wanted to cut a dash, she ought at least to be encouraged to put her money to good use, since she so clearly never put her mind to any use at all.

During her come-out Jessica had often found the social scene boring and unappealing, but somehow it didn't seem so any longer, except upon those rare occasions when Sir Brian failed to escort them. Her popularity had by no means diminished over the years, and she never lacked for a partner or just someone to talk with, but whenever Sir Brian was present, the evenings seemed to pass especially quickly; whereas, when he was not, the time passed with maddening slowness. It did not seem to matter whether he was engaging her attention himself or merely watching her; Jessica found that, in his presence, she enjoyed herself considerably more than she might have expected to do before having made his acquaintance. He made no mystery of his interest in her, but neither did he declare himself, seeming content enough, for the moment at least, merely to enjoy her company. Consequently, she began to relax her guard. He was someone to talk to who entered into her thoughts and seemed to understand them, and he was someone with whom she might exchange a speaking glance whenever someone like the detestable Lady Prodmore did or said something quite ridiculous. Jessica never looked his way in vain. The smiling eyes were always waiting to meet hers, and that fact alone gave her a sense of being looked after that she had never enjoyed before. And she did enjoy it. So much so that the thought of his West Indian estates and his mines didn't so much as enter her head for days at a time.

7

"I DON'T KNOW what's come over my uncle of late," Andrew Liskeard said as he helped himself to a glass of Malaga from a tray that Bates held out to him.

Jessica poured herself a cup of tea. "Do let Bates give you some of these delicious sandwiches, as well, Andrew," she said. They were seated opposite each other in Lady Susan's drawing room, awaiting that lady's return from the Court of King's Bench, where Mr. Hatchard's trial was going forward. When Bates had departed, Jessica lifted a quizzical eyebrow. "What were you saying about Sir Brian?"

"That he isn't himself these days," Andrew replied promptly, helping himself from the tray of crabmeat and cucumber sandwiches resting upon the table between their two chairs. He had renewed his habit of visiting her frequently, and though he never referred to the bogus princess, he seemed to have recovered his spirits entirely. He grinned at her now. "If anyone had suggested that he would spend his days at the King's Bench instead of at Jackson's Boxing Saloon, or his evenings at routs and balls rather than at the Daffy Club, I dashed well wouldn't have believed it."

"But he hasn't been spending his days at court," Jessica protested. "My aunt has certainly done so, and she has scarcely mentioned him."

Andrew wiped his hands upon a napkin and sipped Malaga. "Perhaps not whole days, ma'am, but I know he is there today, and he has kept a close watch on all the proceedings. That is not the way he generally spends his time in London."

"No, Georgie said he customarily spends a good many hours with the Corinthian set."

"I don't know about that. I daresay he don't belong to

any particular set, you know. But in other years he has gone almost daily to Angelo's for fencing practice and Jackson's for sparring, and evenings he is often to be found at the Daffy or in Cribb's Parlor with the back-room set. This year, besides this business with Hatchard, he's been spending an inordinate amount of time just doing the fancy.''

Jessica grinned at him. "Paying too much attention to his nephew's activities?''

Chuckling, Andrew shook his head. "I don't mind. It just seems odd and very unlike him. He actually chatted with that devilish Lady Prodmore for quite ten minutes at Mrs. Drummond-Burrell's soiree last night. And he allowed her to send Albert—her young page, you know—to fetch his wine for him.''

"But he must be accustomed to that sort of thing,'' Jessica pointed out.

"Good Lord, ma'am, why?''

"Well, he has slaves of his own, after all.''

"Dash it, Miss Jessica, young Albert can't like making such a cake of himself, but he's no slave.''

"Indeed, he is,'' she told him. "Lady Prodmore took great delight in informing Aunt Susan of the fact only the second or third time we met her.''

"But slavery is illegal in this country,'' Andrew protested.

"Oh, no, it is not,'' retorted the well-informed Miss Sutton-Drew. "England has seen fit to outlaw the trading of slaves, but not their ownership. And Lady Prodmore purchased Albert in Paris.''

"Well, but dash it, ma'am, you still oughtn't to make it sound as if she and Uncle Brian are cut from the same bolt,'' Andrew said roundly. "He may own slaves, though he never sees them, of course, let alone has them about to wait upon him. And he dashed well don't keep them all tarted up like miniature sultans and use them to puff off his consequence,'' he added in a disgusted tone.

"No, he doesn't do that.''

"You don't approve of him, do you?''

A delicate pink tinged her cheeks. "It isn't that,'' she said, trying to explain the matter without revealing the fact that her emotions were more than a bit confused. "I cannot approve of the exploitation of human beings merely in the name of profit. We see it all the time these days. My aunt will not allow a chimney sweep in the house, though her chimneys desperately need cleaning, simply because of the way sweeps treat their poor climbing boys. And the same is true in other professions. Apprentices are brutalized, like slaves. Your uncle owns mines throughout the West Country, and I cannot reconcile my liking for him with that fact, knowing that in every one of those mines, women and children are crawling about in the dark, doing work that grown men refuse to do."

Andrew cocked his head, regarding her searchingly. "Have you ever discussed your feelings with him?" he asked.

"I've told him precisely what I think of the whole business," she replied with a sigh.

The young man's eyes twinkled. "I am persuaded you were most explicit, ma'am, but did you ask him to explain his position?"

"What can there be to explain? Mining conditions throughout the kingdom are known to be thoroughly disgraceful."

Andrew opened his mouth to say something, but just then the door from the entry hall opened and Lady Susan swept in, followed by a stout dame trailing brightly colored scarves and followed by a slim black boy of approximately eleven, who wore a green silk jacket and baggy trousers and matching turban with a small white plume.

"Only see whom I met upon our very doorstep," Lady Susan said in carefully even tones when Andrew and Jessica stood to greet them.

Jessica stepped forward. "Good afternoon, Lady Prodmore. Have you met Mr. Liskeard?"

The woman gave a hearty chuckle, holding out her hand to the young man. "I cannot pretend that we have been formally introduced," she said in a brassy voice, "but I have certainly encountered Mr. Liskeard at a number of affairs lately. Wherever one chances to see Miss St. Erth, actually. How do you do, sir?"

Andrew's eyes glazed a bit, but his training stood him in good stead, and he acknowledged her greeting with his customary politeness, merely saying that he did very well.

She cast him an arch look. "With a face as handsome as yours, I don't doubt it. But don't be flinging your cap over the windmill for the first pretty face you encounter, eh?"

"No, ma'am." He glanced at Lady Susan, and Jessica was grateful to note that he didn't seem in the least discomposed, not even by her aunt's twinkling gaze. "Did everything go well this afternoon, my lady?" he inquired pointedly.

Lady Susan sighed. "I fear the prosecution was in fine fettle," she said. "Is there any more tea, Jessica?"

"Yes, Aunt, but it has been sitting here growing cold. Let me ring for another pot. I am persuaded that Lady Prodmore would also like some."

"Can't say that I'd refuse," agreed that lady. "We're running into summer if the heat of the day is any indication. Go and stand by the door, Albert," she said tartly. "Do you intend to be mistaken for a statue in my lady's drawing room?"

"*Mais non, madame,*" murmured the boy, abashed. He moved quickly to stand beside the hall door, which opened but a moment later to admit Bates and one of the maids with fresh tea and sandwiches.

As she helped herself, Lady Prodmore demanded to know if Lady Susan had actually set foot in a common courtroom.

"Yes, of course. 'Tis poor Mr. Hatchard, you know."

"I do know, and though I'm aware that you are involved with that Africa Institute, my lady, I'm not one to hide my teeth, and I shan't scruple to tell you that I believe that man has gone too far."

"I beg your pardon?" Lady Susan's tone chilled slightly, but her guest took no notice.

"No civilized person could ever believe that such a series of events as that described can ever have taken place on English soil," said Lady Prodmore firmly. "What gentleman would ever strike a woman, even a black one, who chanced to find herself in a delicate condition? No, no, my lady, I know you believe your heart is in the right place, but I'll wager you was taken in like the rest of them. That Mr. Hatchard ought to have had better sense than to publish such a pack of nonsense."

"Nonsense?"

"Indeed, ma'am. Scandalous, malignant nonsense at that. I'm sure it will be seen for what it is before long—a malicious fabrication."

"You think the Africa Institute, with members like Mr. Wilberforce and the Duke of Grosvenor, not to mention myself, would stoop to such fabrication, my lady?" There was a dangerous note in Lady Susan's cultivated tones. Jessica held her breath, not daring to allow Andrew to catch her eye.

Lady Prodmore, recollecting herself, gave an apologetic chuckle and a dismissing wave of her hand. "How you do take one up. Of course I meant nothing of the sort. However," she added, "I don't doubt you was misinformed, my lady, and with intent. The purpose is clearly to prove to the British public—aye, and to the black population of the West Indies islands, as well—that those who are called to administer justice in Antigua are so debased that no black person can obtain redress at their hands. That, of course, must be pure fabrication. There is no doubt a plot at hand, and you have merely been the victims of it, as has Mr. Hatchard, which is why he ought to have been more sensible than to publish something without first proving the facts."

"A plot, Lady Prodmore?" Jessica asked. "Are you suggesting that members of the Africa Institute would involve themselves in such a thing merely to establish some point or other about the cruelty of slavery?" Involuntarily she found her gaze drifting toward Albert, listening to their discussion from his position by the door.

But Lady Prodmore had mounted a hobbyhorse, and she did not observe Jessica's glance, nor did she spare a thought for the listening boy. "I would not suggest that *all* the members are involved," she said, "though I do find it suspicious that there has been such adamant refusal to name the source of their so-called information. Surely that source could be protected if the British public knew who he was, so it's pure poppycock to suggest that it would be dangerous to reveal his name. Now I come to think about that, I am sure, if the respectable individuals you have mentioned and others whose names I have seen in the list of members of your society had been present when the question of his identity was raised, they would never have refused to name him. Such a refusal can only have proceeded from some person who was influenced more by zeal than discretion in promoting the measures which your society has undertaken to advocate. Furthermore," she went on in grand style, oblivious to Lady Susan's rising indignation, "I would have you remember that not long since, right in the center of those very West Indies, the inhabitants of one of the largest islands rebelled against their white masters, establishing a Negro republic at the cost of many lives. Could there be anything more wicked than to attempt to stir more such rebellion?"

Noting that her aunt was completely incapable of returning a civil reply, Jessica answered hastily, "Surely no one wants that to happen, my lady."

"No, indeed," Andrew added with equal haste and his own weather eye on Lady Susan, whose color had risen alarmingly. "I say, Lady Prodmore, did you ever hear tell of a fellow called Woodfall? Henry Simpson Woodfall was his name, and he was caught up in a libel business very like this one. Printed the infamous 'Junius letters,' don't you know? Happened about fifty years ago right here in London. Poor Woodfall was in the same position as Mr. Hatchard, for no one ever knew who actually wrote the 'Junius letters.' Could have been that Wilkes fellow, or Burke, or even that Mr. Gibbon, who wrote about the Roman Empire. Famous stuff. Read all about it up at Oxford. Created quite a stir at the time, but never came to much. Couldn't get up enough evidence about Woodfall, though they did convict one poor fellow for selling a paper with one of the letters printed on it. Fined him. Expect all this will blow over too, don't you think?"

Lady Prodmore had been staring at him as if she thought he must be demented; however, his intervention had not only given Lady Susan time to compose herself but had also tickled her sense of the absurd.

She smiled at him now. "Pray, have we not had enough talk about trials, Andrew? I cannot think that Lady Prodmore paid her call with any intent of whiling away the afternoon in such serious discussion. Really, dear boy, do have some more Malaga. And help yourself to another cup of tea, Lady Prodmore. Jessica, pour out, my love."

Releasing a long breath, Jessica obeyed, glad to see that

her aunt was sending out no more storm warnings. The conversation drifted along more desultory lines for some minutes longer until the hall door opened again and Bates, with a near-smile of approval, announced Sir Brian Gregory.

Sir Brian came in, dressed casually in a loose-fitting bottle-green coat, cream-colored pantaloon, and Hessian boots. As usual, his neckcloth was snowy white and neatly tied, and his boots were highly polished, but the rest of his outfit was, Jessica had little doubt, the despair of his tailor and excuse enough to send his valet to the nearest corner pub to drown his sorrows in heavy wet. But, sensing rescue, she was very glad to see him.

He bowed to Lady Susan and to Lady Prodmore. "Ladies, good day. I see you are on the point of departure, Lady Prodmore," he added glibly. "I have come to take Miss Sutton-Drew, who has been feeling a bit down pin—though she has no doubt made little complaint of it—for a refreshing stroll through the square garden, so if you like, we shall be happy to escort you to your carriage on our way."

Jessica had all she could do to control her countenance, but she noted with relief that it did not so much as occur to Lady Prodmore to contradict him. Indeed, she was out the door and halfway down the stairs, the slender page like a shadow behind her, before Jessica realized that Sir Brian was waiting for her to join them.

"I . . . I need my pelisse," she said helplessly, "and a hat."

"Rubbish," he retorted. " 'Tis a fine spring day, so bustle about, unless you wish that distressing creature to return."

His voice was low, but Jessica wasn't by any means certain that it hadn't carried down the stairs. She gave him a speaking look, which he ignored while pointedly holding the door open for her. With a shake of her head, she got to her feet, glancing first at Lady Susan, who was grinning openly now, and then at Andrew, who was staring at his uncle and looking a little taken aback. The expression on the lad's face brought a smile to her own, and she moved past Sir Brian with a spring in her step.

They bade a polite farewell to Lady Prodmore from the

flagway, then watched her elegant crested coach roll off down George Street, before turning toward the garden in the center of Hanover Square. Sir Brian waited only until they had passed through the gate in the wrought-iron railing that enclosed the garden before taking Jessica's hand and tucking it into the crook of his elbow.

"I fear you will be giving Aunt Susan's neighbors food for gossip, sir," she protested gently.

"Let them gossip," he replied. "Will it annoy you?"

Jessica was silent. She didn't think it would annoy her at all. Not enough, at any rate, to make her wish to withdraw her hand from his grasp. When she looked up at him in blushing confusion, his eyes were twinkling.

"Detestable creature," she muttered, avoiding his gaze.

"I hope you don't say such things to Lady Prodmore's face, my dear," he retorted, eyes atwinkle, "though I cannot help but agree with your estimation. She is indeed a detestable creature."

A gurgle of laughter escaped her. "You know perfectly well that I didn't mean Lady Prodmore when I said that."

"Oh? You find her entirely charming, I daresay."

Jessica wrinkled her nose, looking up at him again. "She really is detestable, isn't she? How did you realize we were longing to be rid of her? It seemed as if she had been there for hours."

"Even if it had been only minutes, I knew you would be longing to get rid of her. Stands to reason. Anyone would. Besides, your estimable aunt looked ready to chew andirons into horse nails."

The ready laughter bubbled up again, and she responded naturally to the warm little squeeze he gave her hand. "It's a wonder Aunt Susan didn't come to cuffs with that woman. You ought to have heard poor Andrew expounding on some trial or other that took place fifty years ago in an attempt to keep them from each other's throats."

"I should like to have heard it. I collect your aunt mentioned her visit to King's Bench?"

"Yes, were you there?"

He nodded.

"Well, Lady Prodmore doesn't think Mr. Hatchard

deserves to get off. She thinks he ought to have proved the facts of the report correct before he printed it.''

"There is some truth to that view," Sir Brian said seriously.

Jessica stopped dead on the pathway and turned to face him. "How can you say that? Are you implying that those who suggest the report is a fabrication are correct?''

"Not at all," he returned gently. "I am saying, however, that it would not be the first time the Africa Institute failed to get corroboration of certain facts before making them public. Their cause is, for the most part, a good one, but they are a zealous lot, my dear." Seeing the skepticism in her eyes, he grimaced. "Look here, Jessica, I have never been an advocate of slavery, whatever else you may think of me. I inherited my West Indian property from my father. I personally believe that if slavery could be ended with justice for everyone, it ought to be abolished entirely and at once. But that cannot be. There are too many issues involved. For one, the slaves themselves, now that they have been domesticated, cannot go back to their African way of life, and they would not survive on their own without the plantations to support them. Secondly, in order to end the system in the West Indies alone, surely you will agree that some arrangement must be made so that the white landowners are not made to suffer unfair financial losses. Total abolition would mean an end to their livelihood and a tremendous loss of property, and the only way by which their safety could be assured would be to bring them all home. Since many are not even British, a successful solution to the problem would require agreement of action by all the countries involved.''

"But it would not be necessary to end the system in order to abolish slavery," she protested. "Why could the landowners not merely pay the black workers for their services and continue the system without the brutality?''

"It is economically unfeasible," he said, still in that calm, quiet voice. "You forget that the slaves are completely supported by the landowners now. Either that would stop, or the wages would be an additional expense. Whichever way it worked out would be far too expensive for the landowner. At the very least he would have to make do with fewer workers, which would mean a very large number of discontented persons out of work. You've seen for yourself in this country what can happen under such conditions. Riots, violence—it rarely leads to anything healthy."

Silence fell between them again, and Jessica made no protest when he replaced her hand in the crook of his elbow and began walking again. She knew there was much truth in what he said, but it still seemed to her that the major issue was slavery itself. It was a dreadful institution and ought to be ended. At once. But he sounded so very logical and unheated that it was difficult to say such a thing to him without sounding simply bullheaded herself. His words made sense. She glanced up at him uncertainly.

"You said the cause was a good one."

"For the most part, I said. I don't think any civilized person would argue in favor of the brutal side of slavery. I'm not by any means so certain that the brutality is as great an issue as it's been made to sound by the abolitionists, however."

"How can you say that?" she demanded. "Why, there are tales told every day of new horrors."

"And such incidents are undeniably deplorable, but each time something of that nature is reported, it is immediately and heavily publicized, and in truth we do not read those tales every day. Furthermore, I can tell you this, my dear, as a landowner. It takes a very stupid man to destroy a piece of property for which he has paid a long price, merely out of temper or a misplaced notion of discipline. And now that the British slave trade has been abolished, I can assure you that any slave costs a great deal of money, for one must now buy new slaves from other slave owners. And when the supply goes down, the price goes up. Believe me when I tell you the brutality diminishes in a like ratio."

"You're saying that Lady Prodmore might be right, and that the incident in the Institute report was at least an exaggeration?"

"By no means. I have no way of knowing that for a fact, while I do know for a fact that such things are known to happen. However, it is perfectly true in this instance that the Institute's directors did nothing to verify their facts before they delivered the report to Hatchard for printing.

And now there appears to be no evidence to support the fact that the flogging incident ever took place."

"I see. And you say the Institute has done this sort of thing before?" It did not occur to her to disbelieve him.

"So I have been told. With members caring deeply, even passionately, for the cause, it would not be the first time expediency had overruled good sense. Stories like that one stir the public soul, which is precisely what is wanted. Unfortunately, such tactics often lead to action that has not been carefully thought out."

"Is that why you have become involved with the Institute?"

"I believe in working within the system to better it," he said. "I am a justice of the peace, after all, sworn to uphold law and order. And I believe the two, in any responsible civilization, must go together, Jessica."

She wasn't sure at first whether he had answered her question or not, but as she thought about his words, she realized he had. He considered the Institute part of the system now, and if it was going to influence the cause of justice, he wanted to be involved. Understanding that fact gave her a clearer view of the tall man walking beside her. She looked up at him again, but this time she had no thought of politics or causes in her head. He was looking straight ahead, and his profile, against the brown and red brick of the houses in the square, was distinctive. His chin was up, and he moved beside her with athletic grace. He had shortened his stride to match hers, and the slow pace seemed at odds with the vital energy that emanated from him. Jessica's fingers tightened involuntarily on his arm just then, and he looked down at her.

"Warm enough?"

"Oh, yes," she answered, suddenly breathless as his eyes met hers. "You were right. I have no need for my pelisse."

His eyes held hers. "It would be a criminal act to hide that beautiful body beneath a heavy pelisse, my dear," he said, drawing to a halt and turning her body toward his.

Jessica's breath seemed to catch in her throat. They were in a part of the garden that was heavily foliated, but they could certainly still be seen from one or two upper windows around the square. What was she thinking of, to be standing here, nearly in a gentleman's embrace?

Suddenly there was no *nearly* about it. She was in his arms. It was as if he had felt himself drawn by the look in her eye, for he appeared to be mesmerized as his face drew nearer to hers and his arms went with tantalizing slowness around her shoulders. As his lips claimed hers, Jessica forgot to worry about being overlooked from some window or other and gave her complete attention to the sensations coursing through her body. This time it was no simple glow of warmth invading her. This time it was a white heat that seemed to chase every other feeling before it.

Sir Brian's firm mouth moved against her softer one, first caressingly, then more demandingly as his passion grew. Jessica, lost now to the outside world, responded to his demands, allowing his lips to part, thoroughly enjoying the feel of his tongue as it explored the velvety interior of her mouth. His hands moved too, caressing her shoulders, then moving down toward her waist and around to the front of her body. As one hand moved lightly over her breast, she experienced a flash of dancing nerves that sent rippling shock waves clear to her toes. Her eyes opened, widening, and she saw that he had opened his as well. They were twinkling as he watched her. But when she stirred as though she would pull away from him, one of his hands moved to her waist again, tightening, drawing her closer. And Jessica swayed against him, something deep within her refusing to fight the wonderful feelings. The next time his hand touched her breast, she felt the flesh beneath her thin gown swelling to meet him, and she pressed harder against the length of his hard body, her kisses becoming as passionate at his, while she let her hands begin an exploration of their own. She heard him chuckle deep in his throat, and a moment later found herself standing back on her heels, regarding him quizzically.

"You are going to have us both in the briars, my girl, if I don't return you pretty speedily to the safety of your aunt's house," he told her roundly.

"Well, I like that!" she retorted indignantly.

"I could tell that much for myself."

"You know perfectly well that I didn't mean that."

"Didn't you? I had hoped that you did."

"Insufferable."

"And you, my dear, are a pretty little liar if you mean to pretend you didn't enjoy that interlude quite as much as I did."

"Little, Sir Brian?" Her eyes began to dance.

"That's better," he said. "Shall we return to the house?"

They had turned back toward the garden gate, when suddenly Jessica stiffened, staring toward the tall house on the southwest corner. "Look at that smoke," she said, her voice strangling in her throat. "My God, sir, Aunt Susan's house is on fire!"

8

SIR BRIAN'S STARTLED gaze quickly followed her own. There was certainly an overabundance of black smoke billowing forth into the sky from the top of Lady Susan's house. Grabbing Jessica by the arm, Sir Brian began running toward the gate. She pulled away from him.

"You will go faster by yourself," she cried. "Send one of the footmen to St. George's. The vestry fire brigade!"

Each parish vestry in London was responsible for maintaining its own fire brigade, and St. George's brigade had an excellent reputation for both speed and efficiency. Jessica knew that within a very few moments after the bell sounded, the huge fire horses would be racing toward her aunt's house. Right now, though, her only thought was to assure herself that Lady Susan was safe.

Sir Brian, taking her at her word, had dashed off, and a moment later she saw one of the green-liveried footmen running pell-mell across George Street toward the magnificent church. Though she hurried, Jessica did not so far forget herself as to run, and by the time she was mounting the steps to the house, the fire bell had already begun to clang. As she rushed through the open door, Sir Brian strode toward her from the back of the entry hall.

"It is quite all right," he told her calmly. "Only a flare-up in the kitchen chimney, as near as anyone can tell. I sent the lad for the fire brigade, despite the fact that your aunt's cook assures me that they can control it from the basement. It is best to be wise before the fact in an incident like this, I believe."

"Merciful heavens!" exclaimed Jessica, dismayed. "I should have thought of the kitchen chimney."

Sir Brian regarded her curiously. "You mean you ought to have anticipated this fire? Really, my dear, do you number clairvoyance amongst your talents?"

"No, of course not," she replied impatiently. "It is just that every chimney in this house is thick with soot and needs a thorough cleaning, but Aunt Susan refuses to have a sweep in the house because she insists that she cannot support an industry that abuses children. Nevertheless, this is carrying principle entirely too far. Why, we might all have been burnt alive in our beds!"

"Very true. Why does she not hire a man who employs the modern cleaning machines in place of a climbing boy?"

Lady Susan, perfectly composed, came down the stairs in time to hear his words. "What sort of machines do you mean, Sir Brian? I understand there has been a spot of bother belowstairs, but I do not understand why the fire wagon has drawn up before the house, Jessica, or why there are men rushing down my area stairs. Where are Bates and Birdlip?"

Jessica turned toward her, controlling her emotions with difficulty. "They are no doubt in the kitchen, ma'am, where the fire brigade is attempting to extinguish a chimney fire. Surely you knew the kitchen chimney was very likely in the same condition as the rest of the chimneys in this house. Sir Brian says the fire is most providentially contained in that one chimney, which quite fortunately is separate from the others, but what if the flare-up had occurred in one of the bedrooms, where all the chimneys connect not just to each other but to the rooms below? Such a thing would undoubtedly have resulted in a serious conflagration."

"But we do not light fires in the bedrooms these days," her aunt pointed out matter-of-factly.

"On the contrary, Mellin lit one in mine the first night I was here. And, for that matter, one of your footmen lit the drawing room fire that night, as well."

"Well, but that was before we decided the chimneys were too dangerous to use, you know," said Lady Susan, "although I suppose if the kitchen chimney is going to pose a threat, something must be done. We can scarcely do without a cooking fire. You spoke of a sweep who uses only machines, Sir Brian?"

He smiled at her prosaic attitude toward the fact that her house might have been in danger of burning to the ground, but his tone was serious when he answered her. "I did," he said. "It's quite the coming thing, though many people seem to harbor an odd prejudice toward them. They are merely brushes on long poles with a system of levers, ropes, and pulleys, which enables the sweep to control them from the rooms below."

"They do not sound as though they can be very efficient," her ladyship said thoughtfully.

"Not as efficient as climbing boys, certainly," Sir Brian agreed with a wry twist to his lips, "but efficient enough to prevent fires such as the one which your chef and the fire brigade are now attempting to extinguish, my lady."

Lady Susan nodded, then glanced at Jessica. "I daresay we must do something, must we not?"

"Unless you expect to receive a great many invitations henceforth to dine out," Jessica responded unhesitatingly. "Really, Aunt, every chimney in this house needs to be thoroughly cleaned as soon as possible."

The chief of the fire brigade agreed with her when that portly gentleman appeared at the front door some moments later, requesting speech with the owner of the house. His men, having entered the kitchen through the area door, had soon discovered that the fire was still burning merrily away in the chimney.

"There be two of 'em on the roof now, m'lady. They'll soon put things right, but that 'ere chimney's a fearsome menace t' the public safety. Needs cleanin', y' know. Like as not the rest 'o 'em could do with a brushing as well. Needn't tell you what's what, o' course, but a second fire like this 'un could result in a fine bein' levied by the vestry."

"That will not be necessary," Lady Susan told him graciously. "I quite realize that the time has come to clean the chimneys. Merely an oversight, you understand, that they have not been seen to before now," she added with a bland disregard for the truth.

"Figured as much, ma'am. House like this." He gestured grandly. "Bound to take a deal o' care. Figured ye'd know what's o'clock, fine lady like yerself. Be sayin' good day t' ye now. Good day, miss. Sir." He fired Sir Brian a half-salute and took himself off.

"I hope they don't do any damage up there," Lady

Susan said, glancing upward. "The tiles on that roof are shockingly difficult to replace."

Having made up her mind to get her chimneys cleaned, Lady Susan wasted little time after Sir Brian had taken his departure before setting matters in train. That is to say, she gave orders to her butler to see to the business and to make absolutely certain that the person he hired agreed to use only the newfangled machines to accomplish the task. Then, content in the knowledge that she had done her duty to the vestry and seen to the safety of her house, she retired to her dressing room to begin preparations for the evening ahead, which, like its predecessors, was to be a busy one.

Fortunately, in Jessica's opinion at least, they had been invited to dine in Duke Street before going on with Lord and Lady Gordon to a reception at Carlton House. Lord Gordon, though not precisely a member of the Prince Regent's set, made no secret of his admiration for those who were, and he was quite beside himself with pride over having been blessed with the honor of an invitation to the reception. He actually greeted his sister-in-law with the appearance, at least, of familial affection.

"You look charmingly this evening, my dear," he said in his usual pompous tones. "And, Lady Susan, always a treat to have your company, ma'am."

Lady Susan inclined her head slightly. "Very kind of you to invite us to dine, my lord." She turned immediately to his wife. "You have neglected us, Georgeanne. We have not seen you for several days. I trust you have not been suffering ill health."

"Nothing to mention, Aunt Susan. Merely a bilious attack, I believe. I'm feeling wonderfully well tonight," her ladyship said, hugging her. " 'Tis delightful that you and Jessica were able to join us. Your schedule has been so full, I scarcely dared to hope you would honor us."

Lady Susan chuckled. "We have been gadding a bit, have we not? Well, I vow the change has done me good, and I do like to see your sister enjoying herself."

"Oh, so do I," Georgeanne replied, shooting a look brimful of mischief at Jessica. "Come along into the drawing room, both of you, and meet our other guests."

The look warned Jessica, so she was not in the least surprised to see Sir Brian standing near the drawing-room chimneypiece, looking very natty in his evening attire. If it had not required the help of two or three other men to assist him into his dark coat, as Lord Gordon often assured her was the case with himself and any other gentleman aspiring to sartorial heights, it still became him well, and as always his shirt and neckcloth were starched and snowy, and his black shoes shone enough to reflect the light of the cheerful little fire crackling away on the hearth. He was wearing dark pantaloons, as was his nephew, who stood a little distance away in conversation with a thin brown-haired woman, but another, older gentleman, who was conversing in low tones with Miss St. Erth near the front window, was, like Lord Gordon, wearing the knee breeches that were still *de rigueur* for formal occasions.

Jessica was soon introduced to Lady St. Erth, whom she had not had the pleasure of meeting before, and of renewing her acquaintance with General Potterby, a stiffly erect gray-haired old gentleman whom she knew to be a longtime friend of her aunt's. When she had an opportunity to speak privately with her sister, she accused Georgeanne of matchmaking, then flushed delicately when Lady Gordon's eyes involuntarily shifted toward Sir Brian.

"Not that, you goose. I meant the general and Aunt Susan."

"Oh." Georgeanne grinned at her. "I was merely making up my numbers. We've another couple yet to arrive, and I've arranged for Mr. Wellesly Poole to be Lady St. Erth's dinner partner."

"The fortune hunter?"

"The very same. He asked me to arrange an introduction to Miss St. Erth, you see, and though I agreed to do it, I decided it would be as well to hint him away at the same time. This evening should accomplish both purposes to a nicety."

"Georgie, you are a rogue." Her sister's eyes twinkled, but Jessica noticed suddenly that she was looking rather pale. "I say, you are feeling all right, are you not?"

Georgeanne nodded, her eyes still atwinkle. "I am fine, Jess. Truly. Don't say a word to anyone, but I may be in an interesting condition."

Jessica's eyes flew wide. "Good heavens, does Cyril know?"

"No, and he isn't to know until I'm quite certain, so don't say a word to a soul. Promise!"

"Of course. Oh, Georgie, how wonderful if it is true."

"Well, yes." Lady Gordon eyed her speculatively. "You don't think I am too old?"

"Of course not, love. You will make a charming mother. Why, Mama was past thirty when Madeleine was born."

"Yes, but she had had two daughters already. The first is supposed to be the most difficult, you know."

It occurred to Jessica that the topic was a most improper one for the setting, but she took several moments to attempt to reassure her sister before changing the subject to one that would be more acceptable if anyone were to overhear them. A few moments later, in response to an unmistakable look of entreaty in Sir Brian's eye, she moved to his side, greeting him warmly.

"All clear in Hanover Square?" he asked, smiling.

"The smoke has cleared, if that's what you mean," she replied with an answering smile. "And Aunt Susan has given orders for a sweep to be hired. One who will promise to use the machines you told her about. What a day this has been, to be sure. I only hope we do not encounter Lady Prodmore tonight."

He lifted an eyebrow. "Any particular reason why not?"

Her smile widened to a grin. "Well, ailing and weak as I am, I'm sure she would be surprised to see me out and about like this."

He chuckled. "We'll simply tell her that our stroll cured everything that ailed you."

Remembering the high point of that stroll brought a rush of color to her cheeks, and Jessica glanced around hastily to see if anyone was near enough to have overheard him. Everyone else seemed reassuringly engrossed in his or her own conversation. She looked back at Sir Brian to find his eyes dancing wickedly.

"No one is paying us any heed, my girl, nor would they have noticed anyting in my smple words to give them pause. 'Tis merely your own imagination at work. And the roses in your cheeks, I might add, that will cause them to wonder what I've said to you."

Her color deepened, but she managed to answer him with relative calm. "You are quite right. I confess I have lived in dread all afternoon that one of Aunt's neighbors, paying a call to discuss the fire, you know, might say something about having seen us in the garden."

He nodded, his serious expression still belied by the dancing twinkle. "You will be the talk of Hanover Square by midnight."

Jessica shook her head at him, then turned to greet General Potterby, who had stepped up to speak to Sir Brian. A few moments later her own attention was claimed by Miss St. Erth. Jessica had seen the younger girl from a distance upon several occasions since her arrival in London, but until now she had had no opportunity to engage her in conversation. As they moved away from the others toward the window, they made, had they but realized it, a charming picture.

Janet St. Erth was looking her best in a simple white-muslin evening dress, tied with a pink sash that matched the ribbons wound through her flaxen curls. Her lovely blue eyes were sparkling with enthusiasm, and her slim body fairly radiated her youth and good health. Standing next to the magnificent Miss Sutton-Drew, who had chosen a gown of deep-rose-colored silk trimmed with creamy lace, Miss St. Erth looked almost ethereal, while her slim, fragile beauty seemed to underscore Jessica's earthier, more blatant sexuality. More than one eye turned in their direction as they conversed amicably together.

"I'm so glad to have this opportunity at last, Miss Sutton-Drew," Janet said in her mellow voice. "I've never thanked you properly for stopping to come to my rescue that dreadful day."

"Well, I didn't precisely stop to rescue you, you know," Jessica said honestly, but with a smile. "Our coach could not pass, because you and Mr. Hayle were blocking the road."

"I know, but you accomplished my rescue, nevertheless, and I am quite, quite grateful."

Jessica remembered Sir Brian's criticism of her attempted intervention. "I think," she said with a little smile, "that it is rather Sir Brian whom you ought to be thanking, you know."

"Oh, but I have, and Andrew . . . that is, Mr. Liskeard . . . as well. But Sir Brian said I must thank you, too, and indeed he is right, for that dreadful Hayle might well have pushed me over the cliff before ever he and An . . . Mr. Liskeard arrived to save me, if you and Lady Gordon had not come along as you did."

"Well, I don't think Hayle had any real intention of harming you, you know."

"No, I daresay he didn't, though I certainly didn't understand that at the time."

"I collect that everything is all right in that direction now?"

"Indeed, that is why my father has not yet come to London. He had meant to accompany us, you know, but after Sir Brian spoke with him, he went down to that mine himself and discovered, much to his astonishment, that everything was just as Hayle had said. He is overseeing many shockingly expensive changes, but Mama had a letter from him only today, and he will arrive next week. He said it is all going most satisfactorily."

Jessica glanced involuntarily at Sir Brian. He was no longer conversing with the general, and his gaze had drifted in her direction. His look was a quizzical one, which made her realize that her own feelings were very likely reflected in her expression. She smiled vaguely at him and turned back to Miss St. Erth, but her thoughts had been stirred again by the younger girl's ingenuous words. Just as Andrew had suggested to her earlier, Sir Brian had indeed listened to Hayle's complaints, and seemingly he had gone further than that and had successfully acted upon them. Truly, she thought, as she followed the others in to dinner some moments later, there were still a good many things to learn about Sir Brian.

"What were you and Miss St. Erth discussing so seriously?" he asked her once the first course had been passed. He was seated at her right, and she had General Potterby on her left.

Mr. Wellesly Poole sat across the table from her, next to Lady St. Erth, so Jessica did not feel that she could explain the matter there and then. Instead she returned a glib response and asked him if he meant to accompany them to Carlton House.

"Oh, yes. Gordon has assured me that I shall have a splendid time. Upon his word."

Jessica chuckled, darting a quick glance at her brother-in-law, who was deep in conversation with Lady Susan. At least, she amended to herself, Cyril was conversing. Lady Susan looked a trifle glazed about the eyes. Turning back to Sir Brian, she commented that if the Regent were blessed with more supporters like Lord Gordon, he might be a happier man.

"That's not likely to occur so long as the war debt remains as high as it is now, I'm afraid," he replied. "There are men out there in the streets who firmly believe they'd be better off if Napoleon had won. It has not been a good year for Prinny."

Jessica knew his words constituted an understatement of the facts. The year had not even begun well for the Regent. He was so unpopular that when he had opened Parliament the previous January he had had to drive through a hostile crowd, and upon his return to Carlton House that day, it was said by many that shots had actually been fired at him. There was certainly no doubt that gravel and stones had been thrown at the royal carriage, nor that some windows had been broken, and Lord Liverpool's government had seized upon the incident as an excuse to suspend the Habeas Corpus Act, which meant that anybody under suspicion of anything could be thrown into jail and kept there. Indeed, the lawmakers had gone even a step further, bringing out and dusting off an unrepealed act dating back to Edward III, which gave magistrates everywhere the power to send to prison any persons they thought even likely to commit an act prejudicial to public order.

"I cannot pretend that the Regent is a man whom I can admire particularly," Jessica said now, "but it does seem a trifle unfair that he must bear the blame for such stuff as the suspension of habeas corpus, when in fact he had nothing to do with it."

"A fact of royal life, my dear," Sir Brian said. "The common man knows little of the workings of government, but he does know that the Regent is the man at the top. I cannot tell you what wickedness motivated Liverpool and the others to overreact the way they did, but the habeas-corpus business is certainly something to be abhorred."

"I should think so. Why, I've heard of men being thrown into jail for little more than pulling a face or making a rude noise."

"I hope you don't think I would throw anyone into jail for such a reason."

"No, of course not, but most men on the bench these days are not inclined to be very tolerant toward the lower orders, are they?"

Sir Brian could not deny that fact, and his attention was claimed a moment later by the lady on his right, a pretty young friend of Lady Gordon's whose name Jessica could not immediately recall to mind. Jessica herself turned to General Potterby, hoping he had not felt neglected. There was nothing in his attitude to show it if he had, however, and he conversed with her quite charmingly until the second course was brought in. When she turned back to Sir Brian, he was watching Wellesly Poole attempting to charm Lady St. Erth, and there was a glint of unholy amusement in his eyes. Jessica stifled a chuckle, but he realized just then that she was watcing him and turned to face her.

"An interesting display, everything considered," he said, smiling.

"I don't suppose he's making much headway," she murmured.

"None at all, in fact. He's wasting his time, but I daresay Lady Gordon had a wish to entertain his dinner partner. Have you any other deep political topics you wish to discuss with me?"

His question caught her off guard, and her expression revealed her confusion. "I don't believe so. Do you dislike discussing such matters?"

"Of course not. I merely wondered if you will always attempt to steer our conversations into encumbered channels."

"Encumbered channels?"

"I always suspect there may be snags in the water ahead. As if you are waiting for me to trip myself up by taking some route you disapprove of."

"Good gracious, sir, do you suppose I desire you to agree with my every principle?"

"Not every one, perhaps, but the ones you hold most

dear, certainly. And I am not certain I've yet discovered what all of those may be. Hence, my fear of snags.''

"Well, I hope I am not so uncompromising as all that,'' Jessica muttered. "Surely I can allow other people their own opinions on any matter.''

"Even the people you care most deeply about, my dear?''

Feeling the rush of warmth in her face again, Jessica stared at him speechlessly. *Talk of snags in the water,* she thought. General Potterby's voice startled her, but realizing that he was speaking to her, she turned, trying desperately to compose both her countenance and her emotions.

"You have such becoming color in your cheeks, my dear,'' the old gentleman said benignly.

Hearing a choking cough from Sir Brian didn't help matters at all. Jessica smiled at the general and managed a murmur that sounded like an expression of gratitude, but she realized a moment later that she needn't have worried that the general might notice anything out of the ordinary, for he merely wanted to know if her aunt was really changing her ways and getting back into the social whirl.

"Why, yes, I believe she means to go on as she has begun the Season, sir,'' Jessica replied, her voice nearly steady again.

"Excellent, excellent. High time Susan caught herself a husband. Been saying that for thirty years. Thought I'd be saying it for thirty more. Maybe not, though,'' he mused, shooting a speculative look across the table at Lady Susan, who was now speaking animatedly to the gentleman on her right. "Maybe not.''

"Oh, but I don't think . . .'' Jessica broke off, realizing that the old gentleman wasn't listening to her. A moment later, Lady Gordon arose from the table, signaling that it was time to leave the gentlemen to their port, and Jessica followed the others, feeling as if she had escaped from more than one snag in the past ten minutes.

The rest of the evening passed harmlessly enough, with no further opportunity for private speech with Sir Brian, but Jessica found her thoughts returning constantly to various things he had said, as well as to what Janet St. Erth had told her. She wondered if she had become a trifle rigid in her thinking, if she truly did demand that the people she cared about think as she did. Surely not. Surely she could accept dissent from her friends. But a simple difference of opinion and a commitment of any kind to a man whose very way of life was in opposition to all she believed . . .

Her thoughts had a tendency to become confused at that point. No commitment had been requested of her, so what on earth, she asked herself, was she thinking of? Although Sir Brian had once told her she was exactly the sort of woman he had been searching for all his life, he had never actually indicated a wish to marry her. To be sure, he had seemed—before he left Cornwall, at least—to be working himself up to such a declaration. But her responses then had been anything but encouraging. And since they had been in London, though she had given every sign of being willing now to accept his advances, and though that very night at dinner he had as much as admitted recognizing that she held at least a tenderness for him, he had quite failed to take advantage of the situation. If, in fact, he had not been merely trifling with her and still wished to affix her interest, that was all very well and good—at least, she had no objection to such an attempt on his part—but if he *were* to ask her to marry him, how could she possibly give an affirmative reply, knowing that she would be marrying a man who . . .

Here again, her thoughts consistently took a confused twist. Who what? she would ask herself. What did she really know about what he thought? She certainly knew nothing about the way in which he conducted his affairs. Or only what she had imagined from what she knew about coal mining and slavery. Had she perhaps been unjust to assume that he was the embodiment of the wicked men she had learned about over the years?

With all these thoughts in mind, she tossed and turned in her bed that night, and it was with circles under her lovely gray eyes that she faced her aunt over the breakfast table the following morning.

"Shall you accompany me to King's Bench today, my dear? The defense is speaking its piece, you know, and Mr. Hatchard can use any amount of moral support."

"I'm afraid not, Aunt Susan," Jessica replied, stifling a yawn. "I didn't sleep well last night, and I fear I should be poor company."

Her aunt accepted her at her word and soon went away, leaving Jessica with one of her favorite romances to read. But since the heroine seemed particularly stupid and the hero particularly misunderstood, for once, Miss Sutton-Drew found little solace in her favorite pastime.

So it was that when Andrew Liskeard called to inquire whether Miss Jessica might not favor him with her company on a ride through Hyde Park, she decided that a breath of fresh air was just exactly what she needed. Besides, a little voice deep inside whispered, Andrew undoubtedly knew a good deal about the workings of Sir Brian's mind.

9

IN THE TIME that it took her to change into her habit, Jessica's horse was brought around from the stables, which faced onto Little Brook Street, and she and Andrew were soon riding down Brook Street and through Grosvenor Square, where Andrew was able to point out Sir Brian's house in the first block of Charles Street. It was a mere fifteen minutes more to Park Lane and the northeast entrance to Hyde Park.

While they rode through the streets of Mayfair, their mounts required their constant attention, so what conversation there was was desultory. But upon entering the park, where they could simply allow their horses to wander along from one path to another without much thought, Jessica set herself to draw Andrew into speaking about his uncle by asking him to tell her more about Shaldon Park.

The young man followed her lead without hesitation, explaining that he had lived with his uncle for some eight years or so, since the death of his own parents in an influenza epidemic.

"There wasn't anyone on my father's side to take charge of me, and he had named Uncle Brian my trustee, so I came along to him. Of course, I was usually at school, you know, but I spend holidays at Shaldon Park, trotting about after him while he looked over the mines and rode about the estate."

"It must have been difficult for you, losing both your parents so suddenly like that," Jessica sympathized.

"Lord, yes. I was a handful, all right and tight. You should hear some of the tales Uncle Brian can tell. But he understood. Probably better than most men would have— young men, anyway—for you must know that he was only twenty-four or so when it happened. But he had been in my position himself, for his father died when he was nineteen,

113

and though he hadn't had an uncle to take charge of his affairs, he understood what I was feeling."

"Had he no one? What of his mother?"

"Oh, she was about, of course, but she's a bit flighty and not the sort a fellow can depend upon. Shouldn't speak so of one's great-aunt, I expect, but she was quite overcome by my great-uncle's death—he simply fell dead one night while he was preparing for bed, you know. Hadn't even reached his fiftieth birthday yet. Bit of a shock to the poor lady's sensibilities."

"I should think it would be."

"Yes, well, she stayed at Shaldon Park for less than a year before returning to her own folk in Yorkshire. She visits occasionally, but I don't think she cares much for Cornwall. Says it's too damp and windy for her liking."

"And you, Andrew, do you like Cornwall?"

His eyes lit up, and his mouth quirked into a self-conscious little grin. "I think I must love it as much as my uncle does. Of course, my own estates are there, too—on the River Fowey, between Brown Willy and Bath's Plot. That's north of Shaldon Park, you know. And east, too, of course. On the edge of Bodmin Moor."

He spoke proudly, and that alone told her much of the way his uncle had raised him. She knew the area he spoke of, knew too that Bodmin Moor, like most of the higher moors of Cornwall, was more likely to boast vast, infertile wastelands of peaty bogs, wild grasses, and sedges than the fertile, flower-filled lushness that characterized Shaldon Park. Still, those moors, dotted by the castlelike tors of granite that seemed to surge upward everywhere, had their own wild, picturesque beauty, and if Andrew had learned to appreciate it without coveting green lushness instead, that was all to the good. Then it occurred to her that he was no doubt Sir Brian's heir. Perhaps it had never entered his head that he might not have both properties.

"I expect he's taught you all he knows of mining and sugar planting," she suggested blandly.

"Why on earth would he, when I've scant interest in such things? There are two stone quarries on my land, but most of my tenants are small-acreage farmers and sheepherders. He's caused me to learn a deal of what I need to know about wintering sheep, shearing, and such like stuff, for he's taken me along to sit in on his talks with my bailiff whenever it's been possible for him to do so. Let his own sons—when he's got some—learn about tin and copper and sugar when they're old enough to attend to his teaching."

"Tin and copper? I thought he mined coal," Jessica said absently, her mind on Sir Brian's sons.

"Lord, no." He stared at her. "There's no coal mining that I know about in Cornwall. Lead, copper, zinc, tin— that sort of stuff. But coal is mined in the Midlands and the North—Newcastle and Manchester, places like that."

Jessica gave a helpless little shake of her head and cast him a rueful smile. "My lamentable ignorance of geography again, I expect. One hears so much from Aunt Susan and her friends about the horrors of the coal mines that one just naturally thinks of coal when one thinks of mining. Still and all, a mine is a mine. No doubt the danger and the exploitation are the same in all of them."

"I never paid enough heed to the details to deny that," Andrew said, glancing at her quizzically, "but I'd wager every groat I've got that Uncle Brian's mines are safe and his people well cared for."

"Oh, I don't doubt for a moment that his intentions in that direction are better than most," Jessica said, remembering what Janet St. Erth had said about his intervention on Hayle's behalf, "but that doesn't mean that his mines are not dangerous or that he doesn't exploit women and small children in exactly the same way that any other mine owner does. He has certainly never denied that when I've laid the accusation at his door."

Andrew shot her that quizzical look again, but he said nothing further, and some moments later they met some friends of his who fell in beside them, and their private conversation came to a necessary halt. As they rode back along Brook Street some time later, Jessica found her thoughts returning once again to Sir Brian. She tried to imagine him as a nineteen-year-old youth whose father had just died unexpectedly, leaving him vast estates to care for. It was not easy to picture the confident Sir Brian in any light other than the one in which she presently saw him, but she decided he must have felt alone and abandoned at the time. No doubt there had been someone to assist him, a banker or a man of affairs. There generally was, in her experience, someone of that sort around at such times, particularly when the property involved was as extensive as Sir Brian's seemed to be. Nevertheless, it could not have been the same as having someone at hand who truly cared about him. Surely Andrew had been luckier, having Sir Brian to help him over the difficult time after his parents' deaths. Sir Brian, she thought fondly, would be very comforting to have around during a critical time such as that must have been.

When they arrived back in Hanover Square, Jessica invited Andrew to step inside for a bit of refreshment.

"Don't mind if I do," he replied, helping her from the saddle and turning his reins over to her groom.

They went up the stone steps together, but the tall front door opened before they reached it. Bates took a step toward them, his normally benign expression a good deal distressed.

"Oh, Miss Jessica, what a to-do! I don't know what her ladyship can be thinking about. Truly I don't. Good afternoon, Mr. Liskeard. I beg your pardon for blurting such stuff, Miss Jessica, but—"

"I told him, Miss Jessica," stated Mrs. Birdlip righteously, appearing behind the butler, alternately wringing her hands, then wiping them upon the skirts of her black bombazine dress. "I told him just how it would be if he didn't keep an eye on that shifty fellow. But would he listen?" Then she, too, seemed to become aware for the first time of Andrew's presence, and colored with confusion, apologizing for speaking out of turn.

"It's quite all right," Jessica interposed reassuringly when the butler looked likely to defend himself against the housekeeper's accusations. "Mr. Liskeard must be counted nearly one of the family by now, as both of you must know. What's toward?"

"It was that dreadful sweep, Miss Jessica," began the housekeeper as they stepped into the hall. "Just as I had suspicioned, he was not the least to be trusted."

Bates shut the door before asserting his authority by casting a quelling glance at Mrs. Birdlip, who fell immediately silent. "It is as she says, Miss Jessica," he said then in a subdued tone. " 'Twas all my doing, I fear, but the man promised on his mother's soul that he used naught but those modern machines to accomplish his business. I swear, I had not the slightest inkling that he meant to bring that boy along with him."

"Merciful heavens!" Jessica breathed.

"A climbing boy!" Andrew exclaimed, grasping the gist as quickly as Jessica had. "Next you will say that Lady Susan walked in upon them whilst the sweep was still at his work."

"Indeed, she did," said Mrs. Birdlip, nodding her gray head fervently.

Bates nodded. "It was disastrous. I have never seen her ladyship in such a taking. The fellow had somehow smuggled the poor boy into the house without anyone's being the wiser, and they were in the yellow bedchamber on the second floor when her ladyship returned from King's Bench. Evidently the fellow was actually brutalizing the child when she walked in upon them. Oh, Miss Jessica, it was dreadful."

"The poor little boy." Jessica shook her head in sympathy.

"I wasn't thinking of the boy, miss. 'Twas her ladyship. Lost her dignity entirely, and nearly brought the house down around our ears, if I may be so bold as to put the matter in such a common way."

"That disgusting man," put in Mrs. Birdlip, "a standing there in all his dirt bellowing at her poor ladyship that he didn't care what people said about not wanting boys used. Said they always complain their chimneys wasn't cleaned proper with only the machines and such."

"Lady Susan," said Bates, directing another repressive look at the housekeeper, "sent the sweep about his business, without so much as giving him time to clean up the mess or collect his gear."

"Good heavens," Jessica muttered, "we'll have a constable on the doorstep before the sun has set."

"We may that, Miss Jessica," the butler agreed in solemn tones, "but if we do, it won't be on account of a few brushes and bits of canvas. I regret to say that her ladyship refused to let Mr. Crick take the little climbing boy away with him, as well."

Bates fell silent, letting that thunderbolt take its full

effect upon his listeners. The silence went unbroken for several seconds, until it seemed to Jessica that the very walls were waiting for her response. She glanced at Andrew.

"I think perhaps I had better go up to her."

"Well, if you think I mean just to go about my business in a casual gentlemanly fashion whilst you hear the rest of this devilish tale, you've got another think coming, ma'am. Lead the way."

Jessica glanced questioningly at the butler. "She is in the drawing room, miss, with the boy. She has sent for Sir William Knighton."

Jessica had started up the sweeping stairway, but at Bates's last words she turned back. "A doctor! Is she ill, then?" Andrew, behind her, likewise stopped and looked back.

The butler shook his white-fringed head. "No, miss, not her ladyship, the boy. I fear some of his burns are rather severe."

"Merciful heavens!" Jessica exclaimed.

Waiting to hear no more, she hurried upstairs and along the railed gallery to the drawing room, where she found her aunt and one of the maidservants hovering over a settee upon which an old sheet had been spread in order to protect it from the scrawny, soot-covered little boy who crouched there, looking not so much hurt as frightened out of his wits.

"Jessica, my love! At last." Lady Susan got to her feet and strode toward them, her gloved hands held out to take Jessica's. It was clear from the fact that she still wore the high-poke bonnet she had donned that morning before sallying forth to the King's Bench, that her ladyship had not stopped for a moment to take stock of herself since returning to find the sweep in her house. "Did Bates tell you?"

"Aunt Susan, whatever are you about?" Jessica demanded, but her tone was gentle, and the look she gave her aunt was one of compassion if not understanding. "You cannot keep this child. His master will be back with the constable."

"Nonsense, he wouldn't dare," declared her ladyship militantly. "I should have him up on charges so fast his head would spin. And so I told him to his miserable face.''

"Cor, missus, Jem don't be afraid o' no gentry mort,'' observed the tyke on the settee, his gravelly voice reflecting his fear and at the same time making him sound older than he looked. " 'E'll be back, awright, 'n when 'e gits 'is 'ands on me, 'ere won't be but a morsel left t' me backside. Not wiv all this row, 'n all.''

"I've told you, Jeremy, you've nothing to fear,'' Lady Susan said firmly, turning to face him. Her expression softened in response to the abject terror in the child's eyes. "I couldn't let that dreadful man take him away again,'' she said to Jessica and Andrew. "When I walked in upon them, he was lighting brands under the child's bare feet in order to force him up the chimney.''

"I dassn't like goin' up inta the dark,'' little Jeremy muttered. " 'E always gi'es me a 'otfoot. On'y way I'll go up a bleedin' chimbley.''

"Well, he shant' be let to do it again, my dear.''

The boy shook his head in patent disbelief, and Jessica turned to Andrew. "We've got to do something. I don't know what the law is with regard to situations of this nature, but if the boy is properly apprenticed to that sweep, I fear we haven't a leg to stand upon. We shall be forced to give him back.''

The child cowered further into the corner of the settee. " 'E'll gi'e me what-fer, 'e will. Near kilt me t' last time.''

"You are quite right about the law,'' Lady Susan agreed bitterly. "Though I doubt that awful man realized it at the time, there are no real charges I could bring against him that would amount to any more than his having to pay a fine. We shall simply have to make a case of it, use this poor lad to see some changes made.'' Her eyes brightened at the thought. "We can do it, Jessica. I know we can. Just as soon as Sir William has seen him and the child has had a bath''—the boy recoiled from the last word in horror—"I shall call a meeting of the Society to End Employment of Climbing Boys. Someone will know precisely what must be done.''

Jessica stared at her aunt in dismay. Just the thought of such a course struck fear into her heart, for she could easily imagine the sort of scandal Lady Susan might stir. The *beau monde* would rock with it.

Andrew's expression reflected her feelings. "I wish Uncle Brian were here," he said in an undertone when Lady Susan turned back to her charge. "Would you like me to find him? I'm sure he will be at the house or at one or another of his clubs, you know. I could run him to earth in a trice."

"Nonsense," retorted Jessica, her own spirit reasserting itself. "There is nothing he can do that you and I cannot do as well. We simply must think. There has got to be a way to remedy this situation before we all find ourselves in the basket."

"What are you two muttering about?" demanded Lady Susan, patting the boy's filthy head, then removing her gloves when she realized she had got soot upon them. "Do you not think we can succeed with such a campaign? Maybe we cannot, but I certainly think we ought to try. We must help this child. Look here," she added to the boy, handing him a crystal globe containing an intricately carved village scene. "Shake this, and see what happens."

"Cor, I knows wha' 'appens," he said scornfully, his fears forgotten for the brief moment as he took the globe into his grubby hands. "Ye shakes it, like this, 'n it makes snow. Me mum 'ad one like this." But despite his scornful tone, he turned the globe first one way and then the other, seeming to delight in the snowy scene that resulted.

Jessica stared at him. The crystal was not an expensive toy, but she doubted that any climbing boy's mother would possess one. Clearly the child was a prevaricator. She turned back to her aunt.

"I agree that we must do what we can for him, Aunt, but I doubt that using him as the focal point for a campaign against the iniquities of his position will accomplish that. In the first place, you can be accused of stealing him from his rightful master. The laws covering apprenticeship are very clear."

" 'Fraid she's right about that, Lady Susan," Andrew put in. "There's not a court in the land wouldn't turn him over to his rightful owner, same as any other piece of property."

"But he's a child, not a piece of property."

"Well, that's true enough, and perhaps I oughtn't to have put the matter in such a way. 'Tisn't the child the sweep owns, so much as the right to his services as an apprentice. Can't hope to change that. Dashed well been the law in England for centuries, you know."

"Well, it's exactly the same as slavery, and there should be a law against it," declared Lady Susan. "And I think we should use Jeremy here to fight for such a law."

Jessica had been thinking. She turned now to Andrew, her brow furrowed. "Can you purchase an apprentice?" she asked.

"Not like one purchases slaves," he said, "but I suppose the result is much the same. One purchases their papers of apprenticeship."

"Jem jest bought me," contributed the boy on the settee. "Paid two-poun'-ten fer me, 'e did."

"There, you see," said Lady Susan. "Just like slavery."

"I do see," said Jessica slowly, her eyes beginning to light. "Andrew, if that dreadful man paid two-pounds-ten for the boy, wouldn't he be likely to sell him again if the price offered him were higher?"

"Not selling the boy," Andrew corrected her, but when she glared at him, he retreated. "Oh, very well, same thing. I daresay he might accept a good offer if one were made."

"Well, then, we're going to make that offer. Where does Jem live, Jeremy?"

"In Kettle Lane, back o' the Fleet, in Cheapside," responded the boy promptly. "Ye really gonna buy me papers orf 'im?" Jessica nodded. " 'E won' like it, miss. Bit of a brute, Jem is. You watch yerself wiv 'im, y' 'ear?"

There was an anxious look about him now that appealed to Jessica's compassionate nature. She wanted to hug the filthy little waif. Instead, she just grinned at him before turning back to Andrew.

"You'll come with me?"

"I still think we ought to discuss this with Uncle Brian, Miss Jessica. Kettle Lane dashed well don't sound like much a place for a lady. No doubt he would say a gentleman ought to attend to the business. Would myself, only I'd likely make a botch of it, for I've never done such a thing before. He would know precisely what to do, however."

The thought of acquiring Sir Brian's assistance in the

matter was an appealing one. Jessica knew she would be completely safe in his company, safer than she would be in Andrew's, certainly. But a second thought convinced her that Sir Brian would flatly refuse to allow her to accompany him upon such an undertaking, and while she was perfectly certain she could trust him to see the matter ended satisfactorily, she had a great desire to attend to it herself. The notion of purchasing Jeremy's apprenticeship had been hers, after all. Surely she could see it through without assistance. She straightened her shoulders with a little shake of her head and looked directly at Andrew.

"You may come with me if you choose to do so," she told him firmly, "or you may remain behind, but I do not intend to wait until your uncle chooses to pay us a call or for you to search him out before seeing this business at an end. If Jem . . . What's his surname, Jeremy?" The boy looked bewildered. "His other name. Bates mentioned it, but I cannot recall what it was. Jem what?"

"Oh, Jem Crick, miss."

"Well, if Jem Crick is not searching out a constable at this very moment, then he is most likely plotting mischief of another sort, so I don't think we have any time to spare. Ring for a footman, Andrew. Two pulls of the cord just there behind you."

Andrew obeyed, and when the footman arrived, Jessica sent him to gather up all the sweep's belongings and to call for her aunt's carriage. "And request that someone accompany me besides the coachman, if you please. You'll do, yourself, actually," she added, after regarding his tall, well-muscled body with approbation. "Are you coming with me, Andrew?"

"By Jove, I guess I am," he responded promptly. "Uncle Brian won't like it much, I daresay, but I think you've got a deal of spunk, Miss Jessica, and I wouldn't miss this for the world. But should you not have suggested that that fellow carry a shotgun or some such thing?"

"No need, Andrew," she assured him, twinkling. "I shall have my chinchilla muff."

He stared at her, eyes widening, then burst into laughter. "By Jove, ma'am, you are the most complete hand. That ruffian don't stand a chance."

She grinned at him, then hurried upstairs to change out

of her riding habit. When she returned to the drawing room, looking complete to a shade in a carriage gown of peach-colored sarcenet with a matching spencer, Yorkshire tan gloves and half-boots, and carrying her large fur muff, Sir William Knighton was speaking to Lady Susan and Andrew. Of the boy, Jeremy, there was no sign.

"The child is seriously malnourished," Sir William was saying. "It is the same with all those lads, I fear. Their masters starve them in order to keep them small enough to squirm up into the chimneys. Feed him well but with small portions at first until his body adjusts. And put that salve I've given you on the burns daily, being sure to keep them very clean. I don't envy that maid of yours trying to bathe the little devil, since he seemed so set against it, but it is a necessary thing, I assure you, my lady. The burns are not as serious as you might have supposed, but the scarring indicates that he has been burned before, and he has certainly been abused in a good many other ways as well. I shan't ask how he came to be here in your drawing room," he added with a slight smile, "but I wish him well. He's a sturdy lad. Ought to come out of all this without too much damage." He nodded to Jessica and to Andrew and took his departure a few moments later.

Lady Susan expelled a sigh of relief. "I am so grateful that the boy was not seriously injured in my house," she said. "I should have felt so responsible."

"He is being bathed now," Andrew said with a grin. "Must be the first bath he's ever had. You ought to have seen the dust he kicked up when the maid came to fetch him."

"Well, we shall leave him to your tender mercies, Aunt, and see what we can do to free him from Mr. Crick's employ," Jessica told her, bestowing a kiss upon her cheek.

"Wonderful," Lady Susan replied. Then a frown creased her smooth brow. "That is . . . I know we must do something, Jessica, but it really does sound like a dreadful place. Behind the Fleet and all. Do you think you should go yourself? Would it not be better—"

"This was my notion, Aunt, and I intend to see it through. If Kettle Lane is behind the Fleet Prison, then it is also quite near St. Paul's Cathedral. I shall be perfectly safe. Besides, Andrew is to accompany me, and I am taking a stalwart footman along as well, so you need not bother your head about me.''

Lady Susan agreed, albeit with reluctance, and Jessica and Andrew were soon bowling along toward Cheapside, the sweep's gear tucked neatly into the boot, and the large liveried footman standing up behind. Jessica fingered the little pistol in her muff. She had checked before leaving her bedchamber to be certain the weapon was fully loaded, but now she was remembering Sir Brian's words that day so long ago when she had attempted to intervene between Janet St. Erth and the miner, Hayle. If the sweep was as much of a brute as both Jeremy and Lady Susan seemed to think him, perhaps it would be as well if she didn't have recourse to her pistol. Still and all, she told herself, it would be as well to have it there to give her confidence.

The journey to Cheapside took them some time, but Jessica and Andrew indulged in only sporadic bursts of conversation, punctuated by longer periods of silence, during which Jessica's thoughts were taken up with imagined scenes between herself and a burly sweep. All of these were long and drawn out, with the sweep reluctant and recalcitrant and Jessica cleverly using her wits and her quick tongue to best him.

After stopping a number of times so that the coachman might ask directions as they wended their way through streets filled with potholes and the noisome stench of decaying garbage—without once, as Jessica observed to Andrew with a wry twist of her lips, catching a glimpse of even so much as the dome of St. Paul's—they came at last to a halt in front of the narrow, dilapidated, street-hugging, three-story house, crammed into a row of others that were equally disreputable, where they had been told they might find Jem Crick. After all her mental exercise, she would have been disappointed to discover that he was not home; however, while the footman unloaded the brushes and other equipment to the narrow flagway, Andrew knocked loudly upon the door, and it was Mr. Crick himself who answered.

He was not at all the sort of man Jessica had imagined he would be. Thin, wiry, and stoop-shouldered, the sweep bowed and scraped and wrung his hands when he realized they had come to discuss Jeremy. He seemed inclined to offer a number of whining excuses for his ill-treatment of the child until he discovered that they merely wished to purchase any papers he might have that entitled him to Jeremy's further services. So astonished was he by this news that he scarcely haggled more than five minutes or so over the price required, though he did manage to make them stare at the amount he seemed to expect they would be willing to pay. It was not until they had returned to the carriage, papers in hand, that Jessica chanced to remember the little pistol in her muff. She looked at Andrew, grinning.

"That was not so difficult as I had expected it would be."

"Difficult!" Andrew exclaimed. "By Jove, ma'am, it was as easy as kiss my hand. Hard to imagine that craven fellow brutalizing a scamp like young Jeremy, ain't it?"

Jessica disagreed. She could easily imagine Mr. Crick, whose eyes had avoided hers the entire time they had talked, doing just about anything she could imagine. But it was a little easier to understand how it was that Lady Susan had managed to rout him from her house with so little difficulty.

Since she could scarcely wait to describe the circumstances of their victory to her aunt and Jeremy, it was a trifle disconcerting to be met in the entry hall by Sir Brian instead. It was even more disconcerting when she realized, as she did immediately upon allowing her gaze to collide with his, that he was in a towering rage. Andrew, behind her, stopped dead upon the threshold, leaving Bates in something of a quandary, since he could not shut the door until Andrew moved. The butler glanced uneasily from one occupant of the hall to another.

It was Sir Brian who spoke first. He addressed his nephew, and his voice was deadly calm.

"I wish to have a few words in private with Miss Sutton-Drew, but I shall expect to find you in Charles Street upon my return."

"Y-yes, sir."

It was clearly a dismissal, and Andrew fled, leaving Jessica to face his uncle's wrath alone.

10

BATES SHUT THE front door.

"Will you or Sir Brian require anything further, Miss Jessica?" he inquired in a carefully even tone.

"We require nothing, Bates, except a little privacy," Sir Brian snapped before Jessica could collect her thoughts enough to speak. "We shall be in the small saloon, where we do not wish to be disturbed."

"Yes, sir." Bates moved without so much as a questioning glance at Jessica to open the door into the saloon Sir Brian had indicated, a charming little room decorated in pale blue and gold, and overlooking the square through tall, narrow Crown-glass windows.

Sir Brian waited pointedly for Jessica to precede him, and after one quick glance upward to find an expression in his eyes that promptly reminded her of the day Andrew had said his uncle had a talent for turning people's knees to pudding, she swallowed carefully but managed to walk past him with her head high. Inside the room she turned, waiting only until Bates had closed the door again behind Sir Brian.

"You seem a trifle put out, sir," she said, pardonably proud that her voice sounded calm, even though, for the first time in his presence, she could actually feel her heart pounding against her rib cage.

"Put out?" His voice rose a little, and despite the control he was so clearly exerting over himself, there was undue emphasis on the second word. "My dear girl, I have been pacing the floors here, trying to decide whether I ought to go after you or not, ever since the moment your aunt informed me of the ridiculous mission you and my harebrained nephew had set out upon."

He took a step nearer, and Jessica felt a tiny thrill of fear shoot up her backbone, for his eyes fairly glittered with anger, and the fact that his efforts to control his fury were so visible only made him seem the more dangerous. She had no idea how far his anger would take him; nevertheless, she stood her ground, and despite the curious effect his anger had upon her, she found it difficult to control her own temper.

"You need not have disturbed yourself, sir," she said. "We managed the sweep quite successfully."

"By God, Jessica, I believe you are as headstrong and foolhardy as that impetuous aunt of yours," he declared grimly. "It would be an excellent thing if someone were to shake you until your teeth rattled, and I confess, I'm of a mind to do at least that much myself, for you ought to have sense enough to realize that it was not your errand in and of itself that worried me, but rather the danger to your safety. Whatever possessed you to do something so outrageous?"

"There was nothing in the least outrageous about it," she countered, wishing her palms were a trifle drier and that her heart were not fluttering so absurdly in her breast. "Purchasing the boy's articles of indenture, or whatever an apprentice's papers are called, was clearly the simplest way out of the matter once Aunt Susan had taken it upon herself to rescue him. And as for my safety, you may rest assured that I took proper precautions."

"Don't think I didn't consider that fact," he said, glaring. "The knowledge did nothing to alleviate my anxiety, however. Give me that damned muff."

"I do not think it would be wise to do that," she returned warily, "since your senses seem to be somewhat disordered at the moment. There is a loaded pistol in this muff, if you will recall, and I believe I would do better to retain possession of it myself."

"What, are you afraid I shall shoot you with it, or myself?" he asked sardonically. Then he paused, regarding her sternly for some seconds before adding, "Not, mind you, that I'm not strongly inclined to deal with you as you deserve. However, I assure you I have no need of a pistol in my hand to attend to that."

The look of intent in his eyes caused Jessica to take a half-step away from him. "You've no right," she said.

"On the contrary, my dear, I've the right of any civilized

man to protect those who haven't been blessed with enough good sense to protect themselves. You've no more notion of what to do with that thing than the merest infant. First, you shoot my nephew with it. Next, you nearly stir a violent man to further violence. And today you take yourself off to some black slum, expecting that ridiculous toy to protect you, when it was much more likely to turn a bad situation into a worse one. It is therefore my considered opinion that you will behave more circumspectly without that damned gun to lend you false courage." He held out his hand implacably. "Hand it over, Jessica. I've no wish to exert myself."

Understanding that he had every intention of wresting it from her by force if necessary, Jessica bowed to the inevitable and handed him the fur muff. He reached inside and extracted the little pistol, examining it briefly before dropping it into his coat pocket.

"I cannot tell you how much it relieves my mind to discover that it hasn't been fired recently," he said, returning the muff to her.

"Well, of course it has not," she replied with asperity, her temper rallying at once when he showed no further inclination to carry out his threats. "If you had but let us describe what took place in Cheapside, you would know that I had had no reason to resort to such a course."

"If *you* had but waited a half-hour before departing, there would have been no cause for you to go to Cheapside at all," he retorted, the glitter returning to his eye.

"Oh, Andrew said you would say that." Jessica nearly stamped her foot. "I have no patience with such stuff, sir, for I am a grown woman, well past the age of nonsensical missish strictures. Dealing with the sweep directly was my own idea, and I was just as capable of managing the business as any man would have been. Besides," she added, "I had Andrew, my coachman, and a footman to support me. Not to mention that pistol. And you may say what you like, but I do know how to use it, and I should not have hesitated to do so if the situation had called for such a thing. And whether you choose to believe it or not, I do have sufficiently good judgment to have made that decision for myself. There was not the least cause for you to worry that I might have brought anyone to harm."

He did step forward then, impulsively, and Jessica experienced that little thrill of fear again as his hands clamped bruisingly upon her shoulders and he did indeed give her a fierce shake.

"You behaved outrageously," he informed her between clenched teeth as he shook her again. "You had no way of knowing what sort of man you were going to meet or how dangerous he might have been. And as for your *protection*, let me inform you, my girl, that neither my nephew, your aunt's ancient coachman, nor that town-pampered footman you took along with you would have been any match for that sweep if he'd had a few of his friends nearby to incite him to violence. That little popgun of yours would have made no impression upon such a group, believe me."

He released her suddenly, and Jessica was quite unsurprised to note that her knees seemed in iminent danger of buckling beneath her. She stared at him, saying nothing, astonished that he could be so angry with her over such a thing without even wishing to know what had transpired. It was as if he had spent the time while he awaited her return in inventing bogeymen. Nevertheless, just the fact of his anger was doing strange things to her inside, creating sensations she had not experienced before and that she did not know how to counter. Much effort was required merely to maintain her equilibrium.

Watching her, Sir Brian evidently assumed that he had frightened her to silence. A rueful look flitted across his countenance, and he made a strong effort to regain his normal calm. "I should not have lost my temper, Jessica," he said. "I did not mean to do so, and I cannot think how it came to pass. But if I might indulge myself in a bit of plain speaking, you behaved very foolishly. You would have been far wiser to have sent for me, and if Andrew truly suggested such a course, I think the better of him for it. You would have done well to have heeded his words."

Jessica released a small sigh. "You are saying that I ought to have sought your advice before proceeding in the matter?"

"Yes."

"But, pray, why should I do such a thing?"

"Because," he explained patiently, "if for no other

reason, the situation was one that ought to have been handled by a man, not by a gentlewoman. What do you suppose such persons as Lady Jersey or Mrs. Drummond-Burrell would have to say, should they hear of such an escapade?"

"Escapade? Is that what you think this has been, sir?" When he nodded, Jessica felt a sense of frustration. She wanted to touch him, to smooth the irritation from his brow, and somehow at the same time to instill him with an understanding of her motives, her feelings, and her needs. The most she could attempt, however, was to explain her position and hope he would not lose his temper again. "I do not think you understand how deeply I care about certain things," she said slowly. "I love my aunt, and I am accustomed to—how can I put this?—to curbing her higher flights. Perhaps that sounds a trifle impertinent, and I assure you I have never before been put to such a task as the one I took upon myself today. Usually, all that is necessary is that I talk her out of her more outrageous starts. She has an interest in a good many causes, and the social Season seems to bring out her battling spirit simply because there is so much more activity in town then and such a glaring contrast between the members of the *beau monde* and the people she wants to help. Not that I don't worry about her the rest of the year, as well. But I do understand her, because I care about many of the same things she cares about. And today, I was as concerned with helping that poor little boy as I was with protecting my aunt from the worst consequences of her actions. Perhaps I might have called upon you for assistance, but I am not accustomed to resting my burdens upon other people's shoulders." However broad, she added to herself, watching him.

He straightened a little under that look, but his expression remained grim. "You ought to have sent for me," he repeated doggedly.

"Have you not been attending?" she demanded. When he only returned look for look, she had a sudden flash of insight. "I don't believe you have," she said accusingly. "I believe the truth of the matter is that you're merely in a miff because I didn't ask your advice. That's the matter in a nutshell, sir. You weren't worried about my safety. Not in the slightest. You were simply offended that I didn't come to you and beg your assistance. It annoys you that I *was* able to attend to the matter alone."

"Nonsense."

"It is not nonsense. And since you profess to be fond of plain speaking, sir, I shall not scruple to inform you that one reason I did not wish to send for you was that I feared you would prove to be as insensitive to Aunt Susan's needs as you proved to be to Andrew's over the unmasking of his princess. I had no wish to take such a chance. And, for that matter, why you should expect me to come to you for assistance against someone who is exploiting a poor helpless child, I cannot think, for you do the same sort of thing yourself, do you not?"

"Not those old tales," he protested angrily. "Really, Jessica, it is high time we—"

"No, it is not time we did anything at all," she snapped, interrupting him without hesitation. "There is nothing you could say to me at this moment that would make me accept the necessity for exploiting children, no matter how plausible you might make it sound. I confess, I accepted a good deal of what you said about the institution of slavery, but this is a different matter altogether, sir, and one on which we shall always disagree. Therefore, it would be wisest if you were to say nothing further on the subject."

"Very well," he returned stiffly. "Then perhaps it would be as well if I said nothing further at all, except to wish you a good day."

"Perhaps you are right." Jessica was very much upon her dignity, but she could not help feeling a surge of disappointment that he was giving up so easily. And when he gave an angry bow and wished her a curt good day, the disappointment grew to the point where she nearly called him back. But somehow, stubbornly, she held her tongue.

A moment later the door closed behind him, and tears sprang to the back of her throat, causing an ache that she hadn't felt since childhood. She couldn't imagine why his anger should affect her so. Lord knew, no one else's ever did. She remembered Lord Gordon's frequent lectures and scolds. Never had they distressed her in the slightest. As a matter of fact, she realized now, she rather looked forward to his bursts of temperament, thinking they added piquance to an otherwise dull relationship. And her parents had scolded her, of course, from time to time over the years. But although such incidents had been unpleasant, they had never made her feel the distressing ache she was feeling now. That sensation had come only at times of deep emotional crisis, when something happened that she couldn't bear to discuss with anyone else. Like the time her kitten had been run over by a visitor's carriage. Or the time her mother had been so ill that no one had expected her to live. Why, then, should that same feeling come to her now?

Telling herself that she was merely overreacting to the various strains of the afternoon, she took some moments to compose her countenance before leaving the saloon. The entry hall was empty at the moment, so deciding that her aunt was most likely to be found in the drawing room, Jessica went upstairs.

Lady Susan was indeed sitting on a green-striped, claw-footed settee between the tall windows in the comfortable drawing room, working at her tapestry frame. She looked up when Jessica entered.

"Oh, there you are, my dear. I suppose you have been discussing today's events with Sir Brian." Her eyes twinkled. "I fear he thought we had been a trifle precipitate in our actions this afternoon. Was he at all difficult?"

Jessica sighed at the understatement. "Men," she said. "They really have a very small understanding of anything beyond their own needs, Aunt Susan."

"Oh, dear," Lady Susan said, distressed. "I suppose that means he was difficult. I knew he was a trifle displeased not to have been consulted before you left to make your offer to that dreadful man—did he accept it, by the by?"

"Indeed, he did." Jessica smiled, remembering. "You won't credit it, ma'am, but he actually had the effrontery to demand twenty pounds for Jeremy."

"No!"

"Yes, he did. But I told him what Sir William said about the boy's injuries and suggested that he might well bring charges against him for causing such harm, and he nearly groveled after that. Tried on all manner of excuses. You should have heard him. But in the end he settled for ten pounds."

"A tidy profit for him, when all is said and done," her ladyship stated wryly.

"It is that, but it ought to keep him from causing further difficulty. How is Jeremy?"

"Still a little frightened that Mr. Crick will demand his return, I suspect, though we have all done what we can to reassure him. He will be relieved to know that the man is no longer a threat to him. And do you know, Jessica," she added, frowning slightly, "it was the oddest thing. When the maid brought him down after his bath, Sir Brian was here and asked the boy some questions about his origins. Got nothing to the purpose, of course. Poor little tyke can scarcely remember anything before that Crick got hold of him. But while he was talking to him, Jeremy noticed Sir Brian's unicorn signet ring and said his grandpapa had one like it, only with some letter or other carved upon it. Well, Sir Brian was most taken aback, as indeed I was myself, for it's a shockingly expensive piece of jewelry. I told him about the snow crystal then, and he began asking Jeremy all manner of other questions. The child seems to remember a time in the country, with trees and ponies to ride. Before that, Sir Brian had been trying to get him to tell what part of London he had come from, but it now appears that his family must have brought him here from some village or other and sold him to the sweep. It seems very odd to me."

The situation was to become odder yet. When Jessica had dressed for the evening, the high point of which was to be a ball hosted by the Count and Countess de Lieven at the Russian embassy, she went to the little room where the boy had been put to bed to tell him good night. A candle had been left by his bed, but despite its warm glow, his face looked pale and fragile as he looked up at her.

"Cor," he said, drawing the word out in a long breath, "you look sumpin' like, miss. Like me mum used t' look of an evenin'. Smell like 'er, too," he added as she stepped nearer.

Jessica regarded him searchingly. "You remember your mother wearing a gown such as this one, Jeremy?"

"Aye, miss, only not silver, like that 'un. Me mum

mostly wore pink. Like an English rose, me dad used t' say." He looked surprised. "I jest remembered that bit, I did."

She patted his tousled head. "You will remember more, I hope. Can you remember any name other than Jeremy? Like Mr. Crick, you know. Most people have got two names."

But the boy shook his head. "Don't remember nobody callin' me nothin' but Jeremy, miss."

"How old are you?"

"T' man arsked me that this afternoon," the boy told her, "but I dunno, miss. Guess I been wi' Crick six er seven years, 'n 'e says I were four er five when 'e got me."

"Merciful heavens, then you must be at least ten or eleven. You look no older than eight, though I did think from your speech that you must be older than that."

"Guess I am," he said. "Jest a bit small, like. You goin' out, miss?"

"Yes, and my aunt will be wondering where I've lost myself," Jessica said with a chuckle. "But I wanted to be certain you were comfortable."

"Don' remember ever bein' this comfortable afore," he muttered.

"Well, we shall see what can be done to assure that you are not mistreated again, Jeremy. That much I promise you."

"T' gennelmun said t' same thing, miss. I b'lieved 'im."

"Good." Jessica felt the odd tightening in her throat again at just the oblique mention of Sir Brian, and left the boy rather quickly, pausing at the head of the stairs to recover her calm.

Lady Susan awaited her in the entry hall. "The carriage is at the door, my dear," she said, pulling on her long pale pink gloves. She was looking particularly elegant in a gown of mint-green silk with a demi train. Her hair was twisted into an intricate knot at the back of her head, and she wore a becoming little lace cap, which she straightened absentmindedly as she looked Jessica over from head to toe. "Pinch your cheeks," she said. "You are looking a trifle pale this evening."

Jessica obeyed her, but without much hope of putting

any bloom into her complexion. She had attempted to do so with her rouge pot before leaving her bedchamber, but Mellin had thrown up her hands in dismay at the result. And indeed, no matter how lightly she applied the stuff, it made her look as though she had spilled paint in daubs upon her cheeks, so she had scrubbed the rouge off again. The scrubbing had created a momentary improvement, but the blush had faded now.

As the carriage approached the embassy on the corner of Dover Street and Hay Hill, Jessica began to tense with anticipation. Andrew had mentioned that he and his uncle had received invitations to the ball. However, they had agreed to dine at St. Erth House, for Sir Warren had been due to arrive that day from Cornwall, and so there had been no plan for them to accompany the ladies from Hanover Square. Jessica wondered now if Sir Brian would even attend the ball.

He was there. She saw him immediately upon entering the magnificent crystal-and-gilt ballroom. Despite the crush of people, it seemed as if her eyes were directed of their own accord to the tall, broad-shouldered gentleman presently leading a dusky-haired damsel through the paces of a country dance. He even, Jessica noted without favor, seemed to be enjoying himself. As if he had never been out of temper in his life.

Following in Lady Susan's wake, she greeted a friend, stopped to chat with one of her aunt's acquaintances, and finally made her way to a row of gilt chairs along the far side of the ballroom. Thankfully, she took a seat, but her gaze strayed immediately, albeit as covertly as possible, to the dance floor. There he was again, still partnering that fresh-faced girl with the shining dark tresses. The girl looked up at him just then, her rosy young lips parting slightly, her large wide-spaced eyes alight with enthusiasm. Sir Brian smiled at her, and Jessica's teeth came together with a distinct snap. Her aunt spoke just then, startling her.

"I beg your pardon, ma'am," she said, turning away from the scene. "I fear I was not attending."

"Oh, it was nothing of consequence," Lady Susan responded, regarding her with amusement. "I merely commented that these affairs tend to be stuffy."

"We can take a turn in the garden if you like," Jessica suggested.

"Perhaps later. I think you ought to enjoy yourself a little first. Oh, dear," she added with an expression of annoyance, "that despicable Lady Prodmore is headed our way. No doubt she wishes to flaunt that poor little slave of hers under our noses again. If you are wise, you will accept whatever invitation the gentleman bearing down upon us from your left has to offer."

Jessica turned quickly to see a plumpish young man whom she had met at another such affair coming her way, with Lady Prodmore in full sail right behind him. Trailing behind her ladyship, as usual, came the page, Albert, attired tonight in a purple suit and turban, exactly matching his mistress's very expensive gown.

The music ended, and the orchestra struck up for a minuet. Jessica and her partner took their places, and if she was a trifle dismayed to see Sir Brian with a new partner taking his place in the same set, she gave no sign of it. This time he was with a slender blond, who wore the simple white muslin gown that betokened a girl in her first Season. She appeared to be exceedingly shy, and Sir Brian had obviously set himself to charm her into relaxing. Jessica found she did not wish to watch the process. Unfortunately it was difficult to avoid looking at them, for her partner was nearly a head shorter than she was, so she could see Sir Brian even when the shorter man passed directly between them. The view was disconcerting, too, for the first time she caught Sir Brian's eye upon her, he acknowledged her gaze with only the briefest nod, causing her to swallow somewhat harder than usual and look away, but the second time she encountered his glance, she could have sworn that he was amused by something. At that point, Jessica threw herself into enjoying the rest of the evening and ignoring him. But she could not tell if her attitude was affecting him in the slightest, for he made no attempt to approach her, though she did see him conversing briefly with Lady Susan. He departed some moments after that, and the evening suddenly seemed to become particularly dull. Even Andrew's invitation to dance a waltz did little to cheer her.

"Are you feeling quite the thing?" he asked as they took to the floor.

"Now, there's a tactful thing to ask a lady," she teased, making an effort to recover her poise when she realized she must be behaving like a girl fresh from the schoolroom.

The young man's face colored slightly, but he refused to be diverted. "You are looking a trifle pale, you know."

"Yes, my aunt mentioned it earlier."

"Well, I hope Uncle Brian isn't responsible. He certainly seemed out of sorts when you and I returned to Hanover Square from Cheapside. I don't mind telling you, ma'am, I was in a quake of fear when I left you. Expected to have a real peal rung over me when he returned to Charles Street."

"Well, if he said half the things to you that he said to me, your expectations were certainly met," she said, grimacing at the memory his words brought to mind.

"Well, that's just it. Scarcely said a word. Just that I ought to have had better sense than to go trotting all over London with . . . well, with you, I suppose."

"With whom, Andrew?"

His color deepened even more. 'Well . . ." He took the plunge with a rush. " 'With a flea-brained female' was what he said."

"I see. Well, if that was all he said, I suppose I must be grateful. He called me a good many worse things to my face."

Andrew nodded wisely, as if he had expected to hear as much. "I could tell he was in a thundering rage when we first saw him. Guess you dashed well bore the brunt of it, though. Could have knocked me over with a feather when, instead of tearing a strip off me as I'd expected, he apologized for 'humiliating' me, as he called it, in Cornwall. Couldn't think what he meant, at first."

Jessica's eyes opened wide. "He apologized?"

Andrew nodded. "Never known him to do such a thing before. Can't say I wasn't dashed blue-deviled over that princess business, but I never thought he had the least notion of it."

"I daresay it may have risen out of something I said to him," Jessica said slowly.

"Very likely." Andrew showed no disconcertion at the fact that she had discussed his affairs with his uncle. "Must say, he seemed a trifle down pin tonight. Have you spoken with him?"

"No, for he made no attempt to approach me. I daresay he is still furious with me," Jessica said a little forlornly.

"Oh, I shouldn't think so," Andrew replied. "His tempers rarely last long. He'll come about and no doubt be on your doorstep first thing tomorrow, just as cheerful as though he'd never been out of charity with you at all. Mark my words," he added confidently. "It will be exactly as I say."

But Andrew was wrong. Sir Brian did not call in Hanover Square the next day. Or the next. And when Andrew presented himself the day after that to take tea with Lady Susan and her niece, he had to confess that his uncle had left town.

"All he said to me was to mind my manners and keep out of mischief," the young man told her, laughing. "I've not the slightest notion where he went or when he means to return."

Lady Susan shook her head, declaring the whole thing a mystery, but adding comfortably that no doubt Sir Brian knew his own business best. "We shall miss him," she said, glancing at her niece.

Jessica returned what she hoped was a noncommittal smile, but her heart seemed to sink with a thud loud enough for the others to hear. To say merely that she would miss Sir Brian, she realized, was entirely to understate the case.

11

JESSICA HAD LITTLE time to worry about Sir Brian's abrupt departure, for not only were the legal respresentations rapidly coming to an end in Mr. Hatchard's case before the King's Bench, meaning that the justices would soon be ready to render judgment, but Jeremy, the climbing boy, had managed to capture the entire household's attention by means of certain unexplainable behavior.

First, several of the maids observed laughingly that "Master" Jeremy was quite a one, causing Jessica to discover that that boy had taken to having servants at his beck and call as though he had been born to the privilege. His manner of speech rapidly improved, as well, which to Jessica's mind implied that the child was either a splendid mimic or had been accustomed to hearing proper speech throughout his earliest years.

As a result of such details, Jeremy had been in the house for scarcely a week before Jessica confronted Lady Susan over the breakfast table, insisting that something must be done.

"Well, I have made inquiries about a possible school for him, you know," Lady Susan replied vaguely, scanning the *Morning Post* for information regarding Mr. Hatchard's trial.

"Aunt, pray put aside that paper and attend to me. It is not a school which that boy needs, but a proper home. His own home."

"Yes, but I don't think we should keep him here, dear." Lady Susan obediently folded her newspaper and set it down upon the table beside her empty plate, grimacing slightly as she regarded her niece's determined expression. "Remember, love, you will be going back to your parents before long, and I really don't think I should enjoy raising a boy, you know."

"No, of course not."

"Though, perhaps, it is my duty to do so, now that I've rescued him," her ladyship mused.

"No, Aunt, it is not your duty." Jessica smiled, amusement lighting her eyes. "Jeremy belongs with his own family. His real family."

"Well, that would be the very thing, of course, only we don't know who they are, and Jeremy seems unable to tell us. Besides, my dear, anyone who would sell his own child . . . I mean, really, Jessica, could you find it in your heart to return that child to such parents?"

"Not if they had truly sold him, Aunt Susan. But what if he was stolen?"

"Stolen! From his family, you mean?"

"Indeed I do. Only consider, ma'am, all the objects he finds familiar about this house. First the snow crystal, then Sir Brian's ring and my evening gown. Then, only yesterday, the fresh strawberries General Potterby sent you from his succession houses in Sussex. Jeremy said he hadn't had strawberries in all the time he's lived with Crick, but that when he was little he used to have them for breakfast all the time."

"But lots of people eat strawberries, Jessica."

"Not poor people, ma'am. Not unless they live in the country and have access to someone's succession house. Strawberries rarely grow well in this country, you know, unless they have special care. That fact alone puts them generally beyond the reach of the lower orders. And, certainly, he would not have had them 'all the time.' "

"No, I daresay he wouldn't. But he doesn't remember anything to the purpose, Jessica. We can scarcely go about searching for a house which contains a snow crystal, a woman in a pink gown, and a man who wears a signet ring."

"No, of course not. But we can place an advertisement in the papers, Aunt. 'Boy found'—that sort of thing—giving his name, age, and general description. Something might come of it, and I couldn't bear not to make some push to reunite him with his family."

"It might work, I suppose," Lady Susan said slowly, nodding to the maidservant who offered to refill her teacup. "Many persons outside of London read the *Morning Post* and the *Times,* at least."

"Well, I mean to insert an advertisement in every paper I can call to mind," Jessica declared. "We must do all we can."

"Very well," agreed her ladyship. "At least I shan't have to discover a school for him straightaway if you intend to trace his family. I had been feeling as though I must, and today, at least, I mean to attend the session at King's Bench. Do come with me, dearest. You've nothing else to do that can possibly be of greater importance, for I very much fear Mr. Hatchard is going to be convicted, and if he is, he will need all our support."

"It certainly seems unfair to me," Jessica told her, "that poor Mr. Hatchard must suffer merely for printing what someone else wrote."

"For printing the truth," stated Lady Susan grimly.

"But if it was the truth, then why has there been no evidence to support that dreadful story of the flogging?"

To that question Lady Susan could return no acceptable answer, for no one had yet been able to discover a single fact in support of the accusation that the governor of Antigua's aide had flogged any female slave. And, as Jessica soon discovered when she accompanied her aunt to the Court of King's Bench, that lack of support had come to be the chief factor in the case.

After a full hour spent in discomfort in the stuffy courtroom, seated upon a hard pew between her aunt and a gentleman with a noticeable fondness for garlic, Jessica was at last privileged to hear Mr. Justice Abbott, one of the three bewigged black-robed justices at the bench, sum up the case for the jury.

"There is no doubt," Mr. Abbott declaimed in tones more suited to a box at Hyde Park Corner than to the closeness of the courtroom, "that by the law of this country, and of all other civilized countries, a printer or bookseller is answerable criminally, as well as civilly, for the contents of the books he publishes—no less answerable than the authors of them. The fact that the author in this case cannot be determined need have no bearing upon the jury's decision." He went on to explain that the only point of law the jury needed to decide was whether the printed matter itself was of a criminal nature or not. He also gave it as his opinion that the account of the flogging in the

Africa Institute's *Tenth Annual Report,* as printed, was enough to bring not just the one but any of Sir James Leith's aides under suspicion and disgrace, and was therefore a libel. "I am also of the opinion," he added, "that this article accuses Antigua's judiciary of acting improperly by refusing to prosecute. If the members of the jury agree that such an accusation was published with the intention of bringing the criminal justice of the island of Antigua into disrepute by suggesting that criminal justice there is not duly administered on the behalf of slaves, then that statement is likewise libelous."

The jury immediately found the defendant guilty upon both counts, and the judgment was pronounced by Mr. Justice Bayley. Jessica was glad to hear that gentleman say he did not agree that there was the same degree of criminality in a bookseller, who sold material for others under circumstances which implied no want of caution on his part, as there was in an author of such material who distorted facts with the intent of swaying public opinion.

"You did not receive that report from suspicious characters, Mr. Hatchard," said the justice quietly, speaking directly to the scholarly-looking man in the dock. "You received it from persons upon whom you thought you might with propriety and confidence rely." Nevertheless, the law was clear. Mr. Hatchard was fined one hundred pounds. He promptly paid the fine and was discharged.

Jessica was grateful to have the trial over and done. Unfortunately, she realized as she watched her aunt bearing down upon Mr. Hatchard, Lady Susan did not seem the least bit relieved. She was angry.

"I think it is a disgrace that in this day and age an English gentleman cannot find justice in an English court," she declared to the weary-looking Hatchard.

"Dear Lady Susan," the tall, thin man said, smiling slightly, "I cannot tell you what it has meant to me to see your lovely face here throughout this dreadful business, but I cannot allow you to defame the English legal system. By law, every person who publishes a libel is answerable for that libel, and with no one coming forth to prove the truth of what was printed, there could be no other outcome. Indeed, the justices were merciful. They might well have sentenced me to prison.''

"Well, you are generous, sir, but their verdict certainly does our cause no good. If the people of England believe we of the Institute are capable of manufacturing information in order to prove a necessity for condemning the institution of slavery, it will set the cause back fifty years."

"Aunt Susan, surely people will realize that proof could not be put forward without revealing the informant's name. The necessity to protect his safety has been well publicized by the Institute.''

"Yes, that's all very well and good," said her ladyship, glaring at no one in particular, "but if they disbelieve the tale, they will as likely disbelieve anything we print about the source of our information. I cannot imagine, however, that men such as Mr. Wilberforce and the Duke of Grosvenor would have any part in manufacturing the sort of malicious tale this would be if it were not true. At the very least, I am absolutely certain they believe that the informant acted in good faith and not from any other motive which has been attributed to him.''

"I think the problem," Mr. Hatchard said thoughtfully, "lies in the great distances involved. It is most difficult for the average Englishman to comprehend the horrors of slavery and to understand how easily all the evidence in this case might have been swept under the carpet, simply because everyone involved at the Antigua end is a slave owner himself. No one there wants England interfering in the backbone of their economy, and for the most part the average man and woman here at home haven't the slightest notion where Antigua is, let alone what goes on there. If these atrocities were occurring right here under their noses, the reaction would no doubt be quite different.''

"It seems very difficult," Lady Susan said with a sigh, "to understand how a country that outlawed the slave *trade* nearly a decade ago still does not comprehend what an outrage the institution of slavery truly is. Even right here in England, where you say people would care if it were right under their noses, chimney sweeps and their ilk treat their poor apprentices like slaves, and a woman like Lady

Prodmore can trot about puffing off the fact that she does indeed own another human being.''

"Well, if she does indeed own one, she can't have purchased him here, at any rate,'' observed a gentleman standing near enough to overhear the conversation.

"My dear sir, what has that got to do with anything? We say she cannot have bought him here, and we sound very smug when we say it, but fashion or no fashion, she can and *does* own him here, and to my mind that is a much worse thing.''

The unknown gentleman looked a trifle offended by her ladyship's suggestion that he had sounded smug, and Jessica thought it was high time to intervene.

"Aunt Susan, I am persuaded that Mr. Hatchard would like to see the last of this courtroom as soon as may be. And we are engaged to call at Melbourne House this afternoon and to attend the theater with Cyril and Georgie before a late supper at the Clarendon, so we really should be seeing whether your carriage is awaiting us outside.''

Lady Susan, glancing at the little watch pinned to her lapel, exclaimed at the time and agreed that they must indeed be on their way. And within fifteen minutes Jessica actually managed to steer her toward the street.

Jessica found the visit to Melbourne House boring, despite her fondness for Emily Cowper, who greeted her affectionately and treated Lady Susan with all the respect due a wealthy woman who had been about the town even longer than she had herself. The play that evening, too, was a trifle insipid, Jessica thought, finding it difficult to concentrate upon the actors' antics. Lady Gordon glanced at her speculatively a time or two during the second interval, and once they had gathered around a white-draped, silver-decked table at the Clarendon, where one always could be assured of the best dinner in town, her ladyship waited only until her husband had captured their aunt's attention before taxing Jessica about her lack of animation.

"Are you ailing?'' she asked flatly.

Jessica regarded her sister with fondness. "No, indeed, just suffering from a slight case of ennui, I daresay.'' Then, knowing that Lady Gordon often enjoyed flashes of insight, and desiring therefore to change the topic as quickly as possible, she asked if her ladyship had learned anything further about her own condition.

"Indeed, I have. I sent for Sir Richard Croft, the Princess Charlotte's doctor, you know, and he confirmed my suspicions." Georgeanne spoke in an undertone, with an oblique glance to reassure herself that her husband was still holding forth and had not overheard her. Then she added, "I've said nothing yet to Cyril, Jess, nor do I intend to until there's no hiding the matter from him any longer. And I charge you straitly to say nothing either. I do not mind if you tell Aunt Susan, so long as she, too, will promise to say nothing to him."

"But, Georgie, it is his right to know," Jessica protested, her boredom forgotten entirely for the moment.

"Pooh, he has nothing to say to the matter. But Sir Richard said I was to avoid anxiety and to pamper myself. I am persuaded he says the same to all his patients, but only imagine what Cyril will be like if he hears that sort of thing. I shall be wrapped in cotton wool, Jess. He would drive me to distraction in a week."

Jessica chuckled. "I cannot deny it," she said. "The mind boggles when one tries to imagine Cyril in the role of protective husband. He would no doubt lecture you as to how you ought to go on. I can hear him puffing off about the future heir to the Gordon properties. Thank God, Porth wasn't anything like that while Madeleine was increasing. Or afterward, for that matter. A little ill-at-ease with the new arrival until he'd held him for a while, but a sensible man all round, to my way of thinking. Cyril will be entirely different."

"What are you two nattering on about?" Lady Susan demanded when Lord Gordon paused for breath. "Cyril has just been describing all the Clarendon's best dishes to me, and I for one suggest that we allow him to order whatever suits him best."

"Already did," announced his lordship, patting his round stomach. "Stepped in early this afternoon to have a word with the chef, don't you know. Wanted to assure myself that his turtle soup would be available to us. Superb stuff. Wait until you taste it."

He waxed enthusiastic for some moments more before Lady Susan interrupted him ruthlessly. "If you've already ordered, then stop talking about the food, Cyril. We shall see soon enough for ourselves. Besides, I wish to know what Jessica and Georgie were discussing so avidly.''

The two young women stared blankly at one another. Lady Gordon's dismay was reflected by amusement in her sister's gray eyes. Finally Jessica turned back to Lady Susan.

''We were merely gossiping, ma'am, and I shall tell you the whole later, but you know how Cyril detests listening to female chatter.''

Lady Susan knew nothing of the sort, but she pursued the matter no further, contenting herself with a speaking look that informed her younger niece that she would have the whole tale out of her just as soon as they reached Hanover Square. Jessica smiled back blandly.

The turtle soup was everything Lord Gordon had promised, and the rest of their dinner lived up to the Clarendon's reputation. But once the sole with Portuguese stuffing had been removed with a roast turkey, and Jessica had tasted samplings of the raised pie á la française, the beef olives and sauce piquant, and a sauté of sweetbreads and mushrooms, the conversation turned to the play they had seen, and she felt the awful boredom descending upon her again. It was not that the play had not been amusing. She supposed it had had some very comical moments. But the things she had thought funniest had not been the same things that had made the audience laugh, and there had been no one to share her own mirth. Had Sir Brian been there—

But at that point in her thinking she forced her thoughts back to the present and threw herself into the conversation at hand with a will. She would not think of Sir Brian. She would not wonder where he was. Nor would she speculate on why he had gone or when he meant to return. Such thoughts as those, as she had already learned to her cost in the days since his departure, only led to melancholy reflection.

She managed to present what she assumed was the picture of a young woman thoroughly contented with her lot in life until their return to Hanover Square. Even then, when Lady Susan commanded her to step straightaway up to the drawing room, where they could be as private as they chose, Jessica was able to maintain her light humor and even to enjoy her aunt's reaction to her news.

"Increasing? Georgie is in a delicate condition? Truly, Jessica, you are not cutting a wheedle?"

"No, Aunt Susan, it's perfectly true. She only just had her suspicions confirmed by Sir Richard Croft, but she has been aware of the likelihood for some time now."

"Has she written to your mother?"

"Goodness, I haven't the slightest notion. I never thought to ask her."

"Well, she must do so. Gracious, when I think how excited your parents were when it was disclosed that Madeleine was with child. And she their youngest. They have quite despaired of hearing that sort of news from Georgeanne, I can tell you."

"Or from me?" The words seemed to fall from her lips all by themselves, but Jessica suddenly felt heavy and depressed again. She regarded her aunt miserably.

Lady Susan patted her shoulder with a smile. "No, child, that is not the case at all. Why, your father actually wrote me a letter the first time you came to stay with me, commanding me to engage in no matchmaking on your account, but just to allow you to go your own road. He said you'd never allow yourself to be trapped into marriage, that you could be trusted to send the ineligible ones to the rightabout with no help from anyone else, and that when the time came you'd find the right man and marry him. I know your dearest mama hoped you'd get yourself riveted in your first or second Season, but that was only because Georgie had done so well."

"Well, I didn't want a man like Cyril, I can tell you that," Jessica said with a little chuckle. Her aunt's words were like balm to her wounds. There had been many moments over the past years when she had been certain she was a disappointment to her parents. She had literally had dozens of offers during her come-out, and more than a few since, but she had turned them all down for the simple reason that she could not imagine spending two succeeding days, let alone the rest of her life, with any of the gentlemen in question.

"I know your father, at least, never thought you would come home with a man like Cyril on your arm, dear one. I can remember him telling your mother so, right here in this very room, when she was in flat despair after you turned down that young earl—the fidgety one, you remember?"

"Aylesworthy? Of course I remember. He was very persistent. But he is scarcely as tall as I am, and I am sure I must weigh at least a stone more than he does. I couldn't contemplate that match for a moment."

"And so your father told your mother, my dear. 'Mark my words, Thea,' he said, 'young Jess will not want to submit to anyone yet a while, but when she does, she will choose a man who's worthy of her.' That's exactly what he said, my dear," Lady Susan said with an odd gleam in her eyes, "and I believe he was right. The man you've selected is certainly worthy of you, best of my nieces."

Jessica flushed to the roots of her hair. "Aunt! I haven't chosen anyone, and I forbid you even to hint such a thing to anyone."

"As if I would," retorted Lady Susan indignantly. "But it's no use denying your feelings to me, my dear. Or to yourself. They will persist, whether you attend to them or not."

"What feelings?"

"Jessica, do not treat me as if I were all about in my head," Lady Susan said tartly. "I have eyes, and I use them. And I know you. Have done all your life. I know when you are out of sorts, which you are. And I certainly can see when your heart is disturbed. As it is, my dear. Can you, in all honestly, deny that?"

"Oh, you are being foolish," Jessica muttered, refusing to look her aunt in the eye. "As of this very moment, there is certainly no reason for me to be disturbed or out of sorts. I have no right to feel that way," she added dismally.

"He has made you no offer?"

"Oh, once he said I was the very woman he'd been searching for and never expected to find. No more than that."

"I don't know what more you need to hear," her aunt said with a wry twist of her lips. "The man is clearly interested. Why have you not brought him up to scratch?"

It never occurred to either of them that they might not be discussing the same man. Nor did it occur to Jessica to deny any interest in Sir Brian. But the last question stopped her short. She stared at her aunt.

"How can you ask a question like that, when he is what he is and who he is?"

"Fiddle, he is a most agreeable young man who thinks just as he ought."

"Aunt Susan, he owns slaves in the West Indies. He has women and children working down in his mines. How can you say he thinks just as he ought?"

Lady Susan tilted her head, giving the matter some thought. Then she looked her niece straight in the eye and said, "He is the man for you, Jessica, for all that. Neither his plantations nor his mines enter into the business at all. Besides the which I have yet to hear that he mistreats his slaves or exploits his workers. And we certainly cannot do without sugar, copper, or tin. I have never advocated that course, and never will. If I work to outlaw slavery, it is because the institution itself is a despicable one, but that does not mean that, simply as a matter of course, I despise all slave owners. Many of them are good men, trying to make things better for all concerned. I believe your Sir Brian is one of those. In fact, by all I have heard of him, he is one of the most generous and benevolent men in England. I know for a fact that he is contantly on the lookout for newer, more modern equipment to make his mines safer for his workers."

"But the mines will always be unsafe, no matter what modern equipment is used. I've heard they have no idea what causes those dreadful explosions where so many are killed. And the dust. They say that kills, even when nothing else gets them. And the deformities suffered by the women and children from crawling through narrow tunnels and carrying huge loads—*you* know, Aunt Susan!"

But Lady Susan was staring at her now. "Jessica, Sir Brian owns tin and copper mines, not coal mines."

"Oh, Andrew told me that, but I fail to see that there can be a difference," Jessica replied impatiently.

"Nonsensical child, of course there is a difference. The explosions you speak of occur often in coal mines, but rarely in others. And the harmful dust is certainly coal dust, not that from tin or copper. But you should discuss this with Sir Brian. He cannot be aware of these misconceptions or he would have straightened the matter out long ago."

"Is such mining so safe, then? Miss St. Erth was assaulted on the road not long ago by one of her father's miners, who could not get his master to listen to his complaints that the mines were unsafe. Even Sir Brian agreed that they were."

"And so they very likely were," Lady Susan informed her. "I have met Sir Warren St. Erth, and I can tell you the man is an unconscionable pinchpenny who grudges every farthing spent on his mines. Repairs and new equipment are always expensive, and heaven knows there are any number of conditions that can exist in any mine that would make the mine unsafe. The condition of the ladders leading down into the mine, the amount of water that is allowed to collect, the supports for the tunnels—all those things exist in all mines, although coal mining is a particularly dangerous occupation because of certain factors that pertain only to that industry. It is for that reason that while rioting rarely occurs in Cornwall or Devon, it is a constant threat in such places as Newcastle and Manchester. People in coal country fear for their lives and their health even when the conditions are as safe as they can be. That is why we fight to get women and children out of those mines. But with regard to the St. Erth mines," she added, "I've not the slightest doubt that once Sir Brian discovered the dangers, he took the matter up with Sir Warren."

Jessica nodded.

Lady Susan reached out a slender hand to touch her niece's shoulder. "Jessica, you really must discuss all this with Sir Brian."

"Well, I can scarcely do so when we do not know even where he is," Jessica replied with a sigh. "He is furious with me, too. I said dreadful things to him, and he said dreadful things to me. I doubt he will want to discuss anything with me ever again."

"Now you are being as melodramatic as the actors we saw in the farce tonight," Lady Susan told her with a touch of asperity. "I think your best course of action at the moment is to get a good sleep. Once you are thoroughly rested, you will be able to look upon the world with a less jaundiced eye, my dear.''

Jessica went obediently upstairs and found her patient Mellin waiting to put her to bed, but though she was soon tucked under the soft blue eiderdown, sleep refused to come. Instead, her mind's eye seemed to be filled with the sight of a tall, broad-shouldered twinkling gentleman who had once always seemed to be watching her whenever they were present in the same room, and whose twinkling gaze she had begun to search for on those rare occasions when previous arrangements to meet had not been made between them. Clearly, Sir Brian had come to mean more to her than she had allowed herself to realize, she decided. If nothing else, his presence definitely exerted a beneficial effect upon her state of mind. A niggling little voice deep within her seemed to take exception to that wandering thought, and Jessica knew she was hedging. Somehow her mind was avoiding a collision with the truth. Her father had been right. And Aunt Susan was right. Whether Sir Brian had chosen her or she had chosen Sir Brian, and whether the choice had been made purposefully or not, the fact of the matter was that she seemed to have fallen in love. But what she was going to do about that fact was more than Jessica could say.

12

JESSICA HAD HOPED there might be a reply to one of her advertisements regarding Jeremy before the end of the week, but when Friday arrived, there was still no word. Nor had there been word from Sir Brian.

"Not so much as a brief scrawl," said Andrew, having stopped in Hanover Square to pay a morning call, "which must mean that he intends to return soon, Miss Jessica, for otherwise I dashed well ought to have heard from him by now."

With that she had to be content. She had arrived at the conclusion that her aunt was right about one thing. It was time she sat down and had a talk with Sir Brian, explaining her misconceptions about mining and asking him to explain certain matters to her about his own mines. As for the fact that he owned a few slaves on an island far away, well, maybe she could convince him to free them or sell the property, or to find some other way by which her own sensibilities could be reconciled. Then, too, she had to admit in all honesty that, when she thought about Sir Brian, the issue of slavery seemed somehow rather remote.

However, before the weekend was out, Jessica discovered that issue to be having an effect much nearer home than she had dreamed. Having enjoyed a comfortable coze in Duke Street with her sister Sunday afternoon, she returned to Hanover Square to discover her aunt in the drawing room, looking very much like the cat cleaning her whiskers after a venture into the cream pot.

Lady Susan's eyes fairly danced with excitement, and Jessica experienced a sudden sinking feeling. "What on earth—" she began, only to break off when her aunt spoke at the same time.

"You'll never guess what's happened, Jessica," Lady Susan said. Her hands were clasped at the waist of her primrose-colored high-necked afternoon gown, beneath which she actually seemed to quiver with triumphant glee.

"You look very much as though you mean to tell me that a cache of diamonds has been discovered beneath one of the tiles in the entry-hall floor," Jessica said, managing a weak smile.

"No such thing. I think I've discovered the answer."

"The answer to what, Aunt Susan? There are a good many questions being asked in this world, you know."

"Yes, but only one that has been plaguing my mind of late," retorted her aunt.

"A name for Georgie's baby?" Jessica suggested hopefully.

"Don't be daft, girl. Attend to me. Did Mr. Hatchard not say that if the matters of slavery could be made to appear more of an English thing and less the business of unknown men on distant islands, the business could be settled in a trice?"

Jessica did not remember that Mr. Hatchard had put the matter in quite such succinct terms as those, but she was not one to haggle. "He did say that the distance between Antigua and England made it more difficult to illustrate the iniquities of that particular situation," she said carefully.

"I am persuaded he did not intend to define the matter so narrowly," said Lady Susan with confidence. "He made an excellent point, one that I had not clearly understood before. But now that I have done, the matter is in a way to be settled."

"How?" Jessica stared at the older woman. "What on earth do you mean to say, Aunt?"

A strand of Lady Susan's gray-blond hair had slipped out of its coil, and she pushed it back behind her ear with an impatient gesture. "I mean to say that I have done something—really done something, at last—that will make every Englishman face up to the fact that he does indeed allow slavery to exist right here at home."

"Merciful heavens, Aunt Susan," Jessica breathed, "what have you done?"

"I've freed Albert," her ladyship replied simply.

Jessica returned a blank look. "You've done what?"

"Freed Albert. You know, that despicable Prodmore

woman's little black page. Although," she amended conscientiously, "he is not so little. Twelve or so, I believe. At any rate, I asked him if he wanted to be free, and he agreed that he did, so I freed him."

Somewhat distractedly, Jessica found a chair and sat down. "Please, Aunt Susan, I am not following this explanation of yours very well. You say you freed Albert, but since he is not your property, I quite fail to see how that can have been accomplished."

"Well, perhaps it was a trifle premature to say I've freed him, but I mean to assist him to seek his freedom, so it is by way of being the same thing. Still, I daresay it would be more accurate to say that I have rescued him—like Jeremy."

"Oh, I see." Jessica breathed a sigh of relief. "You have purchased Albert from Lady Prodmore. Well, that was indeed kind of you, Aunt Susan, but you can very likely be held up on charges of slave trading, you know. It is not quite the same thing as purchasing Jeremy's apprenticeship."

"Purchased him?" Lady Susan's clear voice rose perilously. "I should say not. I'd never traffic in such a business, Jessica, and you should know better than to suggest such a thing of me. Why, I never. To *buy* a slave. Me? When you know how very abhorrent the entire institution is to me. Besides," she added, recovering some of her customary composure with a little sigh, "I doubt that she would agree to sell him to me, you know. She is a most disobliging woman."

Managing without much difficulty to stifle the smile stirred by the near-petulant tone of these last words, Jessica tried to bring her relative to the point as gently as possible. "I apologize if I misunderstood you," she said, "but if you did not purchase Albert, how on earth have you managed to rescue him?"

"Well, I simply told him he need not return home again when he brought me an invitation from that utterly loathsome woman to take tea with her on Wednesday. As if I would. Take tea with her, that is," she added, her expression daring Jessica to remind her that she had already, upon more than one occasion, done that very thing, in her own home if not in Lady Prodmore's, and certainly in other homes where they had chanced to meet.

When Jessica wisely said nothing, her ladyship's expression relaxed. "When she knows, as indeed she must, how I feel about human exploitation—to flaunt Albert under my nose constantly the way she does. It has been more," she declared, lifting her chin, "than flesh and blood can tolerate. So when I asked Albert if he liked being a slave and he said no, I told him he need not be one any longer, that I would set him free. And I see no reason why he cannot stay here with us and Jeremy until the matter is completely seen to, Jessica. I do not know precisely what must be done in such a case, but I expect Sir Brian can tell us when he returns. He was in such a pucker last time because we did not seek his advice that I am persuaded it will relieve his mind considerably to know that we are learning to depend upon him."

Jessica could not imagine that anything about the matter at hand would in any way serve to relieve Sir Brian's mind. He would no doubt be as dismayed as she was herself. The power of speech seemed to have deserted her for the moment, and she could only stare at her aunt. When she was finally able to speak, all she said, weakly, was, "Aunt Susan, you must send the boy back."

"I shall do no such thing," declared her ladyship, squaring her shoulders. "I promised him his freedom, and by heaven I mean to see to it, and at the same time to let every civilized man in England know what is going forth. I daresay I can find someone who will know precisely how to get the entire tale printed in the newspapers. Why, there are members of the Africa Institute who do that sort of thing all the time. I shall only have to recall a name or two to mind and the matter will be attended to in a trice."

"Aunt, you cannot keep Albert here," Jessica said desperately. "He belongs to Lady Prodmore. You would be guilty of theft."

"Pooh, nonsense. Oh, one might steal a child from his parents, as you believe to have been the case with dear little Jeremy, but Englishmen, proper homebred Englishmen, do not own people, Jessica. Even that awful Crick, though he may have thought he owned poor Jeremy, only owned some papers entitling him to certain services. You will see, Jessica. A good many of our friends, you know, still think poor Albert is merely an ordinary servant, for she does not puff off the fact of his slavery to everyone the way she does to us, and dear Lady Prodmore will not wish to make a name for herself as a slave owner. To parade about with a decorative little black page is one thing, though even that is not fashionable anymore. Why, I would be hard put to it to name five ladies who sport pages these days, and most of them—like the Countess of Carisbrooke, for example— are quite elderly and their pages are in their teens, at least. Those who were purchased, of course, were purchased quite le . . ." She broke off, a puzzled expression on her face. "Everyone used to have them. I wonder what became of them all."

"No doubt they have become properly trained footmen or are quietly earning their keep by occupying various other positions of trust on their masters' estates in the country," Jessica said tartly. "One does not know what became of all the little monkeys that ladies of the *beau monde* were leading about on silken leashes a few years ago either. Not," she added hastily, "that that is by way of being the same thing, of course, or that it is any more to the point than the other, Aunt. The fact of the matter is that Lady Prodmore does own Albert, and she is very unlikely to let him go without a fuss, whether she is keeping him out of some false notion of being fashionable or not."

"Well, even she must have realized that the passion for trailing pages after one has quite gone off," Lady Susan insisted stubbornly, "so I believe she took to the notion because, without requiring the exertion of her mind to the slightest originality of thought, it made her feel that she was being unique, while allowing her to puff off her consequence. I cannot think of anyone more odious than a person who comes into money and does not know the proper way to live with it. But that woman must care what others think of her, when all is said and done. Mark my words, she will be as easily convinced to leave the matter alone as Mr. Crick was."

Jessica didn't believe for a moment that Lady Prodmore cared a whit what others thought of her, so long as they realized how wealthy she was. In Jessica's estimation, a woman who cared what others thought was seldom as outspoken as Lady Prodmore had proven to be. Nor would a woman who cared what others thought take such delight in parading a black page before one who was adamantly opossed to the institution of slavery. And Lady Susan, Jessica knew, had not been overstating the case when she had accused the woman of flaunting Albert. Jessica had seen as much with her own eyes. Every time they met her ladyship, the woman made some excuse to bring Albert to Lady Susan's attention, whether it was by giving the boy some capricious order to carry out or by scolding him and sending him away. Jessica had seen her aunt's growing irritation and knew that Lady Prodmore could not have helped observing it too. Not if she were twice as oblivious to the feelings of others as Jessica believed her to be.

Jessica was as certain as she could be that this time Lady Susan had bitten off more than she would be able to chew, and she did her utmost to persuade her that she must send Albert back to his mistress. But in answer, Lady Susan sent for the boy, and when Jessica realized that he was as adamantly in favor of remaining in Hanover Square as Lady Susan was of keeping him there, she knew she was fighting a lost cause. Still, she made a last-ditch attempt to convince Albert that he was making a mistake.

"Your mistress will be very angry when you do not return to her," she said quietly.

"Is true, ma'mselle," he replied in his careful English. "Me, I have been here two hours now. Mistress say come right back, soon as I give m'lady *le billet doux.* If I go return now, my mistress will punish me. She has a little whip, *n'est-ce pas?*" He raised his dark eyes solemnly to meet hers.

"Good gracious, Jessica, do you hear what the lad is saying? That dreadful woman beats him."

"Aunt Susan, please, there are still a good many people in England who beat their servants, their wives, and their children. I daresay Lady Prodmore does no more to young Albert here than any schoolmaster does to the boys under his charge. Less, in fact. I doubt she is as strong as a schoolmaster."

"My mistress very strong," Albert insisted, his eyes warily upon Jessica, as though he feared she might prevail in her argument.

"Yes, Albert," she said quietly. "I don't doubt that you

dislike it when she punishes you. But she is still your mistress, and you ought to obey her. If you stay here, you may well cause my aunt a deal of trouble. You would not wish to do that.''

"Pooh, don't listen to her, Albert," interjected Lady Susan, straightening her shoulders and glaring at Jessica before returning her attention fully to the boy. "A little trouble won't daunt us, will it? We shall see this business through together. This country will not tolerate slavery within its very boundaries. We'll rout your lady between us, I promise you. Not," she added in a pointed aside to her niece, "that I believe for one moment that there will be any routing to be done. That woman will not pursue the matter. It will be left to us merely to discover the quickest and easiest way to gain the boy his freedom under the law. And I mean to see that every step we have to take is well publicized. It is outrageous that a person can be purchased in another country, then brought here to London and kept in slavery. The very fact that one cannot purchase a slave here proves that England will not stomach such an iniquitous institution.''

Jessica knew that thanks to her easy victory over the chimney sweep, her aunt was well away upon a new crusade and that this time no amount of talking in the world would dissuade her from her course. That Lady Susan so clearly underestimated her opponent was the thing that frightened Jessica the most. If Lady Prodmore were to bring charges, there was no telling what might happen.

For once, she truly wished Sir Brian were present to advise her. Even if he, too, were unable to convince Lady Susan of her folly, at least he would be able to protect her from the consequences. Of that fact Jessica had no doubt. And the consequences could be grave. Remembering how she had feared a scandal over Jeremy's rescue, Jessica shuddered. This matter was a hundred times worse, and she didn't have the slightest notion what she should do about it. She *needed* Sir Brian.

But when, with hope but not much optimism, she sent a footman to Charles Street to inquire whether or not Sir Brian had returned to town, it was Andrew, not his uncle, who accompanied the manservant back to Hanover Square.

"What has happened?" Andrew demanded, hurrying into the drawing room without waiting to be properly announced. "I took the liberty of reading that cryptic missive your man brought round, because my uncle has not yet returned to town, and I thought any message from you must be important."

She explained the matter to him, and he was quite as dismayed as she was herself.

"Hell and the devil confound it!" Andrew exclaimed. "There will be trouble over this, never doubt it. Of all the totty-headed females! Oh, I beg your pardon, Miss Jessica," he added ruefully when he realized his language had gone beyond the line of being pleasing, "but when I consider that you and my uncle caused me to be clapped up in irons because of a mere prank, you can scarcely blame me for suggesting that your aunt deserves to be clapped into Bedlam."

"Andrew!"

"Oh, very well. I should not say such things, I know. But I hope you don't expect me to get her out of this scrape, for I tell you frankly, ma'am, I haven't the least notion how to go about it. Can you not convince her that she is being dashed unwise?" When Jessica favored him with a speaking look, he answered his own question. "No, of course not. I was forgetting how involved she becomes with her causes. That is, I have never really seen it for myself, you know, except a little in the matter of that fellow Hatchard. I say, Miss Jessica, I wish Uncle Brian were here. He'd know how to go to work with her."

For once Jessica had no desire to contradict him. She wanted Sir Brian in the worst way. Not merely because he might be able to manage Lady Susan better than she could herself, but also because she felt a strong need for his emotional support. A smile from those dark brown eyes just now, she thought, would do more to bolster her courage than anything else she could think of.

But Sir Brian was not in London, so they were left to deal with the business themselves. The Prodmore footman who arrived less than an hour later, saying that his lady had sent him to ascertain whether or not Albert had visited Hanover Square that day, was easily dealt with. Bates simply sent him on his way with an affirmative reply and no further information. Lady Prodmore, however, presenting herself at what Lady Susan stigmatized as an unconscionably early hour the following morning, was less easily sent about her business. With a sense of deep foreboding Jessica accompanied her aunt to the drawing room after their guest's arrival had been announced.

Lady Prodmore was standing, waiting for them, her crisp pink sarcenet gown fairly crackling with a suppressed emotion that Jessica was not certain she could define. Her ladyship was either extremely annoyed or extremely excited. "I understand that my page did indeed deliver my invitation to you yesterday, Lady Susan," she said, looking down her long nose at her hostess, as she got directly to the point, "but my footman seems to have neglected to inquire whether or not Albert said where he meant to go from here."

"No," replied Lady Susan carefully, "Albert said nothing about going anywhere in particular."

"I didn't suppose for a moment that he did," the stout woman said tartly. "In fact, my lady, I take leave to doubt that he ever left this house."

There could be no question of it now. Lady Prodmore was not in the least annoyed. She fairly trembled with anticipation as she waited for Lady Susan's reply, and Jessica knew instantly that her aunt's dismayed expression had given her away. But then, before Lady Prodmore could say anything more, Lady Susan's back stiffened, and her countenance took on a look of even greater dignity than usual.

"Your assumption is quite correct, madam. Albert is here, and here he shall remain. I have promised to seek his freedom for him."

"Do you mean to imply that you have formed the intention of attempting to purchase him from me?" Lady Prodmore asked with an archness in her tone that made Jessica long to smack her. "I fear that such a transaction would be utterly out of the question, my dearest ma'am, for surely you must realize that it is against the law to buy or sell a slave in this country. I had to acquire young Albert in France, you know. And as I have already been to Paris this year, I do not think I could agree to making a second trip merely to accommodate your desire to purchase my slave. He will return with me at once, if you please."

"Don't be absurd," said Lady Susan. "I have neither the wish nor the need to purchase that poor child. In this country, madam, you will discover that people will not tolerate the holding of a child in slavery, once they realize that that is in fact what you are doing. I believe you will not wish to figure in the minds of the *beau monde* as a woman who would stoop to such evil."

"Please, Lady Prodmore," Jessica said quickly, "you must see that if you carry this business too far, it will look ill for you. It is one thing to have a black page. People have become accustomed to the fashion over the years. It is quite another thing to inform them that the page is actually a slave. My aunt is right about that. Surely you must realize that the members of the *beau monde* who think so highly of you now would not tolerate having the true facts of the matter brought home to them. Not, at any rate, by means of the scandal that you and my aunt seem determined to brew between you."

"Over the years," pronounced her ladyship in majestic tones, "I have weathered more than one scandal, Miss Sutton-Drew, and I daresay I shall easily weather another. It is you and your aunt who will suffer if you pursue this madness, and it is you who ought to be considering what the more starched-up members of your set will think of it. I think you will find yourself much mistaken in the matter." Lady Prodmore got to her feet and smoothed her skirt. "The *beau monde* tolerates a good deal, you know, but one thing all its members understand is the pound sterling, and Albert is a very expensive piece of property, one that you will never succeed in wresting from me. I shall take steps, Lady Susan, of that fact you may rest assured. Strong steps."

Lady Susan blinked at her. "You cannot know what you are saying," she said quietly. "He is a child, like any child. He is not a piece of real estate."

"Under the law, madam, you will find that you are very much mistaken."

With those words as her parting shot, Lady Prodmore

departed, leaving Jessica to stare, dismayed, at her aunt. "What on earth are you going to do?" she asked.

"Whatever is necessary," responded Lady Susan tartly. "But no matter what else happens, Jessica, Albert must be protected. We cannot allow that woman to get her hands on him again."

Jessica reluctantly agreed, but later that day she wished very much that she had not given such a promise to her aunt. Indeed, it would have made her feel a good deal better to have been able to produce Albert on the spot when two constables arrived, demanding that he be returned to his mistress. When Lady Susan, offended already merely by reason of the constables' presence in her house, refused to accommodate their request, the elder of the two men shook his head sadly.

" 'Tis sorry I am t' ear ye say that, me lady, fer it gives me no recourse. I must place ye under arrest for the theft of the boy Albert, property o' Lady Prodmore."

"No!" cried Jessica.

But Lady Susan was made of sterner stuff. "Never mind, my dear. Just get word to the Institute. Someone will know what to do. I believe the duke is gone out of town this week, but Mr. Wilberforce or one of the others will tell you what must be done to settle this business. On no account, however, are you to give Albert up to these persons or to anyone else."

"No, Aunt Susan, but are you prefectly certain? It will be horrible for you." Tears were burning Jessica's eyes, but when her aunt only glared at her, she did her best to stem them before they could spill over onto her cheeks. Her mind was rushing, so that she had already made several decisions by the time the hackney coach had rolled off down George Street with Lady Susan sitting obstinately erect between the two constables.

First she sent word to Andrew. Next she scrawled a note to the secretary of the Africa Institute, Mr. Harrison, explaining what had transpired and requesting that he immediately inform whomever might best be suited to render prompt assistance to Lady Susan. And finally, albeit most reluctantly, she sent for Lord Gordon.

The latter arrived in Hanover Square within the hour, thoroughly annoyed. "Really, Jessica, I cannot think how you came to allow such a thing to occur. A scandal in the family is the last thing I wish to hear about," he informed her, pulling off his curly beaver hat and puffing out his cheeks in pompous displeasure.

"I am sorry to have disturbed you, Cyril," she returned, nettled. "Had I realized you wished to know nothing of the matter, you may be certain I should not have sent word to you. Please do not hesitate to leave us to deal with things ourselves. I am sure Andrew Liskeard will be along soon, and he will no doubt be glad to assist Aunt Susan in her hour of need."

Lord Gordon snorted. "Confound it, girl, don't be absurd. You know perfectly well I meant nothing of the kind, but upon my word, I cannot like the business. Who could? Nonetheless, I know my duty, miss, and I shall do what I can. Though what business you had to lay a family matter such as this before young Liskeard, I'm sure I don't know."

"Oh, Cyril, don't scold," Jessica said contritely, sorry now that she had snapped at him. "I daresay I shouldn't have sent for him but for the fact that he was here earlier and knows about Albert. Still, you are quite right, for once, to be annoyed. I am, myself. I keep feeling as though I ought to have been able to do something to prevent such a disaster. I did know that Lady Prodmore's constant flaunting of Albert was distressing Aunt Susan, but I certainly never thought she'd get this wretched maggot into her head."

"The woman wants watching," pronounced his lordship ominously. "You'd think she'd have caved in quite sensibly once she knew she was faced with arrest."

But that Jessica would not allow. "How can you say such a thing?" she demanded. "You know how strong her principles are. She would never allow the fear of arrest to weigh with her in such an instance, for she has great courage, and you know it, Cyril. You are merely annoyed," she went on fiercely and without due thought, "because you think nothing is more important than the fact that you are at long last about to produce an heir!"

There was a sudden heavy silence. Lord Gordon had stopped his pacing instantly upon hearing her words, but he stood for a moment, quite still, before turning to face her. In that moment Jessica realized what she had done, and she held her breath, waiting for whatever explosion might come.

"What did you say?" he asked very quietly, much as though he feared he had misheard her.

"I should have said nothing," Jessica said just as quietly. "It was not my news to tell."

"An heir? Georgeanne is . . . is . . ."

" 'Enjoying a delicate condition' is the way we say it in polite circles, Cyril," Jessica told him, tickled by his bemused expression despite everything else on her mind.

"Upon my word," said Lord Gordon with growing astonishment. "An heir."

"Or an heiress," she pointed out.

"Of course." He suddenly looked shaken. "I must go," he said. "At once!" He strode purposefully toward the door.

"Cyril!" Jessica called after him, dismayed. "What about Aunt Susan?"

"Bother Aunt Susan!" he snapped over his shoulder. Then, catching a glimpse of Jessica's outraged expression, he added, "Don't fly up into the boughs, my dear. I'll do what I can. But more important matters must come first." And he was gone.

13

JESSICA STARED AFTER Lord Gordon for some moments before the absurdity of the situation struck her. Then she managed a chuckle and sent a silent apology to her sister for letting the cat out of the bag. She only hoped that his lordship, in his jubilation, did not forget Lady Susan's plight. And that hope became yet stronger when the afternoon passed without a single word from Mr. Harrison of the Africa Institute. When Andrew finally appeared in answer to her summons, Jessica asked him if he thought it possible that the Institute might simply wash its hands of Lady Susan.

"Couldn't say," he replied after a moment's thought. "The Hatchard business put that lot in a bad light all round, you know. Daresay they'd just as lief not have another scandal fresh upon the heels of that one."

"Well, but they've got the scandal whether they like it or not," Jessica pointed out. "My aunt has already been arrested, and by the look of things, she and Lady Prodmore will see the thing through to the end. I fancy Lady Prodmore is actually enjoying herself."

"Feels superior," Andrew told her, nodding sagely. "Your aunt is the one cooling her heels at Bow Street, after all. Must give the odious Lady P. a deal of pleasure to think she's responsible for putting her there."

"Poor Aunt Susan. How her dignity must have suffered today."

"Don't you think it," Andrew told her, chuckling. "Your aunt is no doubt enjoying every moment of her martyrdom thus far, feeling she's doing a *good work.*"

Jessica couldn't deny the possibility that he was right, but she found herself wishing again, and with all her heart, that Sir Brian were in town. Andrew's presence did little to comfort her, whereas she was certain that Sir Brian would know exactly what to do.

The evening seemed interminable, for Andrew soon left her to her own devices, and there was still no word from the Africa Institute or from Lord Gordon. However, that gentleman presented himself the next day at midmorning, accompanied by a dapper little man in a bottle-green coat and dove-colored pantaloons, whom he introduced as Mr. Lionel Wychbold. Jessica received them both in her aunt's drawing room, feeling a large sense of relief that something was at last moving forward.

"Mr. Wychbold, here, is my man of affairs," Lord Gordon told her as they took their seats. "A solicitor, my dear. He will do whatever can be done for Lady Susan." His lordship was looking positively benign this morning, Jessica thought. Learning that he was soon to become a papa evidently agreed with his constitution, but she hoped he was not driving her sister to distraction, as Georgeanne had predicted he would.

Jessica glanced obediently at Mr. Wychbold and nodded, saying she was pleased to make his acquaintance. "Shall you be able to get her out of that awful place, sir?" she asked worriedly.

Mr. Wychbold pursued his thin lips and rubbed his hands together thoughtfully. "As to that, Miss Sutton-Drew, I could not say as yet. However, I must warn you that the indications are against my being able to effect that desirable solution to the problem at hand anytime in the immediate future."

"I beg your pardon?"

"In a word, miss, probably can't be done."

"Merciful heavens, why not?"

"Simple. No Habeas Corpus. Suspended back in January as a result of that dreadful business with the Regent after the opening of Parliament, you know. Habeas Corpus—the act, that is—is what enables us to get a fellow—or a lady, as in this case, you know—out of jail when he, or she, don't belong there. Without it, not much we can do, I'm afraid. Likely to stay there till the trial. Or be moved to Bridewell, of course."

A small moan escaped Jessica's lips. "Bridewell." The

word came out in a whisper. "They cannot send her there."

"No reason to think they will do such a thing," said Lord Gordon, frowning. "Might just as likely keep her right there at Bow Street. Trial should be attended to pretty speedily, I should think."

"Depends," Mr. Wychbold told him. "Does Lady Susan have any compatriots who might be willing to cast a spot of bread upon the waters, so to speak?"

"You may speak as you choose, sir," Jessica told him, "but I fear I, for one, do not comprehend your meaning."

"In a word, miss, to fork over a little of the ready in order to speed things along, don't you know?"

"You mean to bribe someone?"

"Not that word, miss!" Mr. Wychbold protested hastily glancing about the room as though to reassure himself that they could not be overheard. "Merely a tidy something to encourage the clerks to work a bit harder to get her to court a few days sooner than might otherwise be the case. You see, the Court of King's Bench is still in session, but if the justices adjourn before her case is added to the docket, she will be forced to await the next session, which could be a month or more. Another unfortunate result of the Habeas Corpus business, I'm sorry to say. She can be held as long as they like without trial, you see."

"She will be sent to Bridewell then, to await the next court."

"In a nutshell, miss."

"How desperate is her case if she does get to trial immediately?" Lord Gordon asked. When Jessica gasped, he frowned at her. "Don't get yourself into a taking, now. I merely asked a question. That don't mean I favor locking the old girl up. Not but what it might not be such a bad idea," he added irrepressibly. "Keep her out of mischief, at all events."

"Cyril!"

"All right. We'll get things moving. Don't bother your head about the money, either, Jessica. If she needs it, I'll see to it. But how much are we up against it here, Wychbold?"

"Well, I've looked into the matter a bit since you spoke

with me yesterday, m'lord''—Jessica cast his lordship a grateful glance—''and it appears to me that Lady Prodmore and her man intend to argue that since the page —Albert, that right?—well, they're saying since he was legally purchased in France, he represents legitimate property which Lady Susan has stolen. I seem to recall hearing of a similar case some years back, but I couldn't locate it straight off, and I don't recall the particulars. In any event, the laws in this country regarding property are perfectly clear, so we must prove that what is property in France ain't necessarily property here when all's said and done. If we cannot accomplish that, we shall have failed just as Hatchard failed, for her ladyship—Lady Susan, that is—has no intention of denying that she kept the boy here against Lady Prodmore's wishes. She will be found guilty, and I daresay the judgment in such a case will be a deal harsher than it was with Hatchard. Howsomever, that's a wee bit down the road at present, and the man who will speak for her before the King's Bench, Sir Reginald Basingstoke, can make one believe dogs is cats or apples is oranges if he's of a mind to do so.''

Jessica's heart sank, for she could not imagine anyone being able to convince a jury, let alone three prominent justices, that what was property in France, or anywhere else, was not legitimate property in England, as well. But she thanked Mr. Wychbold for his assistance, asked her brother-in-law to relay her best wishes to her sister, and saw them off the premises with a little sigh. Andrew, coming into the drawing room an hour and a half later, had no information to lift her spirits.

''Not a word from him,'' he replied promptly in answer to her first question. ''Can't understand it. And I can tell you I wish we would hear from him, for you'll get no help from Lady Susan's precious Institute, Miss Jessica.''

''What can you mean, Andrew? They must help her. She is one of their most avid supporters.''

''Aye, that's just the problem. The one man who might be able to exercise his influence on her behalf, old Grosvenor, is out of town, and his people insist they don't know where he's got to. Lying through their teeth, of course. Bound to be. Uncle Brian's people do the same thing when he tells them to cover his tracks. But that don't help Lady Susan. And that Mr. Harrison dashed well don't even want to hear about her. Says he cannot have his precious Institute involved at all, that whatever Lady Susan has done is nothing to do with them, and such stuff as that. So I went to see old Wilberforce."

"You didn't." Jessica had never personally met Mr. Wilberforce, although her aunt had spoken admiringly of him many times. Besides being a well-known politician and friend of the late prime minister William Pitt, he was also a philanthropist on an even grander scale than Lady Susan and was undoubtedly one of England's foremost opponents of slavery. He was also a member of the Africa Institute. Jessica was touched but astonished to think that Andrew had actually called upon such a prominent man in his efforts to assist her aunt.

"I did," he returned stoutly, "but it did us precious little good, I can tell you. I believe the man is sincerely sorry about her ladyship's predicament, but his compassion seemed a trifle ironic when you consider that he supported suspension of the very act that would see her released."

"Indeed, people were astonished when he voted with Liverpool and the others."

"No more astonished than when he supported the Corn Laws, ma'am. Uncle Brian said it's because Wilberforce fears anything that might lead to anarchy, and therefore supports any law that will keep the lower classes in their place. On account of the long war with France, you know, and all the resulting shortages of food here. Many people fear that when the poor go about seeing what the wealthy have, their discontent will lead to revolution here, just as it did in France. Uncle Brian says Wilberforce is one of that lot, despite his Christian preaching and his seemingly very real desire to see an end to slavery all over the world."

"But that desire alone should compel him to assist Aunt Susan," Jessica protested.

"Not at all." Andrew's voice was laced with irony. "If you please, Mr. Wilberforce applauds your aunt's courage, and says her martyrdom will do more to assist the cause than any number of speeches in Parliament. Indeed, he says the very fact that she is being held in jail will cause questions to be asked there. He seemed to think that would be a very good thing.''

''Merciful heavens, if he likes having her at Bow Street, what will he say if they move her to Bridewell?'' Jessica asked bitterly.

''Daresay he might suggest the move himself if he comes to think of it,'' Andrew replied with a grimace. ''I don't mind telling you, I don't like the look of this business one bit.''

Jessica didn't like it either. She was of half a mind to write to her father, asking him to come to London, but she could think of no way in which he might be really helpful, aside from the fact that he would sympathize with her position. Moreover, the news that Lady Susan was in Bow Street jail would distress her mother. But there seemed to be no one to whom she could turn. When she visited her sister several afternoons later, even that lady seemed too taken up with her own concerns to lend more than half an ear to her troubles.

''I tell you, Jessica, there is only one good thing about Aunt Susan's having landed in the briars just when she did. Not,'' her ladyship hastened to add, ''that I am not most distressed over her sad state of affairs, but at least it has partially succeeded in keeping Cyril from hovering over me.''

''Dear me, does he hover?'' Jessica asked politely.

''Indeed he does. I do wish you had not blurted the news as you did.''

''Well, I'm truly sorry if I've made matters difficult for you, Georgie,'' she replied sincerely, ''for I certainly didn't intend anything of the sort, and I know you would prefer to have had the news to yourself for a time longer. However, I'm afraid I simply wasn't thinking clearly at the time. Poor Aunt Susan had just—''

''Really, Jess, how could she do such a thing?'' her ladyship asked, shaking her head. ''Surely she must have known it would lead to something dreadful. I declare, it is all I can do to hold my head up when I speak to someone like Lady Jersey, you know, when I'm so well aware that the only reason she is condescending to notice me instead of giving me the cut direct, as the Countess de Lieven did only yesterday, is that she is hoping the latest *on-dit* regarding my aunt will fall from my lips to her all-hearing ears.''

Jessica felt sudden irritation with her sister. "Georgie, do you realize they won't even let me see her? When I took a basket of food and some fresh clothing to Bow Street, they were kind enough to say that they would see that she got the things but insisted that they'd had no orders to allow her to see anyone. Imagine what it must be like for her. And just think what indignities she will be subjected to if they should actually send her to Bridewell. I become frantic, just contemplating the possibility!''

"Well, I said I was sorry, and I am," replied her ladyship, pouting, "but it isn't as if I can do anything, Jessica, or as if I had any part in what happened. And it is a great deal too bad that I must be made to suffer for what is none of my doing. People stare something awful, and I can see them talking behind their hands. And this is only the beginning." The last sentence ended on a wail, and Lady Gordon put her hands to her face. "Oh, I'm most dreadfully sorry. I seem to be on the edge of tears all the time lately. Sir Richard said I must expect to be like this yet a while, but, oh, Jess, I don't mean to turn into a watering pot. I truly am sorry about Aunt Susan, and I wish there was something I could do to help, but . . . but . . .''

She sniffled, much as a child might, and Jessica gave her a quick hug. "Never mind, love. You mustn't upset yourself.''

Lord Gordon, walking in upon them at that moment, agreed. "Upon my word," he said testily, "what's this? You must go straight upstairs to your boudoir and have a good lie-down, my love. No tears, now. I shall send someone up presently with a nice hot posset to calm your nerves. Now, go along," he added more gently as he ushered her toward the door. "I'll attend to everything.''

Jessica stood up and reached for her reticule, assuming he would wish to escort his lady upstairs. "I'll see myself out, Cyril. Take care, Georgie.''

"Not just yet, if you don't mind," his lordship said, glancing at her over his shoulder. His voice was hard, and when he had shut the door behind his wife, he moved back toward Jessica, a glint of real anger in his eyes. "I will not allow this business to distress Georgeanne, Jessica. She is to be kept out of it entirely, which means that you are not to come here babbling every detail to her. Is that clear?"

She saw that he really meant it and thought the better of him for it, knowing he was thinking only of his wife, and that it did not mean he cared nothing for Lady Susan's troubles. Still it was difficult not to show a trace of resentment. "I did not intend to upset her, Cyril," she said stiffly. "I had no reason to think she would not wish to be kept apprised of the facts."

"Well, even if she wants to know, you aren't to upset her," he said flatly. "I'll tell her as much as she needs to hear."

"Very well, only you will have to guard her from the gossips, too. She mentioned Lady Jersey. I daresay there will be others."

"I'm aware of that. I'll deal with it."

He sounded quietly confident, and for once there was no pompous note in his voice. Jessica realized he was truly worried about the effect Lady Susan's predicament might have upon his wife. She had despised Lord Gordon, however cordially, for a number of years, and it had never occurred to her that he might truly love her sister. The notion seemed to present the fussy little man in an entirely new light. For several moments, Jessica felt she might actually be coming to like him.

But then, in the carriage on the way back to Hanover Square, the evils of the situation seemed to close in around her. All she seemed able to think about was the fact that Lady Susan was incarcerated in the most dreadful, noisome place Jessica had ever set foot in and was likely to be sent to an even worse place if something could not be done to avoid it. So far, everything she had attempted had failed miserably, particularly the ill-judged visit she had made to Lady Prodmore in an attempt to convince her to drop her charges. Just to think about that incident now made her grit her teeth.

Facing Lady Prodmore in her opulent drawing room, Jessica had first suggested tactfully that matters would be more amicably settled in a private rather than a public fashion and then, more desperately, had promised to try to convince Lady Susan to agree to return Albert if Lady Prodmore would only be more conciliating.

Lady Prodmore had uttered a short bark of laughter. "She would never agree," she had said tersely, "and, truthfully, I prefer matters as they are, Miss Sutton-Drew. The highborn ladies of this town have despised me from the outset, and few have taken any trouble to conceal the fact. Well, your aunt, for one, won't think so highly of herself, now that she's besmirched with the taint of Bow Street."

Jessica hadn't been able to get out of her ladyship's house fast enough after that, and she had mentally kicked herself more than once in the meantime for ever having set foot in it in the first place. Now, as she thought matters over, lulled a bit by the easy rocking of the carriage, she decided the visit had not been such a bad thing.

Before confronting Lady Prodmore, she had been of two minds. First, she believed that Albert ought not to belong to the woman simply because any form of slavery was an outrage. However, perversely, she wished at the same time that her aunt had never launched them all into the scandal and would agree to return the boy just so she could be set free again. But after the visit to Lady Prodmore, the confusion in Jessica's mind dissipated completely.

She knew that now, no matter what happened, she would support her aunt and do what she could to see that Albert never had to return to his mistress. Even if Lady Prodmore were to come to her that very night, retracting what she had said earlier and promising to drop all charges if Albert were returned, Jessica would refuse to agree. Not, she told herself bitterly, that there was the remotest likelihood of that event ever coming to pass. No matter what anyone did now, Lady Prodmore would be no more minded to drop her charges than she would be to jump off the dome of St. Paul's Cathedral at midday. The woman was reveling in the scandal, cheerfully believing it affected only Lady Susan, and caring nothing for the narrow looks she received herself. Her chief interest seemed to be to achieve some sort of vengeance against those members of the *beau monde* who had slighted her. It seemed rather unfair that Lady Susan should be the scapegoat, however, since Jessica was certain that her aunt had always taken care to be polite to the woman.

Suddenly Jessica realized that everyone she knew had been carefully polite to Lady Prodmore. But somehow her ladyship had deduced that they all despised her, which meant she was not so oblivious as Jessica had thought. Or perhaps the woman merely imagined slights. The current situation might just as easily have arisen out of the fact that Lady Prodmore herself believed she had no rightful place among the members of the *beau monde*.

Not that it mattered what motivated her, Jessica mused. Just the fact that she wanted to make life miserable for Lady Susan was enough. All that mattered now was finding someone, somewhere, who would help. Someone she could depend upon. Someone—preferably a large, broad-shouldered someone—who would understand that she, too, had need of attention and support through this crisis. Andrew was sympathetic. Surely, Lady Gordon—despite her own view of the matter—was also sympathetic. Even Lord Gordon, Jessica had to admit, had shown himself to be dependable in a crisis. But they were not enough. Not nearly enough.

Mr. Wychbold was clearly a competent man. He had also seemed to think there might be a way, despite the clear-cut nature of Lady Susan's offense, to bring matters to a satisfactory end. And he had said, also, that Sir Reginald Basingstoke, whenever he spoke before the bench, could make apples appear to be oranges, or something to that effect. Even Cyril had seemed properly impressed that Sir Reginald would be taking Lady Susan's case to court. But no amount of Mr. Wychbold's confidence or belief in Sir Reginald's talent was sufficient to keep Jessica from feeling anything but despondent as the carriage rolled on toward Hanover Square.

The house would be empty. One needn't consider the servants. Even Mellin would be cold comfort, for she had lately proved to be something of a Cassandra, prophesying doom at every corner. Besides, servants simply weren't like having a friend to discuss matters with. A friend would listen and not only hear the details of Lady Susan's situation but also understand what Jessica was suffering as a result of that situation. He would be sympathetic, not just to her ladyship but to her anxious niece as well. He would offer needed comfort, a shoulder to lean upon, a hug.

Jessica's eyes closed, and she let her body relax against the squabs as she imagined what it would be like to enjoy the warmth and comfort of a hug right then. Strong arms enfolding her against a broad chest. Not just any strong arms, of course, or any broad chest. The vision of Sir Brian floated in her mind's eye. He smiled down at her, and the warmth of that smile sent a glow through her just as surely as though he had been sitting across from her in the carriage. She gave herself a tiny shake, but she didn't open her eyes, and the image refused to disappear on its own. His dark brown eyes were crinkled at the corners, and there were corresponding lines etched beside his mouth, showing that he had made a practice, over the years, of smiling. There was a lock of dark blond hair that had tumbled over one eye, making her yearn to push it back into place. It was odd, she thought drowsily, that just thinking of the man so could send the familiar tingling warmth flowing through her body. She could even hear the sound of his voice in her head, actually hear it, although that was not so unusual, after all. She could make herself hear other voices when she wanted to remember someone clearly. Usually, she simply remembered a phrase they liked to use, like when Lord Gordon said, "Upon my word." She could make herself hear his lordship's voice easily, not that he was a person she generally wished to call to mind.

The difference now was that she didn't need to remember any particular phrase in order to recall the sound of Sir Brian's voice. She could imagine him saying anything she liked, and she could hear the gentle, deep voice speaking in the slow way he spoke naturally. It was almost eerie, and as she let her fantasies run wild, the things he began to say to her nearly curled her toes. For some moments her mind was completely taken up by the fantasies. During those moments she did not think once of Lady Susan. She merely leaned back with her eyes shut, letting the fantasy figure say and do whatever he liked, while a contented little smile played about her lips.

"Miss Jessica." The voice was hushed. "Miss Jessica? Are you asleep, miss?"

Jessica's eyes flew open, and she sat bolt upright, experiencing a guilty feeling as though the young footman staring through the gloom into the coach might actually have been able to see what was going on in her mind. All the warmth in her body seemed to rush to her cheeks, and words stuck in her throat. But, reassured that she was now awake, the footman merely held out his hand to assist her from the carriage. She swallowed, placing her hand in his and stretching one neatly shod foot to the step, the other to the pavement. There was no need to say anything.

She took a deep breath, glad that the deepening twilight made it impossible for the footman to have any notion of her undoubtedly high color, then looked up toward the house. As she did, her despondency returned. There were lights in the windows, but they did not seem to welcome her. Instead they were like beacons, awaiting the return of the mistress of the house. Jessica almost wished she had a social engagement, just so that she would be able to take her mind off Lady Susan for a few hours. But of course that was out of the question, although Lord and Lady Gordon, she realized suddenly, must still be observing some social obligations, or Georgeanne would not have had the difficult meeting with Lady Jersey. But Jessica simply could not gad about while her aunt was languishing in jail. Instead, just as she had done the last few nights, she would face a solitary dinner and then retire to her own bedchamber, where she would attempt to concentrate upon at least one chapter of the Gothic romance she was reading. And then she would go to bed to toss and turn and worry until exhaustion claimed her.

With steps that faltered a little, she approached the door and stepped aside automatically to allow the young footman, who had followed her up the stone steps, to open it for her. Then Jessica walked inside and nodded to Bates as he hurried forward and gently took her pelisse from her.

"Good evening, Bates. How long before dinner will be served, please?"

"That is for you to say now, Miss Jessica, as I've told you," he said with a little smile.

"I keep forgetting," she admitted.

"Well, things ought to be improving right away now, miss," he confided, his smile widening.

Her spirits lifted magically, for despite the fact that he so clearly meant to surprise her, or perhaps because of it, she had not the slightest doubt of his meaning.

"Where is he? Is he here?"

He gestured with his head. "Upstairs in the drawing room, Miss Jessica, and not a moment before he was wanted, I'd say."

She only grinned her agreement of the statement before she snatched up her skirts and, without a thought for propriety, raced up the stairs and along the gallery to the open door of the drawing room.

Sir Brian was standing by the hearth, a glass of claret in his hand. He smiled when she appeared so precipitately upon the threshold, her magnificent breasts heaving, her hat askew, and tiny wisps of loosened hair curling about her lovely face.

"I have been informed that you wish to see me," he said, then scarcely had time to place his glass safely upon the mantelshelf and brace himself before, with tears glistening on her lashes, she flung herself into his arms.

"Oh, Brian, you're truly here at last," she sobbed against his shoulder.

"Well, well, well," murmured Sir Brian to the soft curls tickling his chin as he hugged her tightly.

14

SIR BRIAN HELD Jessica close for some time without speaking, then removed the tipsy hat from her tousled hair and tossed it onto a nearby straight-legged Kent chair.

"My poor child," he said then, gently, "you've been through a difficult time, have you not?" When she nodded against his shoulder, he gave her a gentle squeeze and set her back upon her heels, saying, "Let us sit down, and you may tell me about it. Andrew's version was a trifle sketchy."

"Where have you been?" she demanded instead as he led her to the green-striped settee between the tall windows.

"In Cornwall," he replied, taking his seat beside her. "I shall tell you about it presently. But first, explain to me, if you please, why Lady Susan is residing at Bow Street and why nothing has yet been done to effect her release."

Jessica settled back against the softness of plumped striped satin. "It's that ridiculous Habeas Corpus," she said with a sigh.

"There is nothing ridiculous about the Habeas Corpus Act," Sir Brian replied, turning slightly and leaning back into the side curve of the settee. He crossed his legs with the right ankle resting upon his left knee, laid his left arm casually along the back of the settee, then shifted his weight more comfortably, looking into her eyes in such a way as to make her feel a trifle giddy. "If you are referring to the suspension of the act, however, I must agree with you. I collect then that you have tried and failed to obtain her release."

"Well, Mr. Lionel Wychbold, in whom Cyril seems to repose a good deal of confidence, has attempted all manner of things, I believe, but Aunt Susan is still in that dreadful place, and oh, sir, there is a chance they may remove her to Bridewell!"

"That must not be allowed," he said firmly.

"Mr. Wilberforce would no doubt disagree with you," she told him bitterly, whereupon he demanded to know what the devil Mr. Wilberforce had to do with the matter. Jessica explained in the same bitter tone, "The secretary of the Africa Institute told Andrew that the precious Institute must not be involved in the matter. On account of all the bad publicity they received during the Hatchard affair, you know. So Andrew went to see Mr. Wilberforce."

"Did he, indeed?" Sir Brian seemed properly impressed.

Jessica sighed. "He did, but it was to no avail. Mr. Wilberforce actually said Aunt Susan would do the abolitionist cause more good locked up than if she were free. He would do nothing to help, either."

"And Grosvenor? Did Andrew then beard the duke in his den?"

"No, for he is out of town and his servants say they do not know where he has gone. Andrew says your servants often do the same."

"They do," Sir Brian admitted. "As does the highly trained hall porter at my club whenever I request such prevarication from him. 'Tis a time-honored tradition amongst those of us who would enjoy the occasional odd moment of privacy. But Grosvenor should know of this business as soon as possible. With matters of law suffering the absurd state of disorder our august legislators have managed to create, the best possible recourse in an instance such as this one is a weighty dose of political and financial influence. And the worthy duke wields a good deal of both. As does old Potterby. Odd that he has done nothing."

"The general? We never thought to inform him, and as yet, thankfully, there has been very little in the papers."

"Nevertheless, Potterby enjoys the dubious distinction of membership in the Regent's set, where the mainstay of life is petty gossip. And whether or not the papers have made a nine-day wonder of your aunt's affair, I should certainly imagine the details have been bruited about town by now."

"Indeed, they have. Poor Georgie has already suffered several cuts direct and a most annoying interview with Lady Jersey."

"Silence prodded your sister for the facts of the case, did she?"

"Yes, and she is the most unconscionable gossip. I know

she is well thought of, but she can be a dreadful nuisance. As for the general," Jessica added, "if he is with the Regent, then he is at Brighton, for the Carlton House set left town a day or so after you did."

"Well, never mind, my dear. I am persuaded we shall find a way out of all this business. Who has Wychbold got to speak for your aunt before the King's Bench?"

"A barrister named Sir Reginald Basingstoke."

"Excellent. I know him well. That man can run rings around anyone who speaks for the prosecution. Why, I've seen him make—"

"Apples appear to be oranges," Jessica interjected, smiling for the first time since she had begun explaining matters to him. "I know. Mr. Wychbold and Cyril have said the same thing."

Sir Brian grinned. "It's perfectly true, nonetheless. If anyone can get her off, he can. So you needn't worry anymore."

She nodded, realizing that she already felt better. It was odd, she mused, gazing at him, how his mere presence relaxed her and made her feel as though there were truly nothing further to bother her head about. Lady Susan was still languishing at Bow Street, and all he had said was that she mustn't be allowed to remain there. He had offered no solution to the problem, yet Jessica had faith that he would set things right again, that she could depend upon him entirely. It was a most unusual sensation for one who had been accustomed to depending only upon herself, but she was rapidly discovering the sensation to be a comforting one.

"Shall I tell you now what took me to Cornwall?" he asked gently.

Despite the gentleness of his tone, she thought he was looking rather smug, and her curiosity was piqued. "If you please, sir," she said. "You were gone a very long time."

"I have been to Woodbury Manor."

Jessica knitted her brow. "Is the name supposed to mean something to me? I fear it does not sound familiar."

"Not to you, perhaps, but it may strike a familiar chord in young Jeremy's cockloft."

"Merciful heavens, have you found his family, then? Is Jeremy's surname Woodbury?"

"No, not Woodbury. His surname is Ashwater, but he is the second son of Viscount Woodbury."

Jessica stared at him as though he had accomplished something magical. "How? That is, how did you find them? We inserted advertisements in every paper we could think of, but there hasn't been the whisper of a response."

"Woodbury must not have seen it," Sir Brian replied. "Can't say I did myself. I didn't do anything truly spectacular, however. It was the lad's constant reference to familiar objects that should not have been in the least familiar to a sweep's boy. Saw some of it myself, you know, and then Lady Susan mentioned at the de Lieven affair that there had been other incidents. It was pretty clear that your Jeremy had had experiences that were a deal above the touch of a back-slum climbing boy. Then, there was the name Jeremy itself. That struck a familiar note, but it took me a day or two to remember why it did. It was while I was mulling over something someone had said to me about the exploitation of young children in mines that it came to me."

He paused briefly, and Jessica shot him a rueful look from under her lashes. "Aunt Susan says I must discuss that matter with you more fully, sir. It appears that I have been laboring under certain misconceptions."

"A good many of them, actually," he agreed, smiling. "Not that it was entirely your fault, however. I realized you had got the wrong sow by the ear some time ago, and I did nothing to correct matters. However, we shall attend to that later, and you have little cause to regret those words, for they were directly responsible for stirring my memory to life, causing me to recall a gentleman who came to see me nearly seven years ago, looking for his son."

"The viscount?"

"The same. He labored under some misconceptions too. Although," he added with a grimace, "perhaps he was not so wide of the mark as I then rather naively—and, I fear, indignantly—thought. I do not *buy* children to work my mines. Nor, to the best of my knowledge, does any other mine owner in the West Country. However, I have since learned that it is indeed a common practice with many in the North. Viscount Woodbury—although at the time he was merely the Honorable William Ashwater—thought perhaps whoever had stolen his son had then sold him to work in a mine, and he was visiting every mine owner in the three counties. He also placed advertisements, but there was no response. It never occurred to him that anyone would take young Jeremy all the way to London to dispose of him.''

"Where is the viscount now? I should think he would have come posthaste to recover his son.''

"And so he would have done, except for the fact that his father succumbed to a lingering illness only the day before I located him. That business took me a while, simply because, although I had noted down the child's description and the father's name and address at the time, I just stuffed the information into the nearest drawer afterward, so I had the devil's own time finding it when I returned to Shaldon Park. And there were several pressing matters to attend to at home—as, indeed, there always are when I am available to be pressed—so it was a day or so after that before I was able to set out for Woodbury Manor, which is located in the Brenden Hills in north Devon. The old viscount was to be buried almost at once, and of course Woodbury could not leave until that was accomplished, but though he suggested I remain, I had no wish to do so. I assured him, however, that Jeremy was in the best of hands and would be well cared for until his arrival, which should be within a day or so.'' He paused, regarding her searchingly. "If you like, I can take both Jeremy and Albert to Charles Street with me. You are looking a trifle hagged, my dear, and they must be a sourse of anxiety you would just as lief do without at the moment.''

But although she appreciated the kindness behind the offer, Jessica refused to accept it. She had discovered that the time she spent with the boys each day could take her mind off her troubles more easily than anything else, and she was unwilling to part with either of them.

Sir Brian took his departure shortly thereafter, reassuring her once more that matters would be attended to as quickly as he could manage them. His farewell was friendly, but hardly loverlike, and Jessica felt a nagging disappointment as she saw him on his way. Surely, she thought, he ought to have realized that she would not have spurned another hug or even a kiss. That thought stirred others, as she wondered what his kisses would be like if one allowed oneself to savor them. She remembered the incident in the gardens at Gordon Hall and how quickly and naturally she had responded to him there. The memory was a disturbing one, and she found herself perilously near to falling into a reverie similar to the one that had overcome her in the coach on the way home from Duke Street. But the fact that Sir Brian had failed to take advantage of her exuberant welcome disturbed her, too. She had flung herself into his arms, after all, had cried out his name and as good as sobbed out her frustrations on his shoulder. And all he had done was to hold her much as a big brother might have done, and then he had removed her hat and told her to sit down and tell him all about it. Just like her father. That thought nearly stirred her to stamp her feet in frustration. She did not want brotherly or fatherly assistance from the man!

Suddenly she seemed to have reached the brink of considering those emotions she had before now carefully avoided exploring. Nor should she take the time to explore them now, she told herself firmly, for now that Sir Brian was in London, everything was well on the way to being put to rights again, and that was all that must concern her. Lady Susan's peril must be the primary matter in her thoughts until that matter was satisfactorily resolved. If Sir Brian still meant to make her an offer, he had no doubt had the good sense to realize that he must not press her while she was so vulnerable. Surely that was it. Surely his interest in her had not cooled to mere friendship. Not now that she had finally come to realize how much she loved and needed him.

Annoyed with herself for allowing such a train of thought to continue unchecked, Jessica gave a little shake of her head, picked up her hat from the chair, and strode purposefully upstairs to her bedchamber, where she chatted determinedly with Mellin until that worthy had seen her safely tucked up in bed for the night. Then, however, with the candles snuffed and the golden light from the streetlamps in Hanover Square sending shadows dancing around the room as a light breeze stirred the curtain at the open window, Jessica found her thoughts involuntarily returning to Sir Brian until, with a tiny sigh of frustration, she drifted at last into restless sleep.

All the following day she awaited word from Charles Street, but by the time she had retired for the night, she had yet to hear anything at all. It was, as a matter of fact, nearly three days before her faith in Sir Brian was justified. During that time, she wrote him more than once, demanding information, but all he would vouchsafe each time in reply was that the matter was well in hand and that she was not to bother her head about it any further. When, to one such note, she had added a postscript, recklessly inviting him and Mr. Liskeard to dine with her that evening, the reply was very polite. Sir Brian and Mr. Liskeard regretted that they had a previous engagement.

Jessica actually breathed a sigh of relief over that one. She had been impulsive, too impulsive. Despite the fact that she was an acknowledged spinster, it would have been highly improper for her to entertain two gentlemen who were quite unrelated to her at her dinner table. Two ladies living together might do such a thing. One alone must not. The rules were clear. No doubt, she told herself, Sir Brian had not wished to embarrass her by pointing out that fact and had chosen instead to be tactful. Or, she mused unhappily, he might actually have had a previous engagement.

At last, however, shortly after noon on Wednesday, the third day after Sir Brian's return, his coach, recognizable by the unicorn crest on the door panel, rolled up before the tall house at the southwest corner of Hanover Square, and a footman gently assisted Lady Susan Peel to the flagway. Jessica, hearing the sound of a coach through the open drawing-room window, flew to see who had come to call, and then, with a tiny shriek of jubilation, she picked up the skirts of her dusky-rose silk gown and hurried downstairs to meet her aunt.

Bates was just opening the front door when she reached the hall, and Jessica hurried out onto the stoop. "Aunt Susan! Oh, Aunt Susan, he did it. I knew he would, but it began to seem as if you would never come home."

Lady Susan allowed herself to be gathered into a crushing hug right there on her doorstep in full view of anyone who might chance to be watching from the square or from George Street, and even went so far as to return the embrace with fervor.

When the butler cleared his throat, her ladyship chuckled, releasing her niece, "Do behave, love. You are embarrassing Bates."

"Nothing of the sort, my lady," he countered, grinning at her in a most unbutlerlike fashion. "If it were not to take action beyond my station, I should be tempted to do just as Miss Jessica has been doing. Perhaps, however, not upon the doorstep."

"Oh, Bates, I have missed you," Lady Susan told him, reaching past Jessica to squeeze his hand, which gesture caused the little man to blush right up to the glossy top of his white-fringed pate. "You have been my dear friend as well as my butler for so many years that you seem quite one of the family," she told him. Then, turning a deaf ear to his near-stammering gratitude, she smiled fondly at her niece. "Come along inside, Jessica. We have provided enough sport for the neighbors."

Upstairs in her bedchamber a few moments later, Lady Susan rang for her woman to order a bath and a complete change of clothing.

"I put this gown on fresh this morning," she told Jessica bitterly, "but it is already saturated with the stench of that place. Really, if Bow Street is anything to go by, our jails need a thorough cleaning, and I daresay there are any number of other things that ought to be changed, as well."

Jessica chuckled, clasping her hands upon her knees. "A new crusade already, Aunt? Should you not await the judgment of the court in this one first?"

Lady Susan looked grim and a little fearful. "I do not want to go back there, Jessica," she said simply.

Tears sprang to Jessica's eyes, and she brushed them aside with an impatient hand. "I am certain that Sir Brian will do whatever must be done. After all, he is undoubtedly the man who effected your release."

"Indeed, it was Sir Brian who set matters in motion," Lady Susan agreed, "although he did so first by discovering that the Duke of Grosvenor was in Bath and then by sending a courier to fetch him. Next, he sent word to Brighton to General Potterby, who, as you know, has the Regent's ear. Amongst them all, they managed to stir enough mares' nests to manage the thing. They have also prevailed upon the clerks to set a time for the trial— Wednesday next before the King's Bench." She paused, wrinkling her brow a little. "Sir Brian said it would probably be a speedy business, for there are but few arguments to be made before either our side will prevail or theirs will.''

''I do not know how I shall manage to contain my apprehension until I know what the outcome is to be,'' Jessica said intensely.

''Well, I do,'' announced her ladyship, her expression lightening as she breathed deeply of the scent of roses that began to permeate the room as a footman filled a porcelain tub with perfumed water. ''I mean to be just as busy as I can be. Unless we have ceased to receive invitations, I mean to go everywhere and do everything, just in case right should not prevail. It would be most foolish to have missed what opportunities one had to enjoy oneself before being locked up forever in a noisome cell.''

Accordingly, that very evening, Lady Susan Peel astonished the *beau monde* by appearing at no less than three routs, a musicale, and a veritable crush of a ball at Devonshire House. She was in fine fettle, attired in a magnificent gown of green silk moiré with puffed sleeves, a high neck, and a gossamer gold overskirt. A splendid emerald-and-gold necklace encircled her neck, and a matching bracelet had been clasped around her right wrist over her long white glove. She carried herself with her usual graceful dignity, but the sparkle in her eye showed anyone who chanced to take note of it that she was actually enjoying the sensation she was creating.

Jessica, accompanying her aunt, albeit with some reluctance, was attired with equal splendor in a close-fitting gown of her favorite lavender silk, its high waistline emphasizing the magnificence of her breasts, its softness clinging seductively to the swell of her hips. Her lovely hair was piled into an intricate confusion of curls and plaits, with curly tendrils that had been allowed to wisp about her face and ears and down the back of her slender neck. Her skirt, falling gently to a whispering scalloped hemline, was embroidered with a circle of tiny pink roses and mint-green leaves at each scallop, while a vining of similar embroidery edged the low-cut neckline. She wore diamonds and amethysts at her ears, neck, and wrists, and there were tiny amethyst buckles on her mint-green satin slippers.

Their appearance at the first affair caused quite a stir, but both ladies carried it off with a high hand. Indeed,

Jessica thought, Lady Susan's dignified bearing and artless smile must have caused a good many persons to entertain second thoughts with regard to any tales they might have heard. Her aunt behaved as though there were nothing out of the ordinary at all. Jessica could only admire her courage. As for herself, she cringed a little inside at the looks they received, and only by the third rout was she able to believe that she was playing her part as convincingly as her aunt was. But then, after a dreary half-hour at a musicale, where the conversation had, perforce, to compete with the amateur talent being displayed, they went on to Devonshire House, and even before she saw him, Jessica knew Sir Brian was present.

She could not have said precisely how she knew. Perhaps it was the slight tingling in the fine hairs at the back of her slender neck. Or perhaps it was a tightening in her stomach or the pounding in her breast. Certainly, she experienced all of these sensations, but they might as easily have been caused by the increasing strain of the evening and not by anything more abstruse than that.

The Duchess of Devonshire, known for her unbounded kindness, greeted them with practiced aplomb. Not by so much as the turning of a hair did she indicate that she was surprised to see Lady Susan in her house, or that she was at all distressed by her presence.

"How nice to see you, Miss Sutton-Drew," she said in her cultivated, high-pitched voice as Lady Susan moved on and Jessica followed in her wake. The duchess sounded perfectly sincere, Jessica thought as she returned the greeting. As though she knew nothing at all of any scandal. But then Jessica saw Lady Jersey approaching, and beyond her, leading a slender redhead toward the dance floor, was Sir Brian.

Lady Jersey's eyes registered shock as they came to rest upon Miss Sutton-Drew's lush figure, but Jessica paid no heed to her, having eyes for nothing but Sir Brian and his partner. The musicians were playing a country dance, and the pace was fast and merry, but Jessica's gaze followed only the one couple. They were laughing and clearly managing to carry on a lively conversation despite the music and accompanying thunder of dancing feet. A surge of unmistakable jealousy welled up in Jessica's bosom, surprising her. She actually felt her fingers curl into the palms of her hands as she experienced a strong desire to snatch the red hair out by the roots.

"I can only say that I am astonished! Quite astonished, Miss Sutton-Drew."

Startled nearly out of her wits by the indignant nasal voice, Jessica nearly retorted that she was likewise astonished, that she had never known herself to react in such a fashion in all her life. But then she realized that the speaker was the pretentious, gossipy Lady Jersey and quickly put a guard on her tongue, raising her eyebrows slightly instead.

"Yes, my lady?"

"That Susan Peel should be so blind to all sense of decency," declared her ladyship in tones of strong disapproval. "I have never credited her with more than common sense, you know, but that she should inflict her presence upon us in such a way as this, with the cloud of criminality hovering above her as it does—why, it quite takes one's breath away."

"Not noticeably, madam," Jessica retorted without thinking. Then, realizing it would do no good for her to incur Lady Jersey's displeasure, she added hastily, "That is to say that everyone has been most kind, you know. I am persuaded that all of Aunt Susan's friends must realize that she has done only what her conscience impels her to do."

"That is as it may be," was the haughty response, and Jessica noted the offended expression on her ladyship's aging face with a touch of dismay. "But although that dreadful Prodmore woman behaves as though she has done nothing untoward, until this dreadful business is done, I should have expected Susan to behave more discreetly."

"No, would you really, ma'am?" Jessica asked gently, her eyes glinting now with humor. "Would you truly expect my aunt to hide away in the country somewhere until this all blows over or until she is carted off to jail?"

Lady Jersey gasped. "To mention such a likelihood in civilized surroundings, Miss Sutton-Drew, is not the behavior of one who is at all nice in her ways."

"Good evening, Frances," said Lady Susan, just behind them. "You got away from me, Jessica, when I paused to speak with Emily Cowper." She favored Lady Jersey with a long, measuring look. "You appear to be out of temper, Frances. Has this naughty puss been defending me too fervently to suit your taste?"

Lady Jersey drew herself firmly erect and looked down her nose. "I have merely been telling your niece," she said, making the last two words sound as though she had got a bad taste in her mouth, "that you ought to have had the good sense to remain in seclusion until this unfortunate affair has been concluded. One way or another," she added ominously.

"I see," said Lady Susan in musing tones. "You would sweep me under the nearest carpet, would you? Well, Frances, I have never been one to hide from the truth or from unpleasantness. Nor have I ever been one to seek seclusion. I still have my friends, regardless of my present difficulties, and you may be assured that when this business is done, those are the friendships I shall cherish most. Shall we see who is here, Jessica, who might be trusted to offer us some pleasant conversation?"

Lady Jersey stood like a stock, but as far as Jessica could ascertain, she might as well have been so much ambient air for all the notice Lady Susan paid to her offended expression. Somewhat in a daze, Jessica once again fell in behind her aunt, as that lady swept on through the crush, creating a pathway before them by simple strength of personality. Lady Susan paused occasionally to speak briefly with a friend or to wait patiently while one young gentleman or another signed his name to Jessica's dance card, but at last they reached the far side of the ballroom, where a number of comfortable chairs had been placed for those who had no particular wish to dance. Jessica sank gratefully into one of them, noting as she did that Lady Susan seemed to sigh with relief when she sat down beside her.

"All well, Aunt Susan?"

Twinkling blue eyes met her own, but there was a rueful note in her ladyship's voice when she spoke. "It has been an interesting evening, has it not?"

Jessica chuckled, regaining her own strength of spirit. "It has, Aunt. It surely has. Do you intend to do this every night until the trial?"

"Not if it will distress you, dearest," was the reply. The

look in the blue eyes softened. "This affair has been difficult for you, has it not?"

Jessica nodded, feeling a burning of tears in her throat. "But it doesn't matter, Aunt Susan. You are all that matters to me."

"Not all, I think," replied her ladyship cryptically, glancing at a point beyond Jessica's right shoulder. Then she smiled and held out her gloved hand. "Good evening, sir. Thank you for sending your coach to fetch me this afternoon. It was most kind of you."

"It would have been a deal kinder, my lady, to have come myself," said Sir Brian in his quiet way, "but as I hope my coachman explained, there were other matters requiring my attention."

"I understand, dear boy," she said, her smile warming. "He said you were meeting with Sir Reginald Basingstoke. I trust the meeting proceeded advantageously?"

"We believe so. Several interesting facts have come to light, thanks to the unceasing labors of Mr. Wychbold. Lord Gordon knew what he was about when he acquired that gentleman's services on your behalf."

Jessica had been sitting silently, listening to them, but her nerves seemed to be all aquiver, making it seem as if some sort of electrical field had engulfed her. Every cell in her body seemed alive to his nearness. This time it was not a mere matter of a little warmth creeping through her. This time every fiber of her being seemed to be shouting at him to pay heed to her. It was difficult to believe he could not actually hear the signals her body was sending to him. Even the sound of the music and the constant drone of conversation, punctuated by girlish giggling and occasional bursts of masculine laughter, seemed to fade into the background, so that all she heard was the sound of his voice, interrupted from time to time, distressingly, by the lilting tones of Lady Susan's as they discussed the matter of her upcoming trial.

Neither of them asked Jessica to contribute an opinion, and she was left to sit in musing silence until suddenly Sir Brian's cool voice interrupted her reverie.

"Will you give me the pleasure of your company for this dance, Miss Jessica?"

15

AS HE SWUNG Jessica into the circle of waltzers, Sir Brian said, "I was surprised to see the two of you here, though her ladyship seems to be weathering the stormy looks well enough. How are you faring?"

Jessice found it difficult to concentrate upon his words while his right hand pressed so authoritatively against the small of her back and his left held the gloved fingertips of her right. He was too close, and as always his nearness disturbed her composure. Indeed, his breath stirred the wispy tendrils of hair that curled about her right ear. When his silence indicated that he was awaiting her reply, she glanced up at him from under her lashes to see that he was watching her steadily.

She smiled. "I confess I have felt an urge from time to time to do something of a violent nature," she said. "Some of our so-called friends have strained the limits of my patience nearly to breaking. I don't know which is worse, the honey-sweet words one knows are spoken with the greatest insincerity or the cold looks from persons who have hitherto shown themselves to be well-disposed toward Aunt Susan's reforming crusades."

"I would never have advised either of you to expose yourself in such a fashion as this," Sir Brian replied, his tone surprisingly grim.

Jessica raised an eyebrow. "If we—either of us—had been wise enough to seek such advice, do you mean?"

"I do, indeed." The tone was even more grim.

"Well, but as it happens," she pointed out gently, "you were not at hand to provide us with your opinion. Nor," she added, unable to keep the expression in her eyes from challenging him, "did we believe we required advice upon this particular matter. Aunt Susan has no wish to hide in Hanover Square."

"I said nothing of hiding; however, you would have done better to have remained quietly at home until next Wednesday's business is concluded," he retorted uncompromisingly. Then, before she could take up the gauntlet, he changed course, continuing in a gentler voice, "How are your young charges bearing up?"

"Very well, thank you," Jessica told him, eyeing him warily, since she had expected him to say a good deal more. "Jeremy is a bundle of nervous anxiety and fevered excitement over the fact that his papa will be along shortly to collect him. And Albert is enjoying a pampered sort of leisure he has never known before."

"I hope you are not spoiling that boy," Sir Brian said sharply, "for it would be to do him a disservice. Even if we can bring Lady Susan off, Albert does not look forward to the sort of privileged future that Jeremy will enjoy."

"No, of course not," she agreed, "but Aunt does mean for him to go to school, you know."

They discussed the two boys amiably then until the waltz ended, but when Sir Brian restored her to Lady Susan's side, he paused a moment as though he would say something further to her. With a glance at her ladyship, who was deep in conversation with the mother of a hopeful debutante, he looked down at Jessica. She had not yet taken her seat.

"Would you like some refreshment?" he asked at last.

"No, thank you. If that is a boulanger the musicians are beginning, I have promised this dance."

"I see. Look here, Jessica . . ." He broke off with a frustrated gesture.

"Sir?" She cocked her head, regarding him with bewilderment.

But he had seen her partner approaching, and he merely shook his head. Lady Susan turned just then with an apology for seeming to ignore him, and he responded lightly before taking polite leave of them both. He did not approach them again before they departed for Hanover Square.

In the next few days before the trial, Lady Susan saw to it that they were never idle. From Venetian breakfasts and al-fresco luncheons to afternoon loo parties and carriage rides in the park at the fashionable hour of five, their

activity was so feverish that Jessica scarcely had a moment
to concern herself with her private thoughts. She saw a
good deal of Sir Brian, nevertheless. He stopped in to visit
occasionally, but each time, although his attitude was perfectly cordial, and she even caught his eyes resting intently
upon her from time to time, he gave no indication that he
wished to have private speech with her, and his conversation was directed mainly to Lady Susan.

They also encountered him during the evenings, as Lady
Susan continued her campaign to enjoy herself with as
many as five or six engagements each night, for although
Jessica had feared they might be ostracized, the truth of
the matter was that there seemed to be more invitations
than ever, as though they had become celebrities of some
sort. Though certain scandalmongers were no doubt
merely biding their time, awaiting further developments,
for the most part the ladies and gentlemen of the *beau
monde* had survived the initial shock of seeing Lady Susan
in their midst again, and rapidly became accustomed to
seeing her at all the most fashionable squeezes. And Sir
Brian seemed to be everywhere.

In fact, they encountered him so often that Jessica might
well have wondered if Sir Brian had appointed himself a
sort of guardian to their well-being, had it not been for the
fact that he rarely escorted them and seemed to enjoy
himself thoroughly without specifically seeking out their
company. Though he never neglected to ask her to dance,
if dancing was offered, he likewise never requested the
honor more than twice during a single evening, and if they
met at some other entertainment, he was as often to be
seen on the opposite side of the room as in her immediate
vicinity. And, Jessica noted, he was frequently accompanied by one or another of what seemed to her to be an
unending source of beautiful damsels. When they attended
the play, Sir Brian bowed from a neighboring box, where
he was seated beside a veritable dasher of the first water,
but he did not even avail himself of the opportunity to visit
them during either interval. Though he disappeared for
some moments during the first, causing Jessica to glance
back from time to time to the curtained opening of Lady
Susan's box, he had only gone to procure some refreshment for himself and his companion. And throughout the

second interval he could be seen to be leaning forward, attending carefully to something his companion was saying to him. Jessica's teeth ground together audibly when she observed them.

It was no longer the least bit difficult to recognize the feeling that surged through her each time she saw Sir Brian smiling into another feminine face. Lowering though the knowledge was, Jessica knew full well that she was nearly being consumed by her jealousy. Though she attempted to remain calm and indifferent, her emotions seemed to have leapt beyond all power to control them. She knew she had looked forward with unwonted anticipation to Sir Brian's return to London, but she had nearly succeeded in convin_ing herself that her anxiety was predominantly on Lady Susan's behalf. Now, however, Lady Susan was as safe as she could be under the circumstances, and still Jessica found herself yearning for Sir Brian's continued attention. Whenever they attended the same entertainment, she had to exert a nearly physical restraint in order to avoid watching him constantly. It was nearly as difficult to refrain from walking bang up to him and demanding that he speak to her. And when she caught his eye resting upon her, his expression had a tendency to stir her in much the same way that his touch might have done. Still his attitude remained only friendly. There was undeniable warmth in the dark brown eyes when they met her glances, even sometimes a touch of amusement, but he singled her out too infrequently for her taste, and his attitude when he did remained no more than casual.

When she received word early Friday evening that Viscount Woodbury, having arrived in London but realizing that they would have previous engagements, would call early the next morning to collect his son, she immediately sent word to Charles Street, inviting Sir Brian to call at the same time. However, when Bates stepped into the sunny morning room to announce the day's first caller shortly after nine, it was not Sir Brian's name that fell from his lips.

"Mr. Liskeard is below, Miss Jessica," the old man said with one of his stately bows. "He has come to make Viscount Woodbury's acquaintance, he says."

"Very well, thank you, Bates," Jessica told him, stifling

her disappointment. "I shall go down to him at once."

Lady Susan had not yet stepped forth from her bed-chamber, but Jessica desired one of the housemaids to acquaint her ladyship with the fact that Mr. Liskeard had come to call and to remind her that the viscount was expected momentarily. As it chanced, their second visitor arrived before Lady Susan had completed her toilette. Viscount Woodbury was ushered into the drawing room, even as Jessica was welcoming Andrew.

She turned to greet the newcomer, a gentleman in his mid-thirties, of medium height and coloring, who stepped toward her with alacrity.

"How do you do, my lord?" she inquired, holding out her hand to him. "I am Jessica Sutton-Drew, and this gentleman is Mr. Andrew Liskeard."

"Pleased to make your acquaintance, ma'am," responded the viscount, taking her hand and nodding to Andrew. "Where is Jeremy?" he asked, getting directly to the point.

"My aunt's butler had orders to fetch him as soon as you had arrived, sir. He will be down shortly." She had been measuring the viscount rather narrowly, and she liked what she saw. His smile, though anxious, was warm, and his light brown eyes had a kind expression. Still, she feared he would be in for a shock. "I should perhaps warn you," she said diffidently, "that Jeremy is no doubt a good deal different from the way you remember him."

The viscount sighed. "Don't think I haven't realized it, Miss Sutton-Drew. Gregory warned me how it would be, of course, but I'm not such a cloth-head that I don't realize it's going to be something of a shock no matter how well prepared I think I am. That's why I didn't bring the boy's mother with me. She would have come, but she was already fairly done up over my father's death, for they were very close, and I decided it would be best for her to have time to rest before she has the lad to deal with."

"His wounds are nearly healed," Jessica said gently. "There are still one or two burns that the doctor recommends dusting regularly with basilicum powder, and there will be some scaring, but he has already begun to fill out a bit, so he doesn't look nearly so frightful as he did when he first came to us. Dr. Knighton assures us that there should be no other damage and insists that the best cure for every-thing that presently ails him is fresh air, freedom, and a good deal of love.''

The viscount smiled at her. ''You cannot know how grateful we are that you found him, ma'am.''

''You should be thanking my aunt, sir. It was she who rescued Jeremy from the sweep.''

''A dauntless woman. I look forward to making her acquaintance.''

He was to be granted that privilege immediately, for Aunt Susan came into the room just then with Bates and Jeremy at her heels. Andrew let out a low whistle at the sight of the boy. He had scarcely clapped eyes upon him since the day of the rescue, and the child who entered behind Lady Susan was hardly recognizable as the scrawny, begrimed skeleton of a waif he had seen before. Jeremy had suffered through a thorough bath nearly every day since coming to Hanover Square, and his skin was now pink and white, if still a bit fragile in appearance. His hair had been properly cut and washed, his nails had been cleaned and pared, and he wore nankeen trousers, a frilled white shirt, and a blue jacket with large brass buttons—clothes befitting his station in life. While Jessica intro-duced Lady Susan to the viscount, who could scarcely mind his manners long enough to respond with proper courtesy, the silent boy looked him over narrowly, chewing his lower lip from time to time nervously.

As soon as Lady Susan had been introduced, Jessica turned to Jeremy, gently squeezing his thin little shoulder as she drew him forward.

''Jeremy, dear, this is your papa.''

The boy's eyes widened as though until that very moment, despite whatever Bates may have told him, he had doubted the truth of the matter. But the viscount immediately knelt down before him and held out his arms.

''Come to papa, Jeremy-lad.''

There was a moment's doubt in the boy's eyes before he took one hesitant step and then another. ''Papa?'' The word seemed foreign to his lips. But then he repeated it as though its flavor were becoming more pleasantly familiar, and the next step had less hesitancy. A moment later he found himself crushed in the viscount's arms. Seeing tears suddenly leap to the light brown eyes meeting hers over the boy's shoulder, Jessica felt a stinging in her own eyes.

"It is all right, Jeremy-lad," the viscount muttered, turning his face toward the soft hair curling about the boy's ears. "Everything will be all right now. I'll take you home, and no one will ever hurt you again."

"Cor," the boy said softly a moment later, when he stood back a little and looked at the others in the room, " 'tis like a fella done died and went to 'eaven."

Jessica shot a swift look at the viscount. Jeremy's speech had improved dramatically just in the time he had been in Hanover Square, but he still suffered frequent lapses. The viscount seemed unperturbed, however, and merely stared at the boy as though he could not look long enough upon him.

"Jeremy, dear," Lady Susan said then, "have you the bundle that Mrs. Birdlip made up for you to take with you? Just a change of clothing, my lord, and a few odds and ends that Jeremy has acquired since his arrival here," she added when the boy nodded.

"I left it in the 'all," Jeremy said.

"Well, I've something else for you to put into it," Lady Susan said briskly as she crossed the room to the table near the fireplace. When she turned back, she was holding the snow crystal. "This was our first clue that you weren't what you appeared to be, you know. I feel that you ought to take it with you. To remind you occasionally that you have friends in London, you know."

Jeremy took it from her, turning it slowly in his hands, watching intently as the tiny carved village became engulfed in snow. Then he looked up at her, and when she held out her arms to him, he went straight into them, giving her a hug.

"What will you give Albert, m'lady, to remind 'im of 'is friends?" he inquired innocently as he stepped back again.

The silence engendered by his question caused him to look from one to the other of the adults in the room until Andrew bracingly told him not to bother his head about Albert.

"He'll be well looked after," he said.

"Who is Albert?" asked the viscount. When the explanation was made, he nodded, admitting that he had indeed heard something of Lady Susan's troubles since coming to London. "What do you intend to do with the boy if you win your case in court?"

Lady Susan smiled. "We have not really considered that point, my lord. Time enough when everything *does* go well. No sense getting his hopes up before then."

"My aunt would like to send him to school," Jessica put in.

The viscount's bow knitted thoughtfully. He glanced at his son. "This Albert a friend of yours, Jeremy-lad?"

"Aye." The boy nodded forcefully.

"Would you like him to come home to Woodbury with us?"

"Aye!"

The viscount looked at Lady Susan. "If you agree, my lady, I should be most pleased to take the lad back with me. I'd see him trained to a good trade, and I assure you he would be treated with utmost kindness at Woodbury. I am persuaded it might make things a deal easier for young Jeremy here if he had someone by him who was familiar."

The notion clearly appealed to Lady Susan, but then a thought occurred to her which made her face fall. "But he can go nowhere until after the trial," she said.

"Then Jeremy and I will simply remain in town until that time. Only a few days, after all. Then everything will be settled."

Jessica wished she could feel the same confidence the viscount expressed, but she could not, and it did not help matters when she visited her sister in Duke Street late Monday afternoon, to hear that Lady Prodmore was known to be exceedingly confident of victory.

"You just missed meeting Lady Jersey," Lady Gordon informed Jessica with a deep sigh as she pushed her into a comfortable chair and bade her forget her worries for a moment or two while they indulged in a dish of bohea together. "I'll just ring for a pot and some of Cook's little cakes. I don't know how it is, but I seem to be hungry all the time now, if I am not being disgustingly sick."

"Oh, Georgie, is it awful?"

"Not in the least," responded her ladyship cheerfully. "To be sure, I did think, for some days, anyway, that it was going to be a severe trial. Especially once Cyril began fussing about like a mother hen. I wonder," she added musingly, "if mother hens *do* fuss. Animals always seem so sensible about things that it seems prodigiously unlikely, don't you think?"

Jessica chuckled, beginning to feel herself relaxing. "I haven't a notion. I collect, however, that you are in prime twig."

"Indeed, I have never felt so well, and I am even learning to manage Cyril. There are uncomfortable moments, as I said, but even they are sometimes helpful, as when I can tell callers that I must be excused from the room if I particularly wish them to leave."

"Is that how you got rid of Silence?"

"Oh, dear me, no." She cocked her head quizzically. "Do you think such a ruse would succeed with her? I am persuaded she would merely await one's return if she thought there was more gossip to be wormed out of one. Besides, today she was talking more than she was listening," Lady Gordon confided, "and I felt it was my duty, under the circumstances, you know, to encourage her. I even had out Mama's fruitcake from last Christmas, and we only serve that to really favored guests, so I was able to flatter her, which I think served to encourage her to speak more than she would otherwise have done."

"With as much brandy as Mama soaks into that fruit-cake, I shouldn't wonder if it loosened her ladyship's tongue considerably," Jessica said, grinning. "But what did she have to say that was so interesting?"

Lady Gordon opened her mouth to speak, then shut it again when her butler entered and began to serve their refreshments. After he had gone, she picked up the teapot and poured out two cups, handing one to Jessica with a rueful look. "You will not like what she said."

"No one does, I should think. Though I cannot imagine that she would gossip about me to you."

"Well, you are out, then, for that is exactly what she would do. Just to put a word of caution in my ear, or because she thought I might be able to exert my influence over you, or some such thing as that, you know."

"Merciful heavens, Georgie, what have I done that she wants to warn me about?"

"Why, nothing at all," replied her ladyship. "It was not

you she was speaking about at all. I merely meant she *would* if she had anything of purpose to impart."

"Georgie, for heaven's sake, what *did* she say, then?"

"Only that the betting in all the clubs is on Lady Prodmore, and that that lady herself appears to be in no doubt as to the probable outcome of Wednesday's proceedings. It seems that she actually paid a morning call to Berkeley Square only this morning, and Lady Jersey, though she insists that entertaining the woman was a sad ordeal, felt we ought to know how matters seem to stand."

"But how can they be so certain in the clubs?" Jessica asked, feeling tension creep into her body again. "Surely they do not set such store by what her ladyship—Lady Prodmore, I mean—says."

"Well, you know, dearest, even Cyril says the law takes no notice of a black child, and no one questions that Albert belongs to Lady Prodmore. Evidently, however much Cyril would like to speak confidently to me, he appears to set little store by the fact that Sir Reginald Basingstoke means to prove that since Albert is a person, he cannot be subject to the same disposal as a chunk of real estate. Not that he does not wish Aunt Susan to win her case," Lady Gorden added hastily. " 'Tis merely that I fear he cannot help but be in agreement with the odds-makers. And Lady Jersey said Lady Prodmore is already making plans as to how she will punish poor Albert when she does get him back. She seems to have no doubt, Jess, that she will get him."

So shaken was Jessica by this information that she went home immediately and scrawled a hasty note to Sir Brian, begging him to call in Hanover Square at his earliest convenience. Indeed, the news of Lady Prodmore's confident assumption that the trial would end in her favor so unsettled her that Jessica scarcely enjoyed the sense of gratification she ought to have felt when Sir Brian presented himself less than an hour later. She experienced only relief when Bates pushed open the drawing-room doors to announce him.

Jumping to her feet, she held out her hands. "How good of you go come so quickly, sir."

"I came as soon as I received your note," he said, stepping rapidly toward her, his expression anxious. But just as she thought he meant to gather her into his arms, he took both hands, gave them a hard little squeeze, and led her firmly back to her chair. "What has occurred to put you in such a state, my dear?"

Swallowing her disappointment, she cast him a rueful glance as he drew another chair up close to hers and sat down. "You will no doubt think I am suffering a crisis of the nerves, sir, but my sister informs me that it is all over town that the outcome of my aunt's trial is a foregone conclusion. I confess, I fear for her."

A gleam of amusement lit Sir Brian's eyes before the lids drooped to conceal it. "You sent for me to request advice in this matter?"

"Yes, please," she responded with unaccustomed meekness.

"Merely because I am a justice of the peace and can be thought to know something of matters of law?"

"No . . . that is, yes, I . . ." She broke off, confused. Then, spreading her hands, she said quietly, "I don't know what to do, sir."

"Nonsense," he returned, his amusement turning to sudden briskness as he leaned forward to pat the hands she had folded in her lap. "You will do what you must. It may help you to know, however, that tomorrow morning's proceedings will be merely a preliminary to the main event. There is, it seems, a point of law to be contested before your aunt's case can be argued before a jury."

Jessica cast him a sharp glance. "A point of law, sir?"

He grinned. "Aye, over the business of whether Albert is real property or not. Wychbold and I discovered after a deal of research that the debate is scarcely a new one. It actually goes back centuries, and though I have no notion what Basingstoke means to do with the information we discovered, I do know that there was at least one case within the past century when a chief justice at the King's Bench ruled that a slave became free by being baptized on English soil or even, in certain instances, merely by setting foot upon it. Unfortunately, that ruling was overturned a few years later by two other justices in a joint decision, whereby they declared that property was property and must be treated as such under the law. It's been a devilish seesaw ever since, with individual cases appearing in the courts every fifteen years or so, and that state of affairs will likely continue until slavery is abolished once and for all in this country.''

''So we cannot be certain that Sir Reginald's arguments will prevail,'' she said quietly. ''What then?''

''Then she will have to stand her trial at once,'' he replied grimly. ''But you may safely put your faith in Basingstoke, my dear. He has already accomplished much by arranging for the justices to decide first whether the law has in fact been broken. Furthermore, until a jury is called, Lady Susan's name will not come into the matter and she will not even have to sit in the dock. So tomorrow you will dress with your customary elegance, and you will sit with your aunt in that courtroom as you would sit in Lady Jersey's drawing room. If you take my advice, you will go veiled, and then not so much as the blink of an eye will reveal to any of the common folk who make it a practice to attend such proceedings that you are the least bit frightened.''

His tone was bracing, but Jessica found it difficult to respond with any confidence. Instead, her attention focused for some seconds upon the warmth of the hand still touching hers. Then she looked up at him, her eyes searching his for the reassurance she needed. ''I shall be frightened,'' she admitted in a small voice. ''I don't know if I will have the strength to comport myself as you advise me to.''

''Would you disappoint Lady Susan?'' he asked sternly, removing his hand from hers and bringing it to rest upon the polished arm of his chair.

Jessica swallowed hard. The sternness had reached his eyes, and she felt very much as though he had told her she would be disappointing him instead of Lady Susan if she did not behave properly in the courtroom. She could feel sudden tears at the back of her eyes and an aching in her throat. More than anything, right then, she wanted to fling herself into his arms and sob out her frustrations upon his shoulder. But his attitude did not invite such a liberty. ''I shall try not to disappoint anyone,'' she said at last, stiffly.

Sir Brian's lips folded together tightly, but there was no lingering trace of that sternness in his voice when next he spoke. Instead, it was very gentle. ''You will do what is necesssary," he repeated. "I know you will. You do not have it in you to do otherwise, and it will help if you remember that Basingstoke is never out of the match until the final count is done."

The phrasing made her smile. "I collect that that last bit is boxing cant," she said. "I hope it means he will win his case."

"It means that no one knows what will happen," Sir Brian said.

"Will you be there?" she asked almost shyly, dreading the possibility that he might say no.

"Of course I shall be there. I had thought your aunt would have told you that I mean to convey the two of you to King's Bench in my carriage. Andrew will also accompany us. You will not be left to face any of this business alone, Jessica," he said gruffly.

The tears nearly flowed freely then. She held them back only by a magnificent effort. Still, there was a sense of relief beyond what she might have expected to feel. Somehow if he were going to be there with her, she was certain everything would come right. She gazed at him, wondering what there was about the man that instilled such confidence in her. Only minutes before, she had been in flat despair. Then, when he had made it clear that he expected her to carry on, she had been determined to make the effort to do so. And now, only because he had said he would be there with her, she was confident that she had little to worry about. Was this what love was all about? Being able to place such complete trust in another person? Certainly she had long since come to realize that this man was necessary to her comfort. But would his friendship be sufficient? For surely that seemed to be all he was offering her.

Even at this critical moment Sir Brian was not behaving in the least like a man in love. Oh, to be sure, there had been that anxious look in his eye when he had entered the drawing room, and that one little moment when she had thought he meant to catch her up into his arms. But he had not done so. And if his manner was not precisely offhand, it was still the manner of a friend, not that of a lover. Moreover, a man in love would not go dashing about London on the arm of every beautiful damsel he chanced to meet. Never the same one twice. The man was clearly a libertine.

The last thought made her smile, and when she looked up again it was to surprise a quizzical look on his face. Something in her own expression must have made him wonder what she was thinking, and knowing he was perfectly capable of asking her to describe the thoughts that had just been skipping through her head, Jessica rose quickly to her feet and held out her hand to him. She would be as casual as he was himself if it killed her.

"I must thank you for taking the trouble to come here to reassure me, sir. I see that I have been exaggerating my fears, and I shall take care not to do so in the future."

Rather more leisurely, Sir Brian also got to his feet, then stood looking down at her from his superior height. When he took her hand in his, there was something in his attitude that caused Jessica to regard him closely, but his expression gave nothing away. If there seemed to be a warm glow at the back of his eyes, surely that was only her imagination. And if his breathing seemed more noticeable than usual, what could she make of that, especially when her own breathing was scarcely calm and controlled? When he spoke, his voice was low and carried a note she had not hitherto discerned in it.

"I will hold you to that promise, my dear, once all this business is done," he said.

16

"THROUGHOUT HISTORY, THE courts of this land, with very few exceptions, have ordered the return of escaped slaves to their masters," declaimed Sir Aubrey Totten, the thin, reed-voiced barrister for the plaintiff. As he moved energetically back and forth before the three justices of the Court of King's Bench, Sir Aubrey's black robes swirled around his feet and his periwig displayed a lamentable tendency to slip from one side to the other.

He had been speaking forcefully for some time, pointing out to the bewigged gentlemen at the high bench that there was no law in England prohibiting ownership of slaves, that, moreover, there were numerous records indicating that, like houses and land, Negro slaves had often been offered and accepted in payment of debts, which fact, he said, gesturing dramatically, proved beyond question that they were accepted in the eyes of the law as ordinary real estate.

"I cannot imagine," he declared at last in summation, "what the consequences may be if masters are now to lose their property merely by bringing their slaves to England, though that is, in effect, what my worthy colleague speaking for the defense would advocate as a matter of course. I do know, however, that such consequences would be far-reaching and disastrous. Therefore, it is quite clear, my lords, that that which is a possession in Virginia or in Paris *must* be recognized as a possession in London."

Sir Aubrey sat down with a final swirl of his robes, and Jessica, seated in the front row of the crowded courtroom between Lady Susan and Sir Brian, glanced up somewhat fearfully through her veil at the latter. It seemed to her as though everything Sir Aubrey had said was logical and unanswerable. But Sir Brian smiled down at her reassuringly. Then, with a nod of his head, he drew her attention

to the fact that Sir Reginal Basingstoke was ponderously
rising to his feet to address the bench.

Jessica had met Sir Reginald briefly upon their arrival at
the court, but she had found it difficult to repress the
emotions stirred by the very fact of being in such a place
for such a purpose long enough to pay proper heed to him.
Now that she had been sitting in the courtroom for some
time with her attention focused upon Sir Aubrey, she was
less aware of both her own agitation and the spectators
seated behind her, and able at last to give her full attention
to Lady's Susan's barrister.

Sir Reginald was a good deal larger in every way than his
adversary, but he moved with a stately grace and carried
himself with enormous dignity, much like a famous actor
taking command of center stage. Before he spoke, he took
a full minute to direct his unblinking gaze from one side of
the courtroom to the other, then let it come to rest briefly
upon the two soberly clad, discreetly veiled ladies sitting
between Sir Brian and Andrew Liskeard, before turning to
address the justices. It seemed to Jessica by then that
everyone, the three behind the bench as well as every
spectator, was awaiting his words with bated breath. Not a
sound could be heard except for an occasional noise drifting in from the street outside.

"My lords," said Sir Reginald in a deep, compelling
voice, "the point we wish to make here today is a simple
one. A possession is a thing. A *child,* black or white, is not.
And if he is not a thing, why, then, my lords, as a helpless
child, he is entitled to the protection of the crown and must
be treated as the king's own subject. Furthermore, by the
laws of this country, the theft of a king's subject is more
properly called abduction and requires the use of force. No
one suggests that force was employed in the case which the
plaintiff would bring before this court. Therefore, no law
has been broken." He glanced at Sir Aubrey, who was
looking mildly sardonic. Sir Reginald smiled. "Of course,
my esteemed and learned colleague would prefer that we
ignore the laws of this country. He finds it necessary to
draw instead upon those of other, certainly less civilized
countries, in order to argue his client's position. But what
has England come to, my lord," Sir Reginald went on,
shaking his head sadly, "when we are told that what is law

in the colonies or even, God forbid, in *France,* must also be accepted as law in England? The laws of America, France, or, for that matter, Russia or Turkey, have no authority here.

"Suppose," he suggested musingly, "that a Turkish pasha came here with half a score of Circassian women slaves for his amusement. Suppose these white women were to say to the pasha, 'Sir, we will no longer be the subjects of your lust.' I believe, my lords, that such a man would make a miserable figure before this court on a charge of rape." He paused for effect, and but for a quickly stifled gasp or two, there was still not a sound to be heard in the courtroom. Jessica scarcely dared to stir for fear of missing a single word, and watched, fascinated, as Sir Reginald hooked his thumbs into the folds of his robe where they draped over his massive chest. "I shall describe to you," he said then, conversationally, "what actually did occur in this country in such a case.

"A man called Cartwright, who brought a slave from Russia, wanted to flog the fellow. When he was prevented from doing so, he carried the matter to the courts, where it was resolved that England possessed air too pure for slaves to breathe, that therefore a man setting foot upon English soil was by the very nature of that fact a free man. That event, my lords, took place during the eleventh year of the reign of Queen Elizabeth." He paused again, this time directing a basilisk glare at the three men behind the bench. After a long moment during which Jessica realized her fingernails were digging into the palms of her hands, he went on. "I hope, my lords," he said softly, his voice more compelling than ever, "that the English air does not blow less pure now than it did then."

Sir Reginald took his seat, and Jessica glanced at Sir Brian in time to see a little smile playing about his lips. Glancing next at her aunt, she discovered that Lady Susan was leaning forward slightly, her eyes fairly sparkling in appreciation of the barrister's argument.

Thinking the matter now over and done, except for the justices' decision, Jessica was startled when Sir Aubrey leapt to his feet again. But although the arguments continued for some time, with each side matching precedent for precedent, they seemed now, even to her untrained ear, to be little more than sound and fury. Sir Brian's smile once Sir Reginald had concluded his primary argument, added to the fact that the large barrister was now responding calmly to Sir Aubrey's more agitated pleadings, was enough to instill Jessica with a greater sense of confidence than she had felt since her aunt had been carted off to Bow Street.

Still, once the justices retired to consider their decision, she felt her earlier tension returning a thousandfold. And half an hour later, after little more than desultory conversation with her companions, when the justices filed back into the courtroom, Jessica found that she was holding her breath again. She felt Lady Susan stiffen, and noted, too, that Andrew, seated at her ladyship's left hand, was staring straight ahead, jaws clenched. Only Sir Brian seemed perfectly calm.

Once the black-robed figures were seated, it was Mr. Justice Abbott who spoke, his voice grave. "The question is," he began, "whether the plaintiff in the case pending before this court has returned a sufficient cause for the prosecution of the defendant. The cause returned is that the defendant committed an act of theft by refusing to return a slave to his mistress." Mr. Abbott glanced briefly at his two expressionless colleagues. "We three are agreed that so high an act of dominion as that of one human being over another must derive its force from the law of the country, and if to be justified here must be justified by the law of England. The state of slavery is of such a nature that it cannot be supported by mere reason, moral or political, but only by positive law."

Even without looking at Sir Brian, Jessica sensed victory, and with Mr. Abbott's next words she heard her aunt release an audible sigh of relief.

"Though it is quite true," Mr. Abbott continued, "that there is no law in England opposing the institution of slavery, there is likewise none which defends it; therefore, whatever inconveniences may follow from this decision, we cannot say the case in question is allowed or approved by English law. It is therefore the decision of this court that no law has been broken. The charges against the defendant being herewith vacated, the clerk will read."

The ordeal was over, and Lady Susan's name had not

once been mentioned. Feeling Sir Brian's hand gently upon her own, Jessica looked down and discovered she had been clutching the sleeve of his coat. Guiltily she released it and turned to squeeze her aunt's hand.

"We've won, ma'am."

"Indeed, my love, and Albert is free at last."

"Devil a bit," Andrew put in cheerfully from her other side. "The main thing is that *you* are free."

Lady Susan chuckled. "Very true. However, I was persuaded, you know, that right would prevail. I am merely thankful that Sir Reginald was able to achieve his victory so quickly, and without bandying my name about the courts. He is a very clever man, I think."

A moment later, as the clerk called for the next case, Basingstoke, accompanied by Mr. Wychbold, stepped up to Sir Brian and suggested that they all move out into the vestibule. As Jessica walked beside Sir Brian in the wake of the two lawyers, she noticed a plump, veiled figure slipping out of the room ahead of them, and had little difficulty recognizing Lady Prodmore.

Lady Susan, walking behind the others with Andrew, made a small sound in her throat that made Jessica look back at her quickly. Even through the dark veil shading the older woman's face, she was able to see the triumphant little smile that flickered across her lips.

In the rapidly emptying vestibule, Mr. Wychbold spoke first, to Lady Susan. "I feel it is incumbent upon me, my lady, to inform you that you now have an excellent case against Lady Prodmore for defamation of character. I would be pleased to prepare the arguments for you."

"Thank you, Mr. Wychbold," said her ladyship kindly, "but I have no desire to pursue the matter. We have already provided enough meat to keep the scandalmongers from starving for a twelvemonth, at least. Indeed, were the Season not rapidly drawing to a close, I confess I should be strongly tempted to repair to Paris or Vienna for several months until the furor has died away. However, the Season *is* drawing to a close, and I daresay that dreadful woman will not dare to show her face in polite society, so I expect the rest of us will rub along tolerably well without resorting to drastic measures." The flickering little smile danced upon her lips again, and Jessica knew her aunt wasn't the least concerned about the scandal, but only about the victory she had won. Lady Susan's smile widened as she held out her hand to Sir Reginald. "I must thank you, sir, with all my heart. And you, too, Mr. Wychbold, of course," she added.

"It is Sir Brian," said the barrister, "who deserves your thanks, my lady, for it was he who actually discovered the particular point of Elizabethan law upon which we decided to base our arguments."

Sir Brian immediately denied that he had done anything more than discover a fact that would have been useless to any but the most talented of barristers, and insisted that it had more than likely been the numerous precedents unearthed by the tireless Mr. Wychbold that had tilted the scales of justice in Lady Susan's favor. When the discussion rapidly showed signs of dwindling into an agreeable debate among the gentlemen as to who it was who had contributed the most toward gaining Lady Susan's freedom, it was Andrew who put a stop to it by suggesting tactfully that the ladies were no doubt a trife weary after so long and difficult a morning.

Immediately the other three gentlemen expressed contrition at having kept them standing, and within moments both ladies were tucked up comfortably in the unicorn-crested coach, bowling across London Bridge to Thames Street, up the Strand, then through the Haymarket to Piccadilly. It was then but a short distance to Old Bond Street, George Street, and home. Upon their arrival, Sir Brian and Andrew accompanied the ladies to the front hall but refused to linger, saying they knew both Lady Susan and Jessica would prefer to rest. However, they were not allowed to take their departure until her ladyship had extracted a promise from them to dine that evening in Hanover Square.

"We are going to celebrate," she said cheerfully, taking off her veil, "and I know that Lord Gordon and dearest Georgeanne will want to hear all the details of this morning's business. They did not attend, of course, for Cyril feared that to do so would distress Georgie, and very likely he was in the right of it. But you will need to help us explain matters, sir, and you and Andrew both deserve to have a part in the celebration. I shan't accept regrets."

Sir Brian, his gaze meeting Jessica's, assured Lady Susan that it would be his pleasure to dine with them, but Jessica scarcely heard his words, for there was a look in his dark brown eyes that drove everything else from her head. It was a look so filled with warmth that she knew, for that one brief moment, that he loved her quite as passionately as she loved him. However, he turned back to Lady Susan just then, and the moment was gone. When he bade them adieu, laughingly reminding Andrew that they were pledged to meet Lady St. Erth and her daughter in Rotten Row at five o'clock, Jessica began to fear that she had imagined the look altogether. Nevertheless, for the rest of the afternoon her thoughts seemed to tumble about in her head without direction or logical order.

Lady Susan, having dispatched her invitation to Duke Street, caused a late nuncheon to be served to them in the breakfast parlor, but Jessica could not have said later what she ate or even if she had swallowed a morsel. And when, Viscount Woodbury and Jeremy called a half-hour later to collect Albert, though outwardly she was cheerful and polite, she could not recall afterward what had been said or whether she had even remembered to bid the two boys a proper farewell.

Once they had gone, however, Lady Susan, eyeing her niece in a speculative way, suggested that Jessica ought to lie down upon her bed for an hour or so. "I can promise you, my dear, that I mean to do so. This business has placed a strain upon all of us, but I vow that you have borne the brunt of it, though you have made small complaint."

"I am fine, Aunt Susan."

"Nevertheless, love, it would please me if you would rest."

When it was put to her like that, Jessica could scarcely refuse, but once in her bedchamber, she had no desire to sleep. Instead she selected a book at random from the shelf near her bed and carried it to the comfortably pillowed window seat. But upon opening it, she discovered her selection to be Walter Scott's *Marmion,* and instead of reading, she found her thoughts winging back to the day on the cliff road when Andrew had held up Lord Gordon's coach—the day she had first set eyes upon Sir Brian. How little she had known of him then.

The memories danced through her mind as she curled up against the soft pillows. First, there had been her own reaction to the man, of course, a startling reaction for one who had known so many gentlemen and respected so few. For despite the fact that he could stir her temper more easily than anyone else had ever done, she had been fascinated by him. And he, too, had been fascinated by her.

Smiling softly, she recalled the incident in the garden at Gordon Hall. She had surprised him that day, and herself as well. But when he had made it clear that he meant to pursue her, Jessica had eluded his efforts, and then in the aftermath of the bogus princess, she had begun to believe that his resentment when she had criticized him for interfering had quite overcome his romantic interest in her. And even though his presence in Lady Susan's drawing room upon her arrival in London and his subsequent interest in the Africa Institute had provided Jessica with reason to suspect he had not lost interest altogether, she had been certain that his outrage over her dealings with the sweep had put a period to any of the tenderer emotions he might still have harbored.

More recently, since her aunt's troubles had begun, his behavior had confused Jessica completely. Though she could not doubt that he had been annoyed to discover that she and Lady Susan had chosen to brave the slings and arrows of the *beau monde* rather than remain discreetly in seclusion after her ladyship's release from Bow Street, his anger had been subdued and there had been little sign of his customary arrogance. Indeed, there had been moments since then that she had suspected he was deeply concerned about her. And moments, too, when she had surprised the look of tender affection in his eyes.

Then she remembered the warm glance she had intercepted earlier in the day. In her mind's eye she could see his expression again, clearly, and it occurred to her for the first time that perhaps Sir Brian was unsure of her. He always seemed so confident, so sure of himself, that it had never before crossed her mind that he might be afraid to declare himself. Still, he had shown her more than once that his ego could be fragile. Perhaps he merely feared rebuff.

Straightening suddenly, Jessica laid the book aside and got to her feet, striding to pull the bell cord near the bed. When the wiry Mellin entered the room breathlessly in response to the hearty summons, Jessica ordered a bath and announced that she meant to wash her hair.

"Before dinner, Miss Jessica?" Mellin was shocked. "It'll never dry, miss. Not by eight o'clock, and that's when my Lord and Lady Gordon be expected."

"Well, kindle a fire in here, then," Jessica ordered briskly. " 'Tis cool enough, and at least it won't smoke. And, Mellin, do you go to my aunt's woman and ask if I may use some of Aunt Susan's French soap. Now, hurry!"

17

BY EIGHT O'CLOCK, though she smelled delightfully of French jasmine, despite all of Mellin's strenuous brushing before the crackling fire, Jessica's hair was still a trifle damp when she descended the stairs to the drawing room. Mellin had styled the long, light brown tresses with a central, arrow-straight part leading to a neat, shining coil at the back of Jessica's head, leaving wispy tendrils to curl about her face, neck and ears. Jessica's color was high, for she knew she looked very well indeed in the slim-skirted, puff-sleeved gown of clinging lavender silk. A narrow trimming of gold lace banded the high waist and edged the deep décolletage, and dainty golden slippers peeped out from beneath the scalloped hemline as she walked. She wore long gold net gloves on her slender arms and carried an elegant pink-and-gilt Oriental fan. Besides the gold bobs in her ears, her only jewelry was a simple amethyst pendant on a delicate gold chain.

As she paused upon the drawing-room threshold, her eyes darted swiftly over the room's occupants, and she felt a surge of disappointment. Though her aunt and Lord and Lady Gordon were there, as was General Potterby, whom she had not expected to see, the person she sought was absent.

"Is it your intention to bar the door to latecomers, my girl?"

The words, softly spoken behind her, nearly caused Jessica to jump out of her skin. She whirled, eyes flashing, to face Sir Brian.

"Have you no manners, sir? To steal up on a person in such a way is enough to cause one to suffer heart failure!"

"Or a miscarriage?" he suggested quizzically. His eyes danced. "You may rest assured that I shall not creep up

214

behind Lady Gordon in such a way. Not that I did creep, mind you, but your thoughts were clearly otherwhere, my dear."

Flushing delicately, Jessica favored him with a speaking look, which he returned with a slight lifting of one eyebrow. Much as she had wanted to demand a private word with him, she found now that her courage failed her, and she was grateful to hear her aunt's voice demanding to know whether she meant to keep Sir Brian cooling his heels in the gallery all the evening.

"Thank you, my lady," Sir Brian said, laughing as he stepped past the silent Jessica. "I had begun to fear that, like the porter at Almack's, Miss Jessica meant to refuse entrance to those arriving after the prescribed hour. I beg your pardon for my tardiness."

"And for misplacing your nephew, as well, sir?" Her ladyship regarded him archly. "I seem to recall having issued an invitation to you both."

"Alas, ma'am, he has cried off, having accepted another invitation instead. I promise you, I combed his hair for his poor manners, but he assured me that you would never miss him."

"Well, it is of little consequence," Lady Susan replied with a dry chuckle, "for the general stopped in late this afternoon and has consented to take potluck with us, so my numbers will not be upset. I collect that Andrew's second invitation came from Lady St. Erth. Are we to expect an announcement from that quarter in the near future?"

"Good God, I devoutly hope not!" Sir Brian's dismay was nearly comical, and Jessica, rapidly recovering her equanimity, exchanged an amused look with her aunt. "Miss St. Erth," said Sir Brian, "is scarcely out of the schoolroom, and Andrew returns to Oxford in August." He paused reflectively. "I wouldn't be surprised if they should make a match of it one day, but neither St. Erth nor I would countenance such a thing now."

Lady Susan shot another twinkling glance at Jessica, then turned away to speak to the general, and Jessica looked up to find Sir Brian regarding her with a smile in his eyes. As his gaze rested appreciatively upon her, she felt the disconcerting warmth creeping into her cheeks again, but she did not look away. He recollected himself, and nodded toward Lady Susan and the general.

"That looks promising," he said.

Taking a quick breath to steady herself, Jessica gave a little laugh. "So the general would have us believe," she said, "but I suspect that Aunt Susan merely wishes him to exert his influence to begin a campaign for prison reform. She was appalled by the conditions at Bow Street, you know, and she means for us to do something to see them improved."

"Good God," Sir Brian muttered under his breath.

"Just so, sir. I scarcely dare to imagine what scrape she will next fall into."

"Jessica, you cannot . . . that is, I must . . ." He broke off, looking harassed, and when Bates entered the room just then to announce that dinner was served, Sir Brian's expression changed to one of mingled frustration and relief.

For a moment Jessica had feared that she had somehow said something to vex him, and she wondered what he had been about to say. But the company was too small for formality, and the conversation at the table became general at once, as they discussed the events of that morning. Thus, there was no immediate opportunity for a private word with him. Afterward, however, Lady Susan informed the gentlemen that since they were dining *en famille,* they might have their port served in the drawing room if they liked. This invitation being promptly accepted, the company withdrew to the first floor again.

Jessica could wait no longer. As the gentlemen followed the ladies into the drawing room, she took the first opportunity to catch Sir Brian's attention by the simple expedient of laying her fan upon his sleeve and speaking in a low tone.

"Sir, I must have private speech with you. Will you walk with me in the garden?"

Both eyebrows lifted. "Is the square garden not rather a public place for private speech at this hour, my dear? Surely, even to walk round to the gate would cause comment if we were observed."

"I was referring to my aunt's garden," she said, looking

down at her hands and thus missing the twinkle that leapt to his eyes. "Please, sir. 'Tis important."

"Very well," he replied, "for I confess, I would also like to have a word with you, but I've not the slightest doubt that we shall both be called to account by your aunt for our actions. Come along, then."

He held open the door for her, and glancing back, Jessica saw that her aunt's eye was certainly upon them. But there was affectionate amusement in Lady Susan's expression, and she made no attempt to call them back.

They went downstairs, through the front hall, and along a narrow corridor to the door leading outside to the rear garden. Upon emerging from the house and descending the few shallow steps to the pathway, they discovered a crescent moon and a myriad of twinkling stars overhead that cast an eerie silvery light over the shadowy shrubs and trees. The garden was small but laid out in a formal pattern of gravel paths that wound about through the shrubbery. They had walked for some moments in silence, their feet crunching on the gravel, before Sir Brian said softly that no doubt she would begin, in her own good time, to tell him what was on her mind.

Jessica bit her lip, looking down at the silvery path, quite unable to think what she ought to say first. Suddenly his hand was on her shoulder, and firmly he guided her to a stone bench. Removing his jacket, he placed it on the bench for her to sit upon.

"Oh, sir, I couldn't," she protested, looking quickly up at him. "I would ruin your coat."

"I shan't regard it," he assured her, pressing her to sit. "Or do you fear I cannot afford another?"

"No, of course not." She fell silent again when he sat down beside her. His nearness made it almost impossible for her to think straight.

"What is it that is so important, Jessica?" He spoke quietly, and there was little inflection in his voice. She wished she knew what he was thinking.

"I . . . I wanted to thank you for all you have done to help us, sir," she began, speaking with difficulty. Her mouth was dry. "And . . . and also to apologize for anything I might have done which has vexed you."

"Your gratitude is misplaced, my dear, and I am not at all vexed with you."

"Well, I thought perhaps you were before supper, and . . . well, there have been other times, of course. I know you think I am headstrong, sir, and . . . and willful, but truly I am neither. I merely have little patience with people who do not meet difficulties straight on."

"A gentleman must always hesitate to contradict a lady," he replied gently, "but I do not think you headstrong. Merely a trifle impulsive at times."

She turned her gaze searchingly upon him, and though the moon cast but dim light, she could see enough to tell her that he was in earnest.

"Yet you resented it when I criticized you for unmasking the princess," she pointed out. When he did not deny it, she pressed on. "And you were furious when I confronted that sweep without first consulting you." Sir Brian still said nothing. "Then, too, it must have annoyed you when I was constantly—and I fear, falsely—accusing you of exploiting people in your mines and on your plantations, did it not?"

In answer, Sir Brian put his arm around her shoulders and drew her close. "I believe my temper must be quite as fiery as your own, my dear, for I cannot deny that you have frequently given me occasion to lose it, but you have never given me cause for more than momentary vexation. If I resented your criticism about the devilish princess business, it was only because I recognized truth in the things you said. And if I lost my temper when you ventured into Cheapside, it was truly out of concern for your safety, although you had cause to disbelieve that. As to the mines and plantations, I can only say that, while I do my poor best to make things as bearable as possible for my people, I know of no acceptable way to make things truly right in your eyes. I do not own vast plantations, only one fairly large one; however, I cannot deny owning slaves. I would offer to sell the lot, but I cannot feel that that would be to their advantage, you know, for there is no telling how their new masters would treat them. And I do not feel that I can merely set them free when there is no good place for them to go, and when they are not trained to care for themselves."

"I was wrong about your mines," Jessica said quietly.

"Not entirely. There are certainly dangers, and I do hire both women and children—though not the very young ones—but no one is overworked or mistreated, my dear, and the mines provide quite a good living for my people."

"Still, I was wrong about a number of things."

"Yes."

He was silent, and Jessica felt a niggling exasperation. She had certainly given him every opportunity, if he still wished it, to declare himself. She had not even argued with him over his plantation or his mines. Indeed, she found his explanations completely acceptable. Even with regard to the problem of his slaves, she knew now that they could work together to do whatever was right. Still, he said nothing. She peeped up at him again through her thick lashes.

"Were you wrong, too, sir, when you said you believed I was the exact sort of woman you had searched for all your life?"

His arm tightened around her shoulders, sending little arrows of fire shooting through her veins. "No, Jessica," he said softly, "I was not wrong. I think I fell in love with you that first day at Shaldon Park when you demanded poor Andrew's head on a platter. I knew I was in love the day you planted me in Gordon's rose garden."

"Then why have you never asked me to marry you?" she demanded, straightening indignantly.

"I am not such a fool, sweetheart," he retorted, but in a gentle tone. "You were so damned elusive at first that I feared my suit would never prosper. Later, you showed yourself to be so jealous of your independence that I was certain you would reject me out of sheer contrariness. Then, too, there was a time when I did believe you to be a younger version of your aunt, with your mind too set upon curing the evils of the world to consider marriage. And later, what with the trial looming over us, I could scarcely make a push to convince you to marry me. For one thing, I was afraid you might accept simply because you were vulnerable and needed someone to support your spirits, and second . . ." He hesitated, shooting her a rueful look. "Second, I was worried lest the trial go wrong. If anything happened to Lady Susan, I was afraid you might hold me responsible, say I had mismanaged her affairs just as I'd mishandled the business of Andrew and his princess.''

"Oh, Brian, I do not think I would have said such a thing,'' she protested.

"Perhaps not,'' he conceded. "Nonetheless, when I discussed the matter with Lady Susan, she agreed that any declaration on my part could prove hazardous to our future happiness if I did not first assure myself of victory. She recommended that, with that end in view, I ought to treat you casually. I confess, though I thought it excellent advice at the time, there have been moments when it has been well nigh impossible advice to follow.''

"Was that why you paid heed to other women? To make me jealous?''

He nodded ruefully. "Your aunt suggested that I single out one woman, but I found I could not do such a thing.''

"I'm glad.'' There was more silence. Jessica regarded her hands as they fidgeted with the fan in her lap. Then, in a small voice that she scarcely recognized as her own, she said, "You could, I think, be assured of victory now, Brian. That is, unless you feel, despite my age, that you ought to speak first to Papa.''

He chuckled. "Your age, oh ancient one, is perfect, and I have already taken the liberty of speaking to your esteemed sire. We have his blessing.''

Her eyes flew open at that, and she turned sharply to regard him with amazement. "You have already spoken to my father? When?''

"Before I went in search of Woodbury,'' he confessed, "I traveled into Gloucestershire.''

"Brian, you wretch!'' She remembered thinking he had been gone an unconscionably long time merely to have gone to Shaldon Park and thence to north Devon. Cocking her head, she favored him with a measuring look and lifted her fan as though she would rap his knuckles. "You told me once that you always work within the system to get what you want, sir. If this is an example of your methods, let me tell—''

"This,'' he said, crushing her against him, "is an example of my methods, love.'' His lips claimed hers, and Jessica responded instantly to their touch, letting the fan fall unheeded from her hand, and melting against him as her arms encircled his hard body. Within moments she was lost to her surroundings as his hands gently caressed her breasts, causing them to swell achingly beneath the soft, clinging silk. His tongue probed at her soft lips and soon invaded her mouth, searching its velvet interior as his kisses became more urgent. Jessica's responses were equally fervent. Her pulses seemed to pound, and when his hands and fingers began to move at random over her body, bringing sweet torment with every touch, her breathing became ragged.

"Well, upon my word!"

Startled, Jessica leapt away from Sir Brian, trying desperately to straighten her gown, while her brother-in-law glared disapprovingly through his quizzing glass at her. They had been too involved in each other to hear any sound of Lord Gordon's approach.

"I say, Jessica," he growled, "I'd not have believed it of you."

Sir Brian, chuckling at Jessica's discomfiture as he bent over to retrieve her fan, cast Lord Gordon a lazy glance. "You may congratulate me, my lord. With Mr. Sutton-Drew's permission, your sister-in-law has consented to be my wife."

"Well, upon my word, is that so?" Cyril considered the information for a moment before a welcome thought occurred to him. "I say, that's good news, very good news indeed, for I can tell you, Jessica, I was in a dashed quandary. That devilish aunt of yours is going on something fearful about tearing down all the old prisons and building modern ones staffed with proper servants and furnished with carpeting and I don't know what all. But if you are to marry Gregory here, then Lady Susan can dashed well live with you and he will see to it that she don't—"

"Cyril, what on earth are you doing out here?" demanded Lady Susan, swooping down upon his lordship from behind, followed by the general and Lady Gordon. "Of all the tactless . . ." While she continued to scold, Sir Brian glanced at Jessica, his eyes twinkling.

She grinned back at him, then turned to the others.

"Aunt Susan," she said mischievously, "Cyril was just being so obliging as to suggest that you might choose to live with Sir Brian and me after we are married."

"Well, of all the idiotish . . . Married?" Lady Susan straightened, darting a searching gaze at her niece before turning with a smile to Sir Brian. "So you've got that business all right and tight at last."

"Yes, ma'am," he replied soberly.

"But what," she demanded, casting Lord Gordon a dark look, "would possess Cyril to think I should choose to inflict my presence upon you? I cannot conceive of anything more odious to a pair of newlyweds than to be saddled with an aged aunt."

"I think," Sir Brian said gently, "that he means for us to keep you from falling into any more scrapes."

"Well, of all the—"

"Pack of nonsense!" snapped the general at the same time, moving up to place a calming hand upon Lady Susan's shoulder. "I shall see to it that Susan comes to no harm."

Amazed, Jessica waited for her aunt to contradict him, only to find her astonishment increasing when Lady Susan, looking self-conscious, said nothing at all.

Lord Gordon looked from her ladyship to the general. "Upon my word," he muttered.

"Yes, Cyril," said his lady, taking him firmly by the elbow, "but everyone has heard enough of your words for one night, you know. You come back inside with me." When he hesitated, she gave an imperious little tug to his sleeve. "At once, my lord. I doubt it is doing your heir any good for his mother to be standing about in the chilly night air."

"To be sure," he agreed promptly. Then, collecting himself, he hurried after her. "I say, Georgeanne, that is no way to speak to your husband." As his scolding voice faded into the distance, Lady Susan laughingly observed that dearest Georgeanne was learning to manage her husband very nicely, and then suggested that perhaps they should all repair indoors to the warmth of the drawing-room fire.

General Potterby tucked her ladyship's hand into the

crook of his arm, and Sir Brian, rising from the bench, prepared to follow, but Jessica put a hand on his arm.

"One moment, sir, if you please."

He turned, smiling. "Yes, love?"

"I daresay it has quite escaped your notice," she said demurely, "but you have still not made me a proper offer."

"Have I not? No, you are quite right. Very well." And with that he dropped to one knee and, still holding her fan, spread his arms wide. "My darling girl, will you do me the honor to accept this humble—"

But without waiting to hear another word, Jessica flung herself into his outstretched arms. The results might well have been disastrous, but this time Sir Brian, having come to know his impulsive lady rather well, was not caught off his guard. With a delighted laugh he caught her easily, scooped her up into his arms, snatched up his jacket from the stone bench, and still chuckling, carried her back into the house as though she had been but a featherweight. And he did it all without so much as bending a single delicate stick of the elegant Oriental fan.

About the Author

A fourth-generation Californian, Amanda Scott was born and raised in Salinas and graduated with a degree in history from Mills College in Oakland. She did graduate work at the University of North Carolina at Chapel Hill, specializing in British history, before obtaining her MA from San Jose State University. She lives with her husband and young son in Sacramento. Her hobbies include camping, backpacking, and gourmet cooking.